THE PRICE OF
RESISTANCE

THE PRICE OF RESISTANCE

Book One

JONATHAN CHANEY

HWS

He Who Steps Publishing House

*To the teachers of the world, the illuminators of
darkness.*

Author's Foreword

You could say that the character Remy LeBeau is quite near and dear to my heart. He's not a perfect man but I like him. Will readers sympathize with him? Demonize him? Dismiss it all as a dark fairy tale at best. Time will tell.
Thank you, reader, for your time and attention. Stay frosty and prepare for the unbelievable.

CHAPTER I

USA

"If you go down there, they gonna' chase you down the street."

He nodded casually to the remark, unable to pinpoint the exact source of the comment from the bustling sidewalk and too preoccupied to care. The advice went wholly unheeded as he continued onward through sidewalks pockmarked with loose papers and cellophane plastic, turning this way and that to avoid pools of bodily waste and general filth that covered the ground.

"They'll eat you up," the old woman continued as he walked past. *He don't belong here,* she thought to herself, slowly resuming her duties tending to a disheveled shop along Los Angeles' lower quarters. Skid Row. Official signs at intersections provided the names of streets that few vehicles utilized in lettering too faded to read. Sidewalks choked with tents and sleeping bags and huddles of the poverty-stricken. The young, the old, the sick, criminals and the innocent, Christians, Muslims, Atheists, blacks, whites, Latinos and Latinas, men and women, children, artists, laborers, introverts and extroverts, singers, dancers, do-nothings and did-it-all's, the hopeful and the hopeless, all coalesced seeking shelter and food.

The sun hovered low in the sky, illuminating a horizon choked with tenements and dilapidated motels with promising names. Paradise Inn. Fortune Hotel. Titles standing in stark contrast to reality. It was a clear day in L.A., the sky blue and boastful, the sidewalks predominantly filled with blacks and Latinos with just a sprinkling of white, the stereotypical American demographic turned on its head. Further in, a large group milled at the closed gates of a shelter, staring through the bars of an iron gate at the idea of warmth, a roof, hot water, and food within. Remy arrived with a worn suitcase in tow, wearing a mask of confidence. Around him, destitute men clustered and gossiped.

"A man got stabbed out here yesterday. Got'n an argument and that other man just opened him up. Then he done run away."

"Some guy walked up to me with a knife last week. Said he was paid to watch my back, to protect me. Can you believe that?! I don't even know the man. Just walks up to me and says, 'They pay me to watch your back.' I looked down and he has this little knife in his hand. I said, 'If you stab me, you better kill me 'cause I'll....'"

"I hope they serve somethin' good in there tonight. Last night's was disgustin'."

Smiles, nods. Compassionate grimaces over shared misfortune, laughter at a stranger's.

Others worked the north and south corners, hustling marijuana, cocaine, crack, and crank. "I got those boulders."

"I got that smoke."

"What you need? You good?"

A light-skinned black woman wearing a hot pink wig and a strained smile walked briskly through the scene, arm in arm with a dark-skinned man whose face showed only resolution. Emaciated and trying her best to look sexy, poorly clothed in shorts that covered too little leg and sagged at the waistline with a top that hung loosely off of the shoulders. The whole outfit jostled about her bony form, threatening to fall of completely with each step. She wore the ensemble with head held high as might a baroness, thoroughly stained though it was. The couple rounded the corner and was soon out of sight, leaving Remy with less interesting inhabitants of the city streets to study.

The homeless in downtown L.A. were generally quite familiar with one another and Remy was the freshest of fish. An inch-long, thick, curly, white beard situated about a face framed with high cheekbones and a prominent chin. His eyes, normally bright and on the greener side of hazel, were slightly sunken and far darker than normal. He looked tired and worn and he was. Observing the sights and sounds of the place, judging potential dangers, finding his bearings, life itself, had all taken their toll and while the promise of a dry bed and a hot shower inside was a lovely thing to focus on, he was as prepared as one can be to be refused and turned back onto unfriendly sidewalks to fend for himself, sleeping and living publicly. *If there is a God*, Remy thought, *he does not smile upon me and I have nothing to say to him.*

"Is this the line to the mission?" he asked, knowing the answer, attempting to initiate conversation with a trio of young men that had been eyeing him in the way that hungry wolves eye sheep. They didn't respond to the direct line of questioning and turned away, though they soon began sizing him up once again. "I, say," repeated Remy, "Is this the line to the mission?" using his hands to articulate the question, puffing up and demonstrating that he would not be easy game. Their eyes lowered. "Not even tryin' talk to you," one muttered. Remy accepted this and rolled his suitcase away. He had time to kill before the gates were scheduled to open and with the crowd tightening uncomfortably into a chaotic semi-circle of pushing, cutting, and pressing inward, he left and put some distance between himself and the shelter.

From Fifth Street over to Sixth, to Seventh, he walked in a casual stride, in no hurry, taking in the environment, breathing deeply through widened nostrils, taking in the scents of the street. Urine, perfume, incense, marijuana, human feces, tobacco, the odors of the washed and unwashed alike taken in without prejudice in cool detached absorption, analyzing, trying to make some sense of it all. The crowds thinned and the number of tents lessened as he approached the fishing district on Ninth Street, a region of warehouses where truckloads of seafood were sorted, labeled, and reshipped. Two vigilant seagulls perched along the edge of a rooftop transfixed a steely gaze upon the potential troublemaker until he turned the corner and was out of sight.

He looped his way back to the more densely populated region of Skid Row, circumnavigating those who inserted themselves into his path -- beggars, drug pushers, the inebriated, the fearful and the frightening, the sick and the old -- with disinterest, too exhausted to feel threatened or disrespected or compassionate.

Sweating in the newly setting sun as he hauled his luggage block after block, he stopped for a rest in the shade along the side of a building, unbuttoned his cuffs and folded up the long sleeves of his white and blue striped, button-up shirt. Leaving his belongings resting against a wall nearby, he approached the edge of the sidewalk and surveyed the scene. Shielding his eyes from the blazing sun slowly lowering in the western sky, he took in the surroundings of Skid Row: north to south, east to west. *This is my neighborhood now,* he thought to himself. *For better or worse.* Behind him, the downtown skyline sat poised in the distance as he surveyed the streets, providing the backdrop for a songbird that flitted by, a flash of feather and song.

CHAPTER II

CHINA

Two and a half revolutions around the sun. Ten seasons. Eight-hundred and fifty days, give or take.

Remy LeBeau's life was quite different then. He looked ten years younger two years prior, clean-shaven, haircuts routine and immaculate. He was trusting, open, carefree, optimistic, sure-footed and certain that he was doing important work and that better things were on the way.

He first saw her during a tour of the secondary school that had recently employed him in Nanchang, China. There was something to her, something felt more than seen or heard, something that Remy was immediately drawn to. There was much more to her than the surface, that was obvious to him at first glance. *Much potential in this one,* he thought to himself, breaking away from the guided tour, turning back as she passed him in the hall. "Looks like we're both new here," he called out to her in passing, needing something to say beyond a simple hello.

"Excuse me?" she queried, turning about to face Remy.

He turned back to face his tour guide, a Chinese teacher in her early-thirties, short, bookish, a little stiff but armed with a strong command of the English language. Remy smiled kindly, held out his hand to show he would be right back, and approached the passerby.

"You look as green as me. Will this be your first year as a teacher?"

"We are green?" she repeated to herself cutely, trying to find the meaning in such a statement.

They shared a smile then, and something stirred within him. Something warm and fluttering.

"It's just an expression. Green like young plants maybe. It just means new. Are you a new teacher here?"

"Yes," she replied, the answer coming smoothly and slowly as she looked serenely at both the foreigner and guide. "I am dancer." She paused, searching for the words. "I teach dance."

She possessed a dancer's body, lithe and light. She'd swished down the hallway with the grace of a deer. *A dancer,* Remy's mind echoed, smiling outwardly, planning on how best to pursue her romantically. His guide asked a question in regards to her role at the school, something about assisting the directors. Instead of answering her, she left.

"I will go now," she stated plainly, turning her eyes to Remy for a final glance. Lips upturned casually and then flicked aside with all the expertise of a fly fisherman. Alluring and distant, Remy was transfixed, the hook more or less set already, though he hadn't fully realized how deeply at the time. He was impressed of the expertise she exhibited wielding that pretty face of hers, the poise and control of it all, as precise as clockwork gears.

"Welcome to China."

"Actually, I've been living here for---," Remy was going to include *two years already* but she had already begun striding away. Long, dark, shiny hair swayed in her wake. A colorful ribbon bobbed along.

"My name is Remy," he called loudly down the hallway.

She spun about but continued walking backward, not losing a step in the process. She smiled prettily, spun back around, and was back on her way.

"Who was that?" he asked as much to himself as to his guide.

"I don't know her name. She's just an assistant. Come," she said, "I will show you the computer lab."

"But she said she teaches---," he began, stopping as he realized he was speaking to the tour guide's back. Something had changed in her demeanor, a chilly shift that he couldn't quite put a bead on. He jogged up to his guide and resumed normal questioning of the school: the facilities, the population, the history. But in the back of his mind, one question remained: *Who was that?*

CHAPTER III

USA

Remy found temporary part-time work in a warehouse in east Los Angeles packaging odds and ends along a conveyor belt, saved, and secured a rundown, shared, efficiency apartment in Skid Row within a few months. There was one bathroom on each of the five floors, restrooms which crumbled along the edges and smelled of mold and rot. There was no kitchen to cook in; no refrigerator to store food and drink. The tiniest step up from sleeping in a homeless shelter.

He was reading next to a window in an efficiency room measuring just seven feet by ten - a small, cramped room housing little more than a bed and a dresser - when the party began. Across the street, a neighboring high-rise was boasting its centennial, one hundred years and still standing strong. Well, still standing, despite the earthquakes and the riots and time. It appeared quite similar to the one Remy gazed out of from across San Pedro Street to a rooftop where Latin music emanated from unseen speakers, laced intermittently with yelps and howls of joy. A fiesta in full swing.

Remy's tenement was equally aged, not ancient, but old, wise almost, the walls stoic, the single window in his room stubbornly unyielding. He identified with the window, respecting the sharp twist needed to pivot its handle, the proper stance required to gather the necessary strength to push it outward. The window was closed when the party began because mosquito screens had never been installed and Remy was a magnet for such creatures. But hearing the good times echoing down the poorest stretches of downtown L.A., he stood and, fighting decades of corrosion, heaved the window open. A rush of the final coolness of a fading winter came rushing in accompanied by the magnified sounds of celebration.

He returned to his book but soon his eyes began to droop and his mind wandered from the pages of the novel to possibilities and plans of tomorrow, of things that might occur compared to the probable, the things he wished could be pushed deeply back down, deeper. *Not tonight,* he thought, turning his attention once more to the fiesta across the street.

The party swelled with laughter and banter and proud, boastful statements, the rhythm shifting seamlessly from one hip-hop beat to the next, flowing with the mood of the rooftop partygoers, affecting the cadence of their conversations and the timing of their steps and swigs and howls. The volume escalated, gathering momentum and crashing upon itself only to rise again, its force pushing outward into the night against the backdrop of tents and tenements and cement walls, passed an old window on the fourth floor where he stared off and smiled and forgot about the maybes and what-ifs for a while.

CHAPTER IV

CHINA

By the third date -- dinner prepared at Remy's by Remy, a basic dish of sauce and pasta -- he was beginning to lose interest. He had done his bit to show that she intrigued him, touching her lightly upon the arm during a shared laugh over a minor joke, maintaining eye contact during a shared moment. She had left his home three times without reciprocating, but neither flinching away nor making the moment uncomfortable. She was a tough read. Remy wasn't sure what to make of her. He'd learned little more than her name was Ni Meng Hu and she preferred to be called Monica in the two weeks spent dating her. He didn't ask for a fourth date, though remarks from his colleague Scott in the office they shared expressing interest in her availability did prick his attention. He didn't like that idea at all. Nor was he eager to jump back to a woman so aloof.

She broke the tie and brought up the fourth date. "When you want watch video?" she asked him between classes, a hallway full of Chinese high-school students flowing around them. An older boy, Remy's size, was wrestling rather one-sidedly with one of his mates as a handful of younger students circled and jeered and laughed. He took a moment to absorb the incident peripherally and quickly deduced that all was on the up and up, the wrestling in good nature and mutually desired. *Boys that age are like teething puppies*, he reminded himself. *No cause for concern, no need to play stick-in-the-mud and break it up.* Her stance showed the slightest tell of impatience: left foot out and pointed his way while leaning way back. Venturing into his vicinity while simultaneously backing away. *I'm right here, but I'll soon be leaving,* her posture spoke. She was a piece of work.

"The one with the Monkey King?" he replied, returning his attention to her. "Not too sure when we can work out the time." He had recently begun a correspondence with a manager of a local bar, a good-looking, full-chested lass who hinted of cheap stiff drinks and decent conversation. He planned on visiting her establishment again after work.

She sensed the lack of enthusiasm and moved closer. "No, my dance video. Video of my," she paused thinking of the English word, "performance. In university."

Remy responded eagerly, enjoying the idea of both an artistic showing as well as to see her leap about, beautiful as she was. "Really? You said it would take time for your father to send it." She smiled prettily and provided no explanation. "Well, that is good news but I made arrangements with Scott. We'll spend some time at my place after work today." A pause and then, "But I bet he would love to watch your performance, as well. He may be keen on you, you know."

She smiled knowingly through a veil of ignorance. "Let me know, okay?" Remy nodded and she slipped away. Watching her go, he realized how easily it had been for her to reel him back in. *That one will be trouble,* he warned himself, promptly disregarding the warning as he returned to his classroom and prepared to teach a lesson designed to increase vocabulary.

Hours later, Scott, Monica and Remy sat about Remy's living room. Scott poured a third round of red wine while Monica sipped on her first, mostly untouched. Remy encouraged her to drink more, hoping to glean some insight into what lay hidden beneath the surface, but eventually gave it up and returned to commenting on the dance performance which was all in all quite competent. Few mistakes were made and for the most part the players whirled and pounced in unison. Alternating between complimenting her execution of dance and conversing with Scott about California, Remy slipped into a comfortable buzz.

She listened attentively to the conversation but interjected nothing, speaking only in response to questioning, often answering open-ended questions with one or two word replies. He found her lack of enthusiasm about her own performance a bit disheartening. She didn't seem to care if anyone approved of or disliked the routine, accepting soft criticisms and uplifting compliments with equal detachment. He wasn't sure what to make of all that but he was growing certain that no romance would develop. Their eyes met during a lull in the activities and she made a point of breaking contact to look down at her watch, making a show of it.

"You should probably just go."

"What?" she answered, a hint of anger accenting the tone and wrinkling the smooth contours of her sharp face.

"*Feng shui* states that if someone is looking at the time than they really should just leave. That's why it's recommend to hang clocks above doorways. You're checking the time because you're thinking about departing."

She nodded knowingly, suddenly engaged, "That interesting. I not know that. But you should keep gold in kitchen. Gold in kitchen is good energy."

"I thought that was brass," Remy stated. "I'm not into precious metals. Much ado about nothing, really. Gold is weak; silver needs polishing or it tarnishes. Never cared for jewelry much."

He'd noticed that she wore only one simple band on her left middle finger, white gold or platinum by the look of it, and never wore necklaces, bracelets, or other trinkets. He liked this about her, that she kept the focus on her features rather than her trinkets. He was expecting a grin and an outpouring of agreement with a fellow comrade and indeed it seemed like she had something to say but the words that played on her tongue remained unspoken. Instead, she gave only the slightest of nods. The coyness was excruciating and he had had enough of it. He returned his attention to Scott and easily coaxed another southern Californian tale from his memories. She interrupted mid-story.

"I wonder if I can do split still," she stated loudly.

"Only one way to know for sure," Scott added eagerly, instantly abandoning the anecdote.

And then all at once she stood, taking a deep quiet breath and mastering her environment. She swept the coffee table off to the side briskly, displaying upper body strength Remy had overlooked. Then, without an inkling of stretching, she hurled herself onto the living room floor, left leg forward, right leg back, groin hovering just an inch above the linoleum. She held herself there for a moment before gracefully pushing herself up and back to standing. Remy applauded, impressed with the feat. He decided he would make his move that night after Scott left. If she was into him, great, if not, he would focus his attentions on the bar manager with the ample bosom. A win-win.

She is a bit self-absorbed, though. Doesn't contribute to conversation much. Introverted? Or is it a language barrier issue? Or is it something else? he pondered as he closed the door on the smiling face of Scott.

Buzzed, Remy proceeded to woo and court Monica, drenching the conversation in compliments and appreciations. Leaning ever closer as the evening progressed, gentle touches melded into loose holding of one another and lingering caresses. Face to face with noses almost touching, his face glided forward to steal a kiss. She spoke, breaking the spell, apparently able to hold a conversation after all.

"Do you have girlfriend?"

"What?" he asked, off-balance, the kiss lost.

"Do you have girlfriend?" she repeated, holding onto his forearm and leaning away, keeping both a connection and a distance, a familiar enough ploy that he was coming to know well. A stern demeanor softened into a smile as she observed his dumbfounded features change from shocked to contemplative to presentational.

"A girlfriend," inflecting the statement somewhere between a ponderance and a question, "Why on Earth would you think that? Only I live here. There's no trace of a woman's presence, except of course for you. You don't mean the teacher who guided me about on the day when we met, do you?"

"No, not her. She is, what word?" a pause while she searched her mind for the proper word, bringing the flow of conversation back to her own tempo. "Engaged," she finished.

Remy had always enjoyed a match of wits. *Good. We're moving away from the girlfriend issue*, he thought reassuringly. He shifted his weight back to look upon her full form, creating a little distance. "She didn't act very engaged around me. I thought she was projecting singleness my way. You're not jealous of her, are you?" *The trail should be well lost by now*, he thought with satisfaction.

"I no understand," she stated flatly, exuding confidence in a statement that most certainly should not have inspired such a smug demeanor as the one Remy took in at arm's length across the cushions of his sofa. His puzzlement manifested in a half-smile that played across his lips as he put the issue on the backburner and focused on courting procedures. *Relax and praise the lass. Make her comfortable,* he instructed himself inwardly. He stood and strolled to the kitchen to pour water for the two of them.

"But what I want to ask is if it is girlfriend or wife now?" she asked, undeterred. *She's like a bloodhound on a scent,* he thought, grimacing out of sight as he pulled open a cabinet door. She pressed the attack. "Have you wife?" she called out from the living room.

"A wife! Heavens, no!" chuckling uncomfortably, "No, nothing like that. Came close once or twice, but I'm single. Very single. See? No ring on the finger." He darted into view and held his hands up, waving his fingers in a flutter, "I'm available, if the right woman crosses my path."

"A girlfriend?" she asked doggedly. "You have girlfriend?"

"Ah, well, what is a girlfriend really? A girl that is a friend? Yes, I have some of those." He was losing and knew it, his voice strained with defeat as ice cubes clattered into glasses.

"Some of *those*?!" she exclaimed, shooting up and storming into the kitchen. He stood still, a glass of ice water in each hand. She was all fire and cuteness as she spun about and began marching off for the front door. Remy jogged past and semi-blocked the exit, wielding puppy dog eyes, showing that leaving would hurt him. She paused, affected by such a display. Not knowing what else to do with the awkward silence, he reflected on the back of the hallway that led to bedrooms. "I really should hang up some paintings or something back there. It needs decorating." She cocked her head quizzically and softened. He set down the glasses, took her hand delicately into his own and led her to the kitchen table. They sat on firm, wooden chairs with high, intricately carved backs bathed in bright light.

"I think that we've misunderstood each other. Let me be clear, I have no lover here."

"What about America?" she questioned, "Or in other place?"

Wow, she does not give up, he thought and then voiced, "No lover in the U.S. No lover in Japan. It's just you and me here. Isn't that enough?" he asked, taking her hand again, caressing the back with his thumb, feeling her relax and relaxing himself. They sat that way in comfortable silence for a while, relaxing in stiff chairs bathed in the electric glow of an old chandelier with too many shining bulbs. He brokered the silence, "This feels like the sun shining above us." The mood lightening. "Seriously, it feels like a summer day in my kitchen. I should take some bulbs out of that thing."

"And put something on wall back there," she reminded him.

His eyes sparkled with this rejoinder, at her use of his words reflected back upon him. They leaned effortlessly into one another's parting lips, kissing for the first time, feeling as comfortable as if they had rehearsed it years prior, and yet, with an intensity of a hunger unsatisfied. They tasted each other, wrapped around one another, completely absorbed into the other, and then back again to the reality of two people sitting around a kitchen table.

"Ah yes, back there indeed. There's something I very much want to show you back there in my room."

"What is it?" she asked coyly.

He laughed, "It's best that I just show you, better experienced than talked about." He took her hand and led her down the dark corridor leading to the bedroom, a hallway lacking paintings or photos or mirrors, the entire apartment quite bare. Halfway down the corridor she spoke again.

"So, it is no girlfriend anywhere?"

Ah, that is the million dollar question, he thought. Nowhere else to turn, the elusive fox finally cornered, he turned to face the hounds and huntsmen, a twenty-something Chinese dancer/teacher/principal's assistant. "I have a girlfriend in Chengdu, a city to the west where I lived for the past two years." Knowing this declaration would darken spirits, he followed through with an uplifting distraction without the slightest of delays, "Do you know Chengdu?" knowing she must, "The city with the pandas? Its famous for cultivating pandas, the cutest of all bears. Wait. Are they bears?"

She smiled thinly, halting in her tracks. Remy gave a slight nod and returned to the living room chin down, eyes down, Monica's hand held as if presenting a duchess to royalty, guiding her back to a comfortable seat in the living room. She accepted these movements with refinement, situated herself and posed a question.

"And you are love her?"

"Hard to say, Moni. I want it to work but she must remain in Chengdu another year to complete her university classes. I hope she'll marry me when that's through, but one year is a long time to live apart so we agreed on this, to see others and hopefully return to each other in a year's time. That must sound odd. It's an odd thing to do among my people. Probably odd for Chinese as well."

He looked into eyes that were not as shattered as he imagined they would be. Somehow, for some reason, she was going to stay the evening with him. He could feel it. "You told truth," she stated. "At difficult time. What her name?"

"Daisy. Her name is Daisy. Actually, Xue Ting is her true name. It means The Rain Stops. It was raining while her mother was delivering her. As she emerged, the rain stopped. So, that's her name."

"And does Xue Ting know about me?"

"She will. I'll tell her. I don't lie and we agreed on this sort of thing ahead of time."

"Then let's go back your room. You say have something show me?"

"Right," he agreed clumsily, caught off guard at the abrupt shift. *Who is this woman?* he wondered again as they walked arm in arm toward the back of the flat.

CHAPTER V

USA

After a few months of battling bedbugs throughout the night and apartment managers that had intentionally ruined his wash for kicks, Remy moved out of the efficiency apartment and back into the rotation of homeless shelters and public storage units of Skid Row. Paying five hundred dollars a month for an infested room he was unable to sleep was repulsive.

The weekdays bled into one another until the weekend arrived and brought with it a flood of poor and downtrodden lining up in various cues throughout Skid Row. The weekends were the busiest time for the destitute. It was during the weekends that those with means and a compassionate heart ventured into the slums of downtown L.A. to hand out clothing, food, toiletries, and such. The impoverished often found themselves in a much worse state on the weekends: eviction notices expired, Friday layoffs, family members' generosity worn thin throughout the week. The reasons were vast and varied.

Most waited patiently, though some scourges walked up and brazenly cut to the head of the line, melding with those who didn't argue against the injustice. Observing bullies bully had always rubbed Remy the wrong way, often times resulting in getting himself imbedded into dangerous situations. He was no stranger to such things. Some days he commented. Some days he let it go. That day, after waiting fifty minutes in a line more than a block long, Remy was just too tired to instill justice. He issued stern looks and little else and was eventually fed a decent meal free of charge. With a monthly salary totaling less than a thousand dollars, he was forced into these lines often, though technically housed and employed.

A tall, lean, muscular black man locked eyes with him as he exited the Row, headed north to coffee shops in the nicer parts of the downtown area. "What's up?" he questioned with a sharp upward nod. Remy reciprocated the gesture in passing.

"Not much. Another day."

The man brightened, apparently recognizing him though Remy couldn't place the face. "Cool Breeze, my man," the man called out, the words pouring over Remy like warm sunlight on a prisoner.

He pivoted, keeping stride while walking backward, their smiles meeting and playing out on the sunlit stretch of pavement dividing them. An arm raised, an open hand saluting friendship, returned by the other. The smile unwavering as a few blocks came and went. On the fourth, an older, bald man approached from the south, a thin gold chain of dubious quality and ownership dangling from his hand.

"Brand new. Cheap," he spoke in a hushed voice as Remy moved within earshot.

"Not my thing. I don't do jewelry."

"Broke ass cracker," he retorted, frustrated with his inability to fence stolen goods, angry at the *man*, the faceless entities forcing him to such ends.

"Oh, that's nice," Remy replied sardonically, laughing bitterly as the transgressor's sentiment oozed onto the pleasantries of the day. He pivoted again and walked backward, watching the middle-aged man zig-zag down the sidewalk, approaching the next set of pedestrians. He resisted the urge to attack his exposed back, put a foot through the back of his left leg at the knee, forcing an abrupt kneel and then deliver an inescapable hold of the man's throat, forcing a complete lack of blood flow to the brain that would bring swift unconsciousness. He knew that often such low lives carried knives so he slowed his steps to remain stealthy as he began to creep up silently behind the man.

His would be in his right pocket, being right-handed, he deduced, studying the man as he approached. *I should target the back of his left leg, that's the best choice. Keep the right free for a knife pull, hope for it, in fact, so that I can disarm immediately, dislocating shoulder and wrist through a firm grip and unkind rotation. A further stomp through an arm held taut at the elbow if desired, the bone cracking free from cartilage. He* smiled at the thought, enjoying the idea of removing filth from his streets.

He continued approaching at a slow and steady pace, maintaining a position directly behind the zig-zagging traveling merchant of stolen goods. His pulse began to slow. His eyes darting into the nooks and crannies of the impoverished environment, searching for hazards or cameras or witnesses as he approached his prey. Those on the sidewalks were tending to themselves, in their own tents, huddled in their own groups: smoking, joking, imbibing. No one would miss this guy. A wave of guilt washed over him and there was a release of the stinging pride that had been nipping at his heels like spoiled terriers.

Abruptly, he doubled back, turning his back on the trash and resuming his stride northward from Skid Row to central downtown. *I'll deal with him if I see him again,* he thought with finality. The clouds continued their lazy drifting overhead, spilling light on the scene: a fencer peddling wares; a mother with stroller refusing a purchase; two men speaking animatedly into their phones on intersecting paths, looking up at the last moment, dodging around the other and then back to their conversations; an older lady pushing a cart of tethered personal items asking the world loudly in an irritated voice, "Why can't they see what's happening?"

But Remy did see, was well aware of what was happening. He smiled pleasantly at the unsound woman in need of counseling that she would likely never receive and, remembering a pleasant tune, began to whistle down the street.

CHAPTER VI

CHINA

Monica moved in shortly thereafter and from that night on Remy thought of her, the mystery of her, and knew he needed her close. At first, he told himself this was purely an academic attempt to delve deeper into this mind that fenced with his, finding her mark more often than he was accustomed to. *Besides,* he thought taking in her sleeping form, *she's gorgeous.* She'd turned over in the night exposing her back which seemed to glow in the dim moonlight. A mane of fine wavy curls extended to her shoulder blades. The bedsheet draped loosely across her lower waist. Remy slid his arm under the sheet and across the smooth skin of her hip, continuing upward, gliding across a soft flat stomach. Fingers danced, frolicking on the stage of her body, caressing, embracing, and eventually lying still and warm. He drifted off to sleep without a care in the world.

He loved her. He felt it then as sleep found him smiling absently, enraptured with this gift life had delivered. While he wished Daisy well and would've been happy to share a life with her - kids, in-laws, the whole deal - Monica had changed the whole equation. He'd been given a gift with Daisy, a fair and fine future, but Monica, Monica was a hint of something deeper, a curiosity unexplored, a contentment immovable.

She came piecemeal: a backpack full of toiletries and a change of clothes here, a duffle bag loosely packed there. Within a month, she had repositioned most of the contents of her life into his flat. When he realized this one evening as they lay together hand in hand on a sofa watching a documentary, he smiled and laughed aloud.

"What are you laugh at?" she questioned, and rightfully so, the piece was on the failings of the American education system and didn't warrant laughter.

He turned to her, looking into eyes he found more relaxing than his own reflection, more inspiring than the finest of paintings. "You," he answered.

"Me?" she paused, contemplating, face scrooching up menacingly. "You laugh at my English?"

"No," He looked upon her, joy filling his eyes, his smile. "I'm laughing at your face," knowing this would elicit a reaction, too timid to tell her how much she meant, that she could cause him to laugh for no reason in the midst of a depressing documentary.

"What wrong with my face?" she asked, pouting cutely.

Remy's laughter intensified. "Nothing. Nothing at all," a pause and then, "I love you." It was the first time he'd voiced the feeling that erupted forth from him every time he thought, saw, smelt, touched or remembered her. Bashfully, he looked away after the statement took hold.

She sat and absorbed his words. She didn't respond immediately and for those moments he thought she may flee, might pack her bags and disappear into the night. "I love you, too," she reciprocated.

And so it began.

CHAPTER VII

CHINA

Remy and Daisy kept in touch, calling each other periodically to keep up with current events. A karaoke night here, a friend's engagement party there. In the beginning, he fielded these calls every evening, then every other, eventually fading in frequency to just twice a week as Monica became a more permanent fixture in his life. He would adjoin to the balcony of his flat or take a stroll in order to keep a distance between these two women in his life. True to his word, he told Daisy of Monica, in the beginning adding that the relationship would be temporary, reassuring her of his desire to marry her once college was completed but the certainty of this statement began ebbing the more time he spent with Monica until finally it simply fell flat and felt incorrect.

"Things are becoming more serious with Monica," he began after a weekly update. Daisy had begun her internship and was working part-time as an office worker, something to do with exporting car parts and English translation in Shanghai. "I care for you a great deal. I... I don't know," at a loss, struggling to release the right words. "I think that my idea of seeing other people while we waited this year was wrong. This didn't work out like I imagined it would."

Silence. The seconds rained down upon him like a boxer's blows. "Hello?" he called out into the void.

"It's good, Rem. I'm glad you're happy," breaking the silence gently in her distinctive high-pitched, girly voice. There was an emptiness to it, though. A distance.

"Oh, that's not good. Not good at all. That's what people say when they're hurt, Daze. I hurt you just now. This whole thing is hurting you. I f^%#ed up. Look, I'm sorry. I...," he trailed off, unsure of how to move forward, hating himself for hurting her.

"It's okay. It's okay, Rem," repeating herself as people do in these situations. "I have to go now, okay? I need to go."

"I'm so sorry, Daisy. Can I do something for you? Can I help you in any way? I feel awful. I need to do something for you. You don't deserve any of this."

"It's really fine, Rem. I just need to go now."

"Alright, but don't be a stranger. You're a terrific person and I don't want to be short one terrific person from my life. I'm going to call you tomorrow, alright?"

He could hear her smile faintly on the other end. "If you want to."

"I do. I definitely do. Let's make this a smooth transition. I want to be in your life, give you a hand moving one day, or have a drink and catch up on old times. Don't just fade away on me."

"You don't need to feel guilty."

"I do. I am. But everything I just said is true. I'll call you tomorrow. Bye."

He stared at his phone for a while, not realizing that he was lost in thought, memories of that cute, perpetually happy little fireball, Daisy, dancing about. The girl that literally jumped into his arms squealing during an outing one Halloween night. A woman who ran from frogs. A young lady who pouted in the most theatrical manner, bottom lip extended, cheeks full and rosy, eyes on the verge of scorn. A pout that had a way of bringing him to an immediate, smiling surrender. The woman that brought him into her family's home, a flat the size of Remy's, only worn and cozy. She played the role of translator gracefully and without complaint as her mother scooped endless portions of Sichuan dishes onto his plate. Later that night, her uncle drank strong rice wine with him shot for shot, congratulating Remy on his ability to hold his liquor while trouncing him repeatedly in Chinese chess. They stumbled down the sidewalk later that night as they returned to his hotel room, her arm wrapped in his, hands entwined, a happy couple grinning ear to ear. "I want to marry you, Daisy," he had announced, turning abruptly, holding her firmly and close, kissing her deeply, demonstrating his love.

"I want to marry you, too, Rem. My uncle really like you," she spoke, detaching. Her father had been away, captaining a ship of some sort, the details unclear. In his stead, his brother, Daisy's uncle, had manned the position of father figure. Just one step away in a culture in which the father's approval of his daughter's husband was absolutely necessary. "But I need to finish university first."

A sharp pain emerged, pulling him away from the world of memory and back to the present. Glancing at the source, he found a fat mosquito lackadaisically siphoning blood from his calf. Flattening the creature beneath his palm, he spied two other raised welts around the blood splatter. He straightened, memories of the near past dissipating as heavy, slow steps carried him home.

CHAPTER VIII

USA

His paced slowed to an eventual stop as he entered the beginnings of a dinner line outside of the mission on Sixth and St. Pedro. Some thirty people stood placidly in the hot shade ahead of him, waiting for charity. The line ahead had doubled in size in fifteen minutes while the line behind him had grown five times longer. A young, black thug walked brazenly to the head of the stable queue, inserting himself to groans of dismay. "Hey man, the line starts back here," a bedraggled man shouted somewhere behind Remy. "F^$% you and f$#* your line, ni*^%#!" the transgressor barked. "Clever rejoinder," Remy mumbled. He gave an abnormal amount of thought to repeating this louder to provoke the man, hating that the bad guy dominated the incident. He eyed the line-cutter as the thug waved over a chubby woman, presumably his girlfriend. Her potbelly stuck out from jean shorts that didn't cover what they should in any direction. A sleeveless red shirt, past its prime in the late eighties, dripped from her bony shoulders. The line-cutter wore a massive, white t-shirt that draped to his thighs and bore the face of a murdered rap star. His eyes gleamed with satisfaction, his posture upright and relaxed, hips out, pleased with himself for stealing away position in line. Remy imagined the conversation: *I just told him f%#* you. It's my line, baby. These are my streets.* Disgusted, he turned away, glancing back at a line that extended to the edge of the block and around the street toward Seventh Avenue.

Fifteen minutes later, a tall, shirtless fifty-something crossed Sixth Street, stepping off of the curb and into the street, into a rush of oncoming traffic, forcing a garbage truck and a construction truck to brake suddenly. The shirtless fool waved his arms wildly and laughed at a joke that apparently some others in line nearby Remy understood. Cackles ensued around Remy who stood staring at the near-miss collision disappointedly. *I will have to share a shower and sleep next to that man later,* he mulled. Two younger downtrodden men sat next to two fifty-somethings, a middle-aged couple chatting in drunken slurs about a man named Lil' Mikey and how when they had first met, he had asked if he had a pet monkey, but no, no, he did not. The story repeated itself for ten minutes or so in an incomprehensible dialogue among the four that emphasized the word *monkey* often, which never failed to please the quartet.

"Suckers, any one you want. Twenty-five cents," cried a man peddling past, dreadlocks tightly braided into neat rows atop his head. A clean, laundered white jersey fit properly over red denim shorts. No one in the proximity bothered to say anything, looking slowly to the open bag of pops, to the bicycling merchant's face and then away into nothingness. It was too hot to waste words. The man peddled away slowly and was soon out of sight.

General shouts of displeasure mixed with the din of an old, white Ford pick-up truck stranded on the side of the road, its owner failing to turn the engine over, pistons clacking uselessly. As the driver struggled, the gates to the mission finally opened and the hungry scampered in. The thugs that crowded the head of the line pushed heedlessly through. The line stopped, moved forward, stopped again. A short, fat woman, ball-like in appearance, pressed in behind him. "I haven't been in no line. I haven't ate. I just wanna throw this away," she motioned to a cup of yogurt, foil jutting out, yogurt oozing out from over the lip. Remy hugged the wall, allowing her room to pass. "Excuse me," an older, well-dressed gentleman rushed forward, walking briskly to the middle of the line ahead and cutting. "Old man shouldn't cut!" a lady called out. Remy nodded, finding even that exhausting.

Thirty minutes later, a Latina Remy's age shuffled in hauling two trash bags filled with old clothes and two containing various recyclables. A man nearby perked up, his posture straightening, joy brimming over as he proceeded to relieve her of her burden. "Can I get that for you?" he asked pleasantly. She didn't respond and at first Remy took her glazed eyes and slack expression to be a product of the heat or of drug abuse, but looking deeper into the dispassionate face, he found a stroke victim. She entered the lunch line on clumsy, heavy legs while the man doted and cared for her, asking questions about her day that remained unanswered. He was used to this, his smile uncompromised. He grabbed her tightly from behind and hugged her, whispering just loudly enough for Remy to make out the words, "I love you" through the commotion.

The line continued to press onward, a trickle at a time, as it wrapped its way around the tightly packed dining hall. Remy placed his closed fist at the base of his nose, diminishing air intake into overworked nasal passages, a trick of the senses developed to maintain his appetite. He focused on timing the last man working on the food service line, an older sixty-something, as he deposited a drink and napkin-wrapped plastic fork onto each tray. *One, two, three, four, five, six.... five, six, seven, eight, nine... six, seven, eight nine, ten. About eight seconds each,* he reasoned. Multiplying this by the thirty-five people ahead, he calculated a five-minute wait unless the old man dishing out food was to stop for some reason, which he soon did in order to chat with a regular in the queue.

"Thank you," Remy muttered later, mostly out of duty and not feeling particularly grateful. He took his tray to a seat next to a large woman in a wheelchair at the end of a long table, who gobbled down old salad voraciously, as if it might be lost to her forever if she delayed. A lithe, short man spoke loudly to himself in a singsong manner, a random bunch of words that had the good fortune of rhyming. Remy pegged him for a non-medicated schizophrenic and kept a weary eye on him as he suddenly rose and bounded into the seat directly across from him. "Hot sauce?" he offered, glee shining forth from all the angles of his radiant face. Before Remy could answer, the man began drowning his own meal -- shredded chicken in gravy that looked suspiciously like wet cat food over rice -- with the stuff. Remy took the bottle afterward and drizzled a bit atop the meal. "*Gracias,*" he said through a forced smile. "You're welcome," the man beamed back. Remy took a tentative portion into his mouth and began coughing violently, overcome by the spice. "Wakes you up, don't it?!" the man laughed as Remy guzzled the contents of his milk carton before desperately searching the neighboring table for more to drink. Teary-eyed and burning, he froze, realizing that half of the table had stopped eating and was enjoying the show. Accepting the absurdity of the situation, he began chuckling to himself and for a little while, everything was okay again.

CHAPTER IX

CHINA

The front door closed more abruptly behind him than he'd intended, startling him back to his senses. He looked about, ready to apologize for disturbing her at a late hour, but she was no longer in the living room. He listened for the sounds of her tapping away on a keyboard in the computer room or of water draining in the shower. He strained his ears, listening intently to a completely empty flat. On the coffee table, he discovered a handwritten note:

Dear Remy, it began. *Office call me back. I want waiting you but I no keep director waiting. Don't waiting me. I sleep in dorm room tonight.*

--- Monica

His eyes turned upward to a plain white clock the size of a dinner plate set onto the beigest of walls. *God, this place needs some character*, he thought absently reading the time: 10:25. *Ten twenty-five? I haven't been gone an hour. No one worked that late in Chengdu*, he thought, remembering the assistants' comings and goings of the school he worked at a year prior, how they would scramble for the office door, key in hand, a minute prior to five. *That's way too late for office work*, he thought, puzzling out the oddity. Possibilities swam through his open mind: an important document misplaced; a frantic mother calling about an ill or injured student; a student unaccounted for during attendance at bed count before sleep; preparations for an important visitor to the school. Remy would hear all of these and more in time, one rarely duplicating the other, but on that cool early autumn night, they were of his own making, his own imaginings of what could have been.

Closing the refrigerator door with a cool beer in hand, he stood and drank in the darkness of his flat, the outside world gradually emerging into view as his vision adjusted. Four stories below, a quiet street void of both cars and pedestrians separated his apartment from the high school. It spread out below him cloaked in the blackness of night save for one lone window on the third floor glowing brightly.

The top floor of the secondary school, the entire third floor, was the realm of the directors, principals, and vice-principals, the *higher-ups* as Remy called them, named for the physical location they inhabited as well as their social position in the school's hierarchy. Some occasionally arrived a few minutes before the first bell of the school day rang, but more often than not it was well into the first period, or even during the second, before a higher-up straggled in and began delivering morning announcements. The majority of the elite bunch arrived a touch before lunch or even afterward, sometimes missing days at a time.

The higher-ups consisted of some twenty individuals all told: a mix of mostly investors who funded the construction of the school and continued funding its operations, a handful of former teachers who worked their way up the ladder, and a handful of government-appointed communist party representatives whose job it was to ensure the party's interests were being handed down to the future generation.

The investors had no formal training in education management or pedagogy. The party representatives seemed to have had some training in scholastic management but little or nothing in the realm of actual teaching experience, their role being that of overseer, making certain that the teachers didn't lead the younglings astray with wild ideas. All of the foreign staff had been told stories in hushed voices of the fate of those who had failed to abide by the Rule of the Three T's. Teaching of, mentioning, or allowing students to study or ask without reprimand of Tiananmen Square, Tibet, or Taiwan was grounds for immediate dismissal without pension for Chinese instructors, and immediate deportation for any foreign staff. Remy utilized English textbooks in which every copy, teacher and student alike, had pages 41-44 sliced out neatly from the spine. Doing a bit of research online, he discovered these pages involved an excerpt from an interview with the Dali Lama, an excerpt that contained nothing whatsoever regarding China or Tibet. The removed pages were almost immediately the most popular aspect of the new course, the censorship having had the exact opposite effect as intended. A perfect example of irony. He dropped hints into the lessons and gently prodded student conversations after class toward the truth with an arsenal of kind eyes, nods, winks, shakes, coughs, and chuckles.

The select few higher-ups that worked their way up from teaching to the third-floor were the nearest of the clique to competency, experienced in leading classrooms and usually still part of the day-to-day operations of the school. They were also the least numerous and least powerful. Furthermore, the majority of this division of the higher-ups hadn't really worked their way up so much as flattered and praised their bosses more than their colleagues and ultimately were simply implementers of the investors' and government officials' will, contributing little or nothing to policy-making decisions. Yes-men and little more. The least experienced, the least knowledgeable in the field of education, made the vast majority of the decisions.

A very thin line separated investor from government representative. Only the very wealthy held the capital necessary to invest in schools such as those which existed all throughout China and it was that same wealth that bound them inextricably to the communist party, the only party, the government a conglomeration of the wealthiest citizens and the spokesmen they purchased to represent them in the oligarchy of the People's Republic of China. A common theme found throughout most governments the world over. America being no exception to this cold truth.

Such was the way of the third floor of Jiangxi Attached Middle School in Nanchang, China and of all the figurative third floors of upper-level private Chinese schools. But of all the third floors in China, Remy was concerned with only one that night. He opened his kitchen window and looked out across the silent road to that solely glowing window, slowly drinking his beer in silence, listening intently to the sounds of the night, straining for a clue, staring off, lost in thought. So began his ultimately very costly new hobby: sleuthing.

CHAPTER X

USA

"One lonely Sheriff," he said motioning to a pack of the cheapest of cigarettes, handing a pleasantly plump African-American lady a dollar bill. Remy removed the smoke on his own from the pack she opened. She handed him back three quarters as they exchanged a smile.

He strolled a little farther down the sidewalk, deeper into Skid Row, searching for a stiff drink. A sidewalk merchant looked up at his arrival. "How much is that E & J?" he asked the man, motioning to a tiny bottle the same size as the ones doled out by airline attendants. "A dollar?" he added hopefully.

"Two dollars."

"Brings me back to my high school days. Erk and Jerk," he reminisced aloud, stretching for time while he mulled over the price.

They all sort of nodded together in the shared knowledge of the nickname to the brandy, dubbed for the response of the body after downing a shot. Remy crouched to one knee on the sidewalk, the early evening sluggish, most of the inhabitants bedding down, preparing to sleep. The air was cool and still.

"Where did you go to school?" the man asked.

"Over in Florida. Central Florida. Orlando. Class of '96."

"You're a young man, then. Florida, huh," replied the merchant openly.

"Yeah. Can't be much younger than you, though. We look the same age. Thirties, forties. Something like that."

"Let me ask you something. What brings you out here?"

Remy looked around before conjuring a truth that avoided the sharp sting of memory. "L.A. seems to have a decent homeless scene and I burned through all of my money. Work hasn't been easy to find. Decent work I should say. But it's kind of nice out here really. The hustle and bustle of city life. I dig it."

"I don't know about that," the man said.

Remy let that hang rather than disagree. "One seventy-five for the Erk and Jerk?"

"Yeah, I can do that," the merchant turned to another man approaching. "At least this motherf&$^%r's got some money, not trying to borrow everything on credit." Chuckles all around from a crowd that knew an inside joke when they heard one, Remy slightly uncomfortable at the praise. He placed the money into a clean cardboard box that served as a do-it-yourself cash register and retrieved a tiny plastic bottle from something akin to a shelf. Cracking the lid, he crouched once more, checking his peripheral, downing the shot after a car passed. The flavor danced down, a sour spike that snaked its way to his stomach. He shook his head tightly back and forth, similar to the motion of a dog drying off from a drenching, as newly thinned blood began rushing throughout his circulatory system.

"Brings back those high school memories, don't it?" the merchant asked cheerfully. Remy nodded and gave one more shake to clear his head before walking off. Two blocks later, he passed new sidewalk occupants having gathered on the street to socialize.

"I know you don't feel well, that's why I'm talking to you motherf*%^$r!" hysterical laughter all around.

"Nebuchadnezzar blasphemed and for blaspheming he was turned into a beast, into an animal." A middle-aged man preparing for church the following day, spoke passionately with his own group.

"You better wash that shit! Wash it! Don't you make me..." a woman yelled across San Pedro, furious and unable to finish the sentence. A couple strolling toward Remy arm in arm, shoulder to shoulder, turned to each other. "Do you know her?" He asked his partner, referring to the screaming woman. "No," she replied calmly as they continued their stroll.

More dialogues of the city streets washed over him as he walked on, enjoying the warming temperatures spring had brought, feeling more rejuvenated with each passing day. He was acclimating to America, albeit in absolute squalor.

He returned to his spartan cell on another day in the late afternoon, walking uncharacteristically briskly as opposed to his usual slow and steady pace. He maneuvered through Skid Row crowds with an ease that came from having learned to negotiate the confines of tightly-packed Tokyo, having mastered the art of striding through sidewalks as densely populated as a rock concert without brushing shoulders or trampling on toes.

He glided past a young man engaged in an adamant conversation, arms waving about, timing the steps and positioning himself correctly through the swings, passing him smoothly, well out of range of his movements and directly into the course of a fist headed straight for his nose. Remy ducked the oncoming arc, pivoted and raised his arms up in the typical pose of those being robbed or commanded by police at gunpoint, the initial stance of the *Wind* style of ninjutsu, the surrender pose.

"Whoa!" he uttered, as much a command as an exclamation. His eyes darted around the area, a congested bit of sidewalk where a dozen African-American males, mostly twenty-somethings, now circled, making a clearing around Remy and a muscular middle-aged black man who was clearly psychologically troubled. Flitting eye contact and wide dilation of pupil indicated a drug-fueled high. Two of the larger males on the outskirts of the ring began jeering something antagonistic. Remy assessed he could overcome his opponent without resorting to permanently damaging him. The larger, younger black males that had formed a ring jeering and encouraging a fight were another story completely. The situation warranted alarm but for an unexplainable reason, Remy felt things would end well. Was certain of it, actually. He didn't take a deep breath to steady his heart and mind. He didn't need to. There was no quickening of the heartbeat. No adrenaline. A strange calm overtook him.

"Control your man," Remy stated flatly in an authoritative voice, speaking to the loudest and most animated of the antagonists. He kept his hands up in wind/surrender pose and continued along his way toward the crazed streetfighter who threw his right fist back to deliver another punch. Remy neatly placed his open palm against the man's right shoulder and gave a sharp push, fifty-percent or so, causing the man to stumble back a bit, the form of his potential punch disrupted from shoulder and throwing him off balance. He swung awkwardly, connecting with nothing and stumbling to find his footing again. Using this newly formed opening, Remy continued onward through his opponent's guard and dipped out of the ring in a suddenly different direction, choosing a weak link in the ring that had formed, glad to have broken free of the incident. Slow, easy strides took him back to one of the homeless shelters he frequented.

A week later, another situation arose. Leaving the confines of a local shelter early one morning, he opened the exit door to find a man sitting just outside the exit. A cardboard box turned upside down played its usual role of displaying usual wares. Remy spied cigarettes and approached, intent on a morning smoke.

"One cigarette, please."

The man stood and, looking upon him, Remy sensed something amiss in his eyes: a reluctance to hold eye contact; a firm squinting caused by neither sunshine nor wind; bloodshot whites; a strange darting. He just seemed off.

"I don't have any change. Is a dollar okay?" Remy queried. *In for a penny, in for a pound*, he thought to himself. *I've already begun the transaction and I want a smoke.*

The man nodded, grunting an affirmation as he rose. Remy glanced right and left and noticed no one supporting the man, no one paying any attention at all, in fact. Turning his attention back to the shorter, thinner tobacco merchant he suspected no true danger would be forthcoming. He handed him a dollar bill from his wallet, stooped, and retrieved one cigarette. He rose and waited for seventy-five cents in change. Instead, he received two quarters and a nickel.

"Ah, this is a nickel. It looks a bit like a quarter, both shiny and whatnot, but I need a quarter for this," he stated, holding the nickel up and thrusting it forward. The man smiled elusively, like a man shy on a first date, eyes downcast as he took a step back.

"A quarter," Remy repeated, moving forward until the merchant's back touched the outer wall of the shelter. The man kept his gaze down, eyes tethered to the sidewalk, the dollar locked in his clenched fist.

"Alright, well here is your cigarette back," Remy began, returning to the cardboard box and placing the smoke back in its pack, "And here is the change that you handed me so..."

He was cut off from the conclusion as a dark-skinned man pressed forward through his peripheral vision. Remy side-stepped a bit to face both men, prepared in detached coolness for either a knife attack or a handshake. The three men formed a mistrusting triangle on the early morning sidewalk. The newcomer broke the silence, turned to the salesman and said, "You owe me from yesterday," and with one smooth motion removed two quarters from Remy's open hand and was once more on his way. Remy looked to the merchant who looked even more startled than Remy. He didn't resist as Remy cleanly jerked the dollar bill from his clenched fist. Remy turned and was on his way almost in the same step as the newcomer but moving in the opposite direction.

Behind him, he heard, "Hey! Come back! Stop!" Remy pivoted, walking away backward.

"Learn your math!" Remy called back "I didn't take a cigarette, you had the change, you owed a guy who is now repaid, and I have my dollar back. We're good." The merchant made a move forward on uncertain, jerking feet, defiance in his eyes. Remy stopped, knowing it wiser to continue moving away, wiser still to accelerate his pace, and yet, something in him beckoned him to return to the scene. *He tried to steal from me and he's not a problem physically. Why not?* He eyed him from head to toe, finding chinks in his armor, identifying his opponent's rhythm. A smile played across Remy's face as the short-changing sidewalk merchant began approaching, intent on causing trouble. Remy moved forward to intercept.

It was then that the unexpected happened. Another man, an older black guy, a blur of red shirt, materialized from an unknown niche. This fourth player kept his back to Remy and grabbed the incoming merchant by his shoulders, halting the tobacconist in midstep saying, "He's cool. He's alright." Remy responded to this with a cocked head, clearly puzzled by the interruption. The merchant obeyed this new player and the danger passed as swiftly as it had begun. Remy turned about and headed back, on his way, northward, out of the slums and into the nicer parts of downtown, toward the library and coffee shops. *I narrowly avoided a violent encounter,* he thought to himself, maintaining a quick pace away from the unpleasantness. *At least today.*

CHINA

The rice was overcooked, soft and clumped together in great mounds, accompanied by wedges of eggplant flavored with thin slices of pork, resulting in a palatable dish. Remy pinched a morsel of rice and balanced a wedge of eggplant between two chopsticks with graceful ease attributed to decades using such utensils. He ate slowly, in no rush to consume the dish. He chatted amiably with those that surrounded him, as was his way, speaking slowly with the Chinese, intentionally choosing simple words to describe stories and ask probing questions. The conversations, if he could navigate them out of the bounds of pedagogy and student behavior, were the best part of the school cafeteria experience.

"Sure are a lot of Maos," Remy mumbled loud enough to be heard during a lull in conversation. He flipped through the bills in his wallet. "One hundred. Fifty. Twenty. Ten. Five. I mean the ones and the tenths are different, but it's mostly Mr. Zedong, Mr. Zedong. Over and over."

Half of the group of six or seven Chinese teachers sharing the table with Remy shied away as if the air had suddenly become poisoned. The other half's eyes brightened and they engaged.

"He was great man. Leader of country." A pause as he searched for the correct English. The gentleman shrugged, unable to find what he was searching for in the foreign vocabulary section of his brain. "He make us strong. Alone." His face soured. "No that word. There is better word."

"Yeah, I know. I get it. China stepped up as a world player under his leadership. Doing your own thing. Independence. I'm an American. I get that. Independence is important to us, too."

"That the word. Independent. He made us independent."

"No doubt due to your atomic bomb development in the fifties. But I get it. I would've done the same if I were ruling China. World War II had just ended. Russia and America seemed to be intent on conquering the entire world. You needed to protect yourself. I get it. I don't dislike Mr. Mao. He gets a bum rap in most American history textbooks, but I see the good he did." Remy looked up half-smiling. "I mean, there was some bad, too, though. Political dissidents who mysteriously died, that sort of thing. I mean, no one's perfect, right?"

The first half was hurriedly finishing their meal and preparing to leave. The other half, the engaging half, remained though discomfort showed plainly on their faces. Remy was enjoying the conversation immensely and hoped to prolong it by exposing his own people's weaknesses, to rebalance the conversation.

"George Washington owned slaves. Don't get me started on Andrew Jackson and the Native Americans. Teddy Roosevelt, I love Teddy, but he probably shouldn't have been killing Spaniards in Cuba as a rough rider. I'm just saying people are flawed, you know. Leaders, too."

Another man chimed in proudly, "China no have slaves."

"Yeah, well, that's debatable. Every east Asian nation was forced to pay your empire yearly tribute. Protection money, more like it. Japan. Cambodia and the Khmers. Thailand. Vietnam. The Mongolians. Every year, year after year for a thousand years, they sent jewels and gold and silver and silk and coin or soldier-servants or horses in as tribute under fear of the repercussions if they did not. That's why Japan lashed out at you back in the thirties." There were many fascinated eyes on him. Remy smiled knowingly. "They have long memories, the Japanese. I mean, they should have forgiven and forgotten, but that's a whole other topic."

One man, stammered out, "I, I no heard this."

"Well, it's true. Look it up." Remy looked away, "I mean, if you can look it up. The government blocks quite a few websites. Might be hard to research."

Another man chimed in, one of those who had gobbled down his meal quickly to make an escape, having reengaged in the conversation he thought to flee from. "He is right. That happen. Many years Chinese empire do that."

Another man added, "Mao Zedong end that. He stop old king and queen."

Remy looked to the five men and one woman listening and participating in the conversation. *Their minds are full,* Remy deduced. *This has already been a lot to digest.* He smiled widely, "I appreciate you all speaking with me. Your English is very good and it's nice to discuss interesting things in my language. I don't always get to do that. Can't talk to my students like this. *Xie xie.*" Remy bowed a bit, a Japanese gesture of appreciation and one deeply ingrained in his own mannerisms. The listening party roundly welcomed the thanks he gave.

Remy returned to his wallet. "I just thought I'd see some other Chinese people on the money. Where's Confucius?" The small gathering in the school cafeteria chuckled a bit at this. "Lao Tzu. That was a wise man with a lot to say. But nope, he doesn't even get a coin." The mood had softened, the people relaxed. "I think Jackie Chan should be on the five-yuan bill."

A lady teacher Remy's age spoke fluently in Mandarin. The group broke out laughing.

"What did she say?" Remy asked.

"She say, 'Jackie Chan should be on five-dollar America money. He left. He American now.'" They laughed together, unified, loud enough to draw most of the attention of the cafeteria.

She entered the cafeteria as the laughs cooled into chuckles, adorned with a red ribbon tied into a bow that held her hair back into a ponytail that draped across her right shoulder. He turned to look at her, eyes wide, openly pleased at her arrival. He motioned with his head at an empty seat catty-corner to him. She smiled thinly and turned away, returning to the solitude of waiting in line. He kept her in his peripheral while he distractedly engaged in dialogue with those around him. Monica shifted her weight from side to side as the line progressed. *Antsy,* he thought.

Remy's jovial smile faltered a bit as she sat down at the opposite end of the table. Remy's side consisted of a lively group chit-chatting away; Monica's was vacant. She sat alone and began to eat, intentionally avoiding eye contact. Her posture was that of a ballerina, perfect and poised, head held high as eggplant wedges moved methodically from metal tray to mouth. Remy bid his party farewell and took a seat across from her. She barely glanced his way.

"Hi. I guess you didn't see me there." he began, walking a fine line between truth, lies, and sarcasm.

"Hello," she replied, still looking off to the side.

He traced a path with his index finger following the direction of her gaze, turning around in his seat to see that it led to the ceiling of the adjoining room. He spun around in his plastic chair, tracing her focal point: two rectangular compartments on the ceiling housing long fluorescent bulbs, only one of which glowed. A white, rectangular panel, like all the other panels lining the ceiling of the cafeteria.

"Pretty boring. Are you seeing something I'm not?"

She cracked the beginnings of a smile, caught herself swiftly and placed another bland bite through thin, soft lips that Remy lost himself in.

"Or is this an ancient Chinese thing?" he continued, "If you're meditating, just let me know. I think you're supposed to cross your legs and chant for that though."

"I not meditate," she spoke through a mouth of half-chewed eggplant pulp.

"You just love ceiling panels?"

"What? I no understand you."

Swallowing the mixture, she turned and fixed a cold gaze on him. *She's not even trying to understand me,* he thought. There was no joy in her features. She obviously wasn't enjoying his presence so he left shortly thereafter and returned to the office to grade quizzes taken earlier in the week.

She's likely trying to shield our relationship from the public eye, he thought as he tallied student scores. He was upset by her sudden disappearance the previous night, troubled further by the gothic indifference he'd recently endured in the cafeteria. He felt mistreated and it was with a mischievous heart that he took comfort at the frustration that played across that beautiful face of hers when Remy rejected her offer to speak with him privately later that day and instead retreated to a bar for drinks after work. They did battle, Monica and Remy, right from the start, an intricate game without end, victory perpetually fleeting.

CHAPTER XII

USA

Spring turned to summer, and while the desert heat baked and burnt his skin as he walked miles to and from bus stops and train stations in southern California, he was able to earn some income background acting in various television shows. It was a rewarding experience: being on set with the major studios; outfitted by wardrobe; spruced up by hairstylists and makeup artists; adopting the proper mannerisms per assistant directors' commands. The catering was phenomenal, and being homeless and lacking decent nutrition, Remy found it difficult not to overindulge in freshly-juiced vegetables, goat-cheese croissants, and the like.

Extras were often prepared and then sat off-camera for a few hours, waiting for the stars to deliver lines needed to secure a scene before the background actors would be called in for the following scene. Some extras read from books, mainly books written on developing acting skill. Others read from scripts or spent the time developing their own writing. Most stared into their phones, checking social media for posts by friends and family. Remy spent this time introducing himself, getting to know the others, and generally bringing some sort of cohesion to the group. He learned that he could make a crowd of strangers laugh and made a few fleeting friends.

It was through this crowd that he learned of a small theater off Hollywood Boulevard that was open to showcasing background actors. A week later, he had secured a position in an artistic portrayal of Pink Floyd's *The Dark Side of the Moon* which consisted of one long, interpretive dance as the album played without stop from beginning to end. The forty-five-minute exhibition took on many forms as the songs ebbed and flowed from track to track, and after a month of preparation, he was proud of the performances he and his troop delivered. He learned to play most of the roles over the following couple of months.

After a season, he transitioned into a traditional play of a comical fantasy genre in which various fairytale characters competed with one another over princes and princesses. This role led him to another in a superhero spoof that, while mostly comical in nature, surprisingly turned to darker social elements such as suicide and the hardships of putting the many over the few. He enjoyed his character, a buffoon of a hero named Cpt. Marvelous. Narcissistically blinded to the obvious, he provided many of the laughs of the play and held the distinct role of interacting with the audience. It was a good fit for Remy.

A far better fit than stand-up comedy. While charismatic and not frightened by the stage, he unfortunately found it difficult to connect with the audience. His material was based on everyday observations, a place where most comedy originates. Living in homeless shelters in the heart of Skid Row, his material was unrelatable to the audience: showering with ex-convicts, dodging punches from strangers, waiting in line for an hour to eat. They didn't want to think about any of that and so his material fell flat.

Neither of these two roles provided much in the form of income. He pressed on until winter began creeping in, marking one full year of living down and out in Los Angeles, California. He had a few bigger than average shows at some of the major comedy clubs of L.A. but nothing really stuck. Tired of earning barely enough money to eat and returning to a shelter at the end of the day where he would sleep next to a hundred men of various odors on cots, he began to consider a move. He loved acting on stage. Enjoyed rehearsals and the occasional chance to direct when the main director took a day off. He didn't even mind bombing on stage with unrelatable material as a comedian, though receiving chuckles from the crowd was far better. He just couldn't handle the poverty any longer. After a year, he had met some popular actors, performed stand-up for a crowd that had contained one of his favorite screenwriters, and had honed his acting skills to a reasonably adequate level. He had also come to grips with the fact that he just couldn't make ends meet where he was so he left L.A. and returned to Florida both gladdened and with a heavy heart.

CHAPTER XIII

CHINA

"I'm glad to see you, Moni," he said, opening the door.

She lowered her gaze and just stood there. Remy waited. Monica waited. Shifting her weight back and left, she looked up and directly into his eyes, "Are you going let me in?"

He held the stare. She smelled clean. Hair curled. Dark, royal blue eyeliner lightly accented small, sharp Asian eyes that held an iris so dark the pupil was indistinguishable. Just a touch of the white of the eye around the edges. One was left with the feeling that a shark was wearing a beautiful mask when she was in one of her moods, which she was.

Lowering his gaze and taking a step back, he parted the door open wide and returned to the depths of his apartment. She followed. From the living room sofa, he adopted a comfortable position, legs stretched before him, the arm closest to his guest open wide trailing along the back of the couch. He motioned for her to sit, tapping twice gently. She turned to him glaring.

"Why you leave me out hallway so long?"

"You were out there for less than a minute, Moni. What's really on your mind?"

The glare sharpened. Her face contorted into fine, jagged lines of cruelty. "You no care about me. What I to you?"

"First of all, let's not raise our voices. Sit down. Relax."

"I no want sit down," she retorted, crossing her arms to emphasize the point.

"And yet, you came here today of your own volition carrying a large purse which undoubtedly contains a change of clothes and toiletries. You plan on spending the night here Monica Hu and honestly that sounds great. I miss you. I love you, you know. But don't think for an instant that I will endure negative nonsense. Sit down and talk to me."

She was shaking visibly as he began to speak, but recovered and seemed calm by the time he finished. She looked down on that smiling, knowing face of his with a mix of scorn and tenderness. She relaxed her shoulders and the large heavy bag slumped clumsily down to the crook of her elbow. She let it continue its downward descent and it crashed lifelessly to the floor. She crossed the living room and sat down at his side, eyes lowered to her own lap. After she had settled, he moved his head slowly towards that treasure of a mouth and they kissed passionately, no words spoken, caressing each other gently as the laden purse noisily collapsed to one side on the floor.

Later they lay entwined, warm and glowing. Neither one rushed back for their clothing, both content in their skin. Remy had never met her equal. He smiled smugly as he held her and wondered what had caused her such dismay a day earlier.

"You don't want your clothes?" he asked, speaking softly into her neighboring ear, gently nibbling a lobe to accent the question.

She stretched, holding one wrist and pushing her arms outward to arch her back, and then relaxed into him purring a bit in the process. He readjusted his head to keep loose hair from tickling his face and closed his eyes. There they dozed until hunger roused them back into clothing and conversation.

"That was excellent. You and I tonight. Top notch."

"Really?" she queried.

"Yes, really. I was deeply moved. Primally. Is that a word?" his voice softened with uncertainty. She smiled a bit at this and turned a steady gaze to Remy as he left for the kitchen and soon began fishing through a cabinet, pots and pans and trays banging and clanking. He located the cutting board off to one side and banged a few more pans together in the process for good measure, just to be noisy. He stood erect again and she was already there alongside him, close enough for him to feel the heat pulse from her. In one quick motion, he placed the cutting board on the countertop, grabbed her distant wrist swiftly and firmly spun her about in a tight circle, as a lead dancer does to a partner. She resisted halfway into the maneuver and Remy released her. She looked to him awkwardly. He moved in and began dancing slowly with her, hands clasped, chest to chest.

"You are an odd one, Monica Hu," he said through a smile so wide it danced on laughter.

"So are you, Remy LeBeau."

They kissed in a dancer's embrace and released from one another with mutual agility, Remy to his cooking, she to her phone. Remy cocked his head as a sudden thought emerged.

"You ever study martial arts, Moni?"

"What is martial art?"

"You know," he began, repositioning himself to the cutting board. "Fighting, but skilled fighting. Kind of like dancing. Ninja stuff." She looked more puzzled. "Look it up on your fancy smartphone. You love doing that at opportune moments such as this." The last sentence spoken at barely a whisper and with an open mouth void of lip movement.

"What is *opportune*?"

"Now, I am impressed!" he set down the knife and walked briskly toward her, kissing her squarely on the mouth with pride. "I am so glad to be with you! How was your day? And why were you acting so strangely earlier?"

She retired to the living room pleased with herself, escaping quietly on deft feet while Remy was in mid-question. Remy looked up and over after failing to hear a response and found her sitting comfortably on the sofa. Muttering a small curse upon her ancestors, he continued dicing and cubing vegetables while she began typing away on her laptop in the living room.

That really was incredible this evening. The first few times were lovely but stiff, formal almost, Remy thought, sniffing the simmering aroma of spaghetti sauce. He added a pinch of salt. *Actually, that was black and white, night and day. She didn't gradually become a better lover; she suddenly became one. That's never happened before.* He thought back, swimming through the stream of memories of past lovers. *Nope, definitely never happened before. Always a long, slow learning curve even with direct assistance and solid communication, neither of which apply to her and me. Never had a lover suddenly perform well.* He turned down the heat. *Put it all together, Rem,* he instructed himself, turning over a pot of boiled water onto a strainer, the noodles disappearing in the hot steam. As the cloud rose upward, he dodged back to avoid the heat, taking pleasure in maintaining good form. *She was out late, leaving in the middle of the night, a worknight no less. Gone for a couple of days. Hot and bothered about waiting at the doorstep. She's somehow instantly five times better at sex. At least five times,* he thought, stopping with dinner preparations just to grin and remember details. *Does this mean anything more than she's high maintenance?*

Unable to procure an answer, he took a deep breath and assembled two plates of pasta and sauce. With outstretched arms and a slight bow, he presented one heaping plate of spaghetti drenched in sauce. She sat upright at its delivery, slipping a smart phone she'd been texting with into a pink purse as she straightened.

"Should we eat at table?"

"Sure," Remy replied. "Good idea. We should chat anyway." The last bit caused a slight stutter to her step and a half-glance toward Remy. Plates were placed on two sides of a rectangular, wooden dining room table. They sat in unison.

"Let's eat," Remy suggested, inhaling deeply through his nose and savoring the upcoming meal. Seeing Monica forking into her noodles, he began eating, the sounds of sucking and slurping the only noise in the home, until, "Why were you so upset today?"

Dark eyes shifted his way without the slightest hint of a response, but eventually she answered, "Because you make me wait outside."

"You weren't really waiting very long, princess," a term he chose when she was being overly-demanding. "It's you that's been keeping me waiting. You haven't been here in days. And last time I saw you, you were cold and distant. I should be the one upset, not you."

She shrugged noncommittally, Remy hating the gesture.

"Why do you care about waiting on the doorstep for a moment? Are you afraid of the sunshine? Do you hate the fresh air?"

"What is *sunshine*?" Questioning vocabulary was a method she used to turn attention away from something undesirable. Remy did not appreciate the deception.

"You damn well know what sunshine is," speaking louder than he wanted to and eliciting a pleased look from her. "You drive me crazy. Does that work with most guys? 'What is sunshine?' Please. What is respect, how about that?" She frowned a bit and with their expressions reversed, Remy happily dug into his mound of pasta.

Slurping. Sucking. He looked to her taking a forkful with gusto, adoring his lover and opponent. He set down his utensil and held her hand. She swallowed hard and they sat looking upon each other. Remy brought her tender hand to his lips and kissed. Both smiling now, returning to supper.

"What does sunshine mean, Moni?"

She laughed.

"No really, I want to know. I use the word sometimes but I don't know what it means. It's a type of small dog, right?"

"Yes, Remy. It small dog."

"It's so weird because I know that you've used the word *sun* and *shine* correctly a few times since I've known you. If you're going to try to trick me, you've got to step up your game. Oh, I hate and love you, Moni," she stiffened at the word *hate*. "Not really hate, babe. Just jokes."

With tensions eased, he pressed on.

"Are you embarrassed to be seen with me?"

"No," she replied curtly. A silence while she congealed the proper words in English. After ten years of teaching students that spoke English as a second language, Remy knew the telltale signs. He waited patiently for the necessary five seconds or so and she continued, "Other people, neighbors, will talk bad things. They will say bad things each other and leaders of school. I no want us find trouble."

"We're adults, babe. We make decisions like this on our own. The leaders of the school are not our parents. Even if they were, we're adults and we live independently of work." She looked legitimately puzzled by the word *independently*, unlike the sunshine query earlier. "Alone. Separate. Just you. Just me," he added as her puzzlement gave way to certainty.

"No in China."

"I don't accept that. People are basically the same at heart. Chinese, Japanese, Americans: we all want freedom and peace. We all laugh at funny things. We all cry at funerals."

She shrugged again and returned to the spaghetti unfazed. But the idea of foreign intrusion into his love life did not sit well with him. He slid his chair back, stood and walked to the bedroom, produced a duplicate key to his front door and slid it next to her mostly empty plate. "This is yours now."

"You sure? We only know each other one month."

"Monica, I want to share my life with you. That includes this place. Come and go as you see fit."

"What about other girls?"

He laughed, caught off-guard, coughing hard on half-chewed noodle bits. "What other girl could there possibly be, Moni? 'What is sunshine?' Our little dance there in the kitchen. It's just you, love."

The softest smile took her face as her fingers closed over the small, metal key. "What about Xue Ting?"

"Gone now," his features tightening. "I loved her but we never danced like you and I dance. Back and forth. Still, I feel bad about all of that. I let her down, I suppose. Didn't fulfill my responsibilities," he trailed off, hoping Daisy was finding happiness in her new life. He snapped back, feeling contempt swell from Monica's side of the table. "Are you finished with the meal?"

"Yes, Rem. It very delicious. I will wash dish."

"Very nice of you to lie to me like that. An excellent cook I am not. But the dishes can wait. I cannot," taking her hand in his and pulling her into the hallway towards the bedroom. "Have you seen this painting in my room back here?"

"You don't have painting."

"Too true, love. Help me plan where one should go. It's just back this way," he said with a wink moving alongside her slowly and holding her close to him, loving her, kissing her, and then merging together as one.

CHAPTER XIV

CHINA

Each new visit brought with it that same pink bag filled with those delicate necessities of hers. Shelves were cleared and claimed as Monica's territory, a sovereign state with borders all throughout the flat. Each time she walked through the front door hauling another heavily laden purse, Remy would grin knowing more of her was with him.

She was gone some nights, mysteriously disappearing after sunset to return to the school office. He would find his way to the kitchen window each of those nights, drinking in the cool air, nursing a local beer, and gaze across the street to that same distant well-lit room on the third floor, the curtains firmly shut. Sometimes she would return later that same night. Most times she did not. She was generally colder than normal afterward, requiring more silliness before she opened up to him, blooming only after the most careful of attention was given. As the weeks passed, he grew tired of dancing around the issue, weary of going so far out of his way to put her into good spirits.

"Talk to me," he stated bluntly as they walked hand in hand around the neighborhood after dinner one night.

"Okay. What you want?"

"Oh, surprise me, Moni."

"Chinese make gunpowder but we only use for firework. We use for festival, for wedding, and what the word…?" she began thumbing through a dictionary app on her mobile. "Ceremony. In ceremony."

"I said surprise me, not tell me something every third-grader already knows."

"Really?" looking honestly puzzled. "Your people learn that about China?"

"Yeah, it's all part of our master plan to create future citizens who know the intricacies of Chinese culture so we can more easily conquer you and cast you into submission. Better watch out," he added somberly, halting in place and making the peace sign with two fingers, then placing them to his eyes and forking the gesture towards her. *We are watching you closely*, the gesture said.

She was pulling him forward before he could complete the menacing motion. "Come, come, walk, walk."

"That's not funny?" he asked with a chuckle.

"A little. That is small funny."

"You're small funny."

"I am not funny, but I am small."

"High maintenance, though," he added as they pressed onward. "You require a lot of energy to keep happy."

"You are used to Japanese women," she replied.

"Yeah, maybe. I did live there for years. But Chinese and Japanese are all the same anyway, right?" delivering the sarcasm with a poorly concealed grin. She exhaled loudly at this, preparing to retort, unaware of his jest. He continued, "I mean all Asians are the same. Chopsticks. Rice. Weird squiggly symbols. I get it."

Her eyes lit up, "Chinese no same! We very different. We people with culture and his---" Remy's outburst of laughter cut her off in midsentence, grunting noises forcing his way through his nose as he tried to breathe and laugh simultaneously.

"You no laugh!" she commanded. "We very different from Japanese, f&%* Japanese."

"Whoa, babe! Ease up! I know, I know. It's a joke. Definitely different, that's what makes the joke funny. Relax, babe," he moved forward to kiss her mouth but she turned and he had to compromise with the jaw. Neither of their paces were altered in this process, both maneuvering deftly on spinning heels and tips of toes.

"Your jokes are very small."

"Yeah, I get that sometimes. Pretty sure that one was funny, though," he recounted the last minute again, beginning to laugh once more. "Yep, definitely funny."

Her pensiveness dissipated as they rounded the last corner around the block. At the bottom of the stairwell leading to his flat, he pulled her close to him.

"I love you."

"I love you."

They kissed passionately. She broke away first and began leading the way up the steps, Remy lackadaisically following in her wake. There was a jingle of keys on a ring followed by the sound of a bolt striking through a locking mechanism and a yawning creak of old hinges bearing the weight of the door against wall's edge. She entered like the winds of spring push away winter; he entered as autumn winds cool the summer. He dropped his keys into a large bowl by the door, a bowl that she perpetually neglected to use. *That woman works hard to keep her distance*, he thought absently. *Which reminds me...*

"Hey, Moni."

She was blowing by him, returning from the bedroom, toothbrush in one hand and a papery facial mask in the other. A glance up was her only response.

"We still need to talk."

"So talk."

He crossed his arms and leaned against a clean portion of the doorway, shifting most of his weight to one leg and crossing the other leg comfortably. Defensive posturing 101.

"What's the deal with your late-night rendezvous?"

"Hwat d'you mean?" she asked through tooth-brushing strokes.

"With work. What's going on with that? You leave here around eight some nights, sometimes later. Some nights you return, some nights you don't."

"I tell you. Director of school call me. When he call, I go." Her voice flattening out and lowering at the end. *Sounds like the truth. Doesn't feel like the truth, though.* He nodded as one who has had a sudden deep understanding, pushed off the doorway and strolled to the kitchen, not bothering to turn on any lights in the small chamber. Across a dark, empty street the school sat in solitude, still and lifeless. He opened the window and listened to the darkness. *All quiet on the western front*, he thought. *Don't know what I'd be hearing anyway. Even when that damned light is on when she's away, sounds within don't make their way back to this window. No voices, no music, no squeaks of desks moving, no footsteps.*

He leaned against the countertop, peering deeper into the darkness until he heard a lengthier than normal shower come to an end. He closed the window and retreated to his home office to check emails. She entered, a towel twisted into an encircling turban about her head, dressed in comfortable silken pajamas, glistening and damp. She rested her newly-cleaned hand on his right shoulder, pivoting around him gracefully and coming to rest on his lap, perching solidly, comfortably, secure. Remy wrapped his hands around her waist and nestled his head against her small bosom inhaling deeply of her, immersed in her. He closed his eyes, smiling at visions of a potential future projected on the back of his eyelids: her nails scraping across his back in ecstasy, mutual moaning and clutching, lips barely meeting, his hands on her bulging belly months after, later, a child that cooed and crawled atop a soft rug. He opened his eyes and hugged her warmly, kissing a shoulder. Grudgingly, he retracted, looking up into her eyes with an apologetic expression.

"We need to talk."

She rose immediately, "About what?" a louder than needed tightness in her voice. He looked to her and remained silent until she softened, "About what?" she asked again as she situated herself into the neighboring chair.

"What happens when you leave this place, our home, some evenings? Why do you leave our flat and what do you do when you're gone?"

"Oh, Rem," she looked to him pleadingly. "I told you I ..."

"I know, I know. I heard you. Felt like total bullshit, Monica."

The pleading expression turned cold and cusped on something worse. He fought through the desire to shrink back in his seat but instead tightened his own eyes, cowboy style, and glared right back. There their expressions met each other in cold defiance, unflinching. She stood and sauntered off to bed.

"Just going to walk away?!" he heckled to her retreating back. "It's just me, so who cares, right?! Why would you care at all?" She collapsed onto the mattress with an audible *whoomph*. He mumbled unpleasantries to himself, while in the bedroom down the hallway she did much the same in Mandarin. He shifted his anger, cursing his computer's slowness in opening a webpage, a dull rumbling that rose in caliber until the walls shook with obscenities cast in rage. He slammed an empty beer bottle down on a wooden coaster, cracking it into four bits though the bottle remained whole. He cleaned up and retired for the night keeping well to his side of the bed, tossing and turning, breathing too quickly and deeply to signal the body that the time for rest was imminent. The blood flowed in his veins like liquid ore.

"The director of school like me, Remy," she began, her words cooling him.

"Finally. How long ha---"

"You want hear this or no? I talk now."

They shifted on the mattress, pivoting to face one another in a pitch-black room, "Tan. Principal Tan," she continued. She looked to him in the darkness of the bedroom with eyes that pleaded, *Stop. You don't know what you're getting yourself into.* "You should leave alone. No worry. This Chinese thing."

"This is my life which happens to be in China right now. This involves me. This is my life we're talking about. Our lives. You live with me. We share a home. What happens to you happens to me. Keep going, my dear, and leave nothing out, no stone unturned. The principal of the school? The big man on campus? Isn't he married?"

"Yes. He marry."

"What an asshole. F#%* him. Even if you and I weren't doing our thing, that's just an awful, disgusting thing to do. Marriage is sacred. What a wicked little f^%#er!" He took a slow, deep breath, exhaled and spoke more calmly. "How often does this happen?" A follow up thought came later, "Wait. Your job isn't threatened, is it? I mean, you could turn him down and that would be the end of it, right? He can't fire you for not having sex with him, can he? I mean that would be wrong."

She looked at him quizzically, surprised by his naivete.

"When I leave here at night, I go to office. I file papers for next day. He talk me. He say one night I look like his daughter and---"

Remy broke into a maniacal laughter, razor sharp. "His daughter? He has a daughter and his pick-up line is to say that you look like her?" More mirthless laughter followed. Chuckling through snarled lips, he felt her discomfort and calmed himself.

"Don't do anything," she said as he said, "I'm going to go speak with him tomorrow." Both hearing each other, feeling each other really. Remy smiled, strengthened by their synchronicity.

"This may not even be an issue," he chimed. "Maybe you misread the situation. Why do you think he wants you sexually?" She grimaced at his bluntness, at the lack of couth.

"He do. It true."

He waited for her to go on but she took the pause as acceptance, rolled over and began to fall asleep.

"How are you sleeping right now? Finish it up, Moni. What happened that gave you the impression that he's interested in you sexually?"

She turned swiftly, a complete 180 degrees in one fluid motion, holding onto his eyes with the tenacity of an angry pit bull. *Let it go!* she thought at him. *Let me handle this. You don't understand this place, the things I must do.* She turned her back to him again.

"Fine, Monica. Perhaps, everyone I speak with at school will be able to provide some sort of insight into the perverted old principal's life. If he's fooling around with you, then he's likely doing this with other teachers, too. I'll start talking to the attractive teachers and assistants---"

"You no do that!" she cut in, flipping back.

"Oh, but I will. I will not allow a wicked old man to interfere with my happiness. I will fix this with or without you."

She smiled as a mother smiles at her child. *You will fix this? Just you?* she thought, smiling wider.

He fumed at the expression he could only barely make out in the faint light. "Stop mocking me, Monica. Just stop. This is your life. Maybe you don't care about your honor, about respect, about dignity, but I sure as hell do."

"What is *honor*?" she queried.

"Good question, actually. It's important, I'll tell you that. Life is precious and beautiful but honor rises above even that. What is honor? Well, I suppose we could define honor, fundamentally, as the--- wait a minute! You got me going off on one of your tangents again." he chuckled, cooled down by this private trickery, her way of changing the subject by asking for a definition of a word she already understood. She smiled and kissed him fully on the mouth and they found peace on each other's lips.

She related the full tale as tensions eased. Tan, a married man with two children, one son and one daughter in a country with laws against the creation of a second child. An esteemed member of the communist party, the only party, the principal of Jiangxi Middle School in Nanchang, China. Principal Tan had barricaded Monica in his office one night using a sofa to brace the only door. He had Monica sit upon his lap and talk with him of her past boyfriends and romances. A week later, he visited her dorm room and thumped on the door until she let him in, whereupon he proceeded to take off his pants, and only his pants, and approach her lecherously. She raised her voice then -- *"Only then?!"* Remy had exclaimed, before being shushed -- in protest, repeating what a tragedy this would be for his wife and family until he clothed himself and staggered out, evidently in fear of the attention such a loud voice would bring.

Remy listened attentively, literally biting his tongue at times when she paused to search for proper words or to gather the strength needed to relate such an embarrassing event, careful not to interject his own thoughts into her retelling. He listened attentively, dismissing devilish imaginings of the suffering of the old fool as best he could. At the story's end he queried.

"Have you told your parents about this?"

"Yes, my father say I try no alone with him."

"That's it?! Try to not be alone with him? That's not an option. He calls you up whenever he wants. And what about the others? You need to bring this man down or he'll surely do this to others if he isn't already. You're not the only one, I'm sure."

"I think I only one. He told me that I am remind him of his daughter."

A shiver rolled down Remy's back and his stomach recoiled. "That is a line he speaks to every woman he does this to. A horrid, grotesque line, but a line nonetheless. Your tale describes a man whose actions are predetermined. There is a certainty to his actions that tells me this is an old hat for the bastard. He's comfortable in his routine." *Dear Lord, I want to kill this man,* he thought, quelling bubbling rage. "You're a first-year teacher in a new school. You know no one here and have barely more clout than me, a foreigner to your nation. You will be unable to avoid his advances indefinitely without it affecting your employment." He repeated this portion in simpler terminology until it made sense to her. She agreed reluctantly. "Your word against his. You'll lose, love. What you need is evidence."

"Maybe I just stay away."

"Maybe you could but the good shouldn't make way for the wicked, rather the opposite. Hand me your phone."

He rolled out of bed and flipped on the light switch, blinding them both. "I'm serious. Do it." She complied solemnly. Changing the menu into English, he found what he was hoping to find. He thumbed the app into the upper right corner of the screen, far removed from any other clickable icons, easily accessible without having to stare at the screen first.

"Next time the two of you interact, day, night, alone or even in a crowded room, the second you see him, you click this app, ok?" He looked to her with a steadfast resolution. She nodded firmly and he passed the phone back to her, their thumbs lining up symmetrically on opposite ends of the *Audio Record* icon.

CHAPTER XV

CHINA

"I did it!" she sang triumphantly, breezing through the open door. Remy paused the game and looked up with a contented half-smirk. "You did it? You recorded?" he asked unbelievingly. *This is far more interesting than teaching*, he thought, *whatever this is.* "Well then, let's hear it. Let me listen."

"You no understand what say."

Good point. I have a passing understanding of basic expressions in Mandarin, enough to order food, command taxi drivers and muddle through the smallest of small talk but that's it, nothing more. "Doesn't matter. I want to hear the quality, the volume, the clarity. Translate as best you can along the way." Pausing intermittently, they worked their way through a rather tame conversation involving the scheduling of a future meeting that would involve various directors of the school. According to the translation, nothing was mentioned of the previous no-pants encounter at her dorm room. No sexual overtones whatsoever. His voice came through clear and crisp, professional actually, in a perfunctory conversation between a leader and his assistant. Remy listened carefully for the many subtleties in a voice that unmasks a speaker's true intent. He had grown quite capable of such things while living overseas over the years. Pitch, tone, speed, and volume were perhaps the only universal languages.

"Are you sure this is the same guy?" he asked. "There's no shame, no tension in his voice at all. Was he so drunk that he didn't remember?" He stared at the microphone/speaker that was just a phone the day before trying to make sense of the ease in the man's voice. When no answer popped up, he turned about sharply and began to pace the flat. fixing his gaze downward at his steps, fixed on visions of this older man and Monica in Tan's office, her seated and taking notes attentively, he issuing tedious commands pertaining to the meeting. The details of the office became clear: loose papers, a pen under an open textbook, an office phone with a worn keypad, the lower wires grimy due to an underpaid cleaner's neglect. Flat facial expressions and minimal body gesturing as he spoke. Monica dutifully complying with instruction. Vocal inferences, Monica's translation, and Remy's memory of the office he had once glanced at while walking by one day, merged into one. The audio cut out and he detached from the imagery.

Is he truly ignorant of the fact that she would be uncomfortable around him? he questioned himself softly. *Rising to power as he did must have required a fair degree of skill in human relations,* pausing, searching. "So he just tunes it out completely? Perfectly, I would say." He replayed the message once more in his head, listening for any sign of apprehension or nervousness in the man's voice, finding none. "Spooky."

"Not really," Monica chimed in. "No in China. This China. Chinese find many way get to same place. We twist. Turn, up and down."

Remy halted in midstride and turned to her perplexed. "What does that mean?"

She shrugged a response unsure how to answer.

"What is apparently normal behavior for you is blessedly abnormal for me," he timed the following sentence so his back would be turned to her, in the outer fringe of the dining room, on the threshold of the kitchen, ten meters away, whispering the last bit, "He sounds like a psychopath to me."

He turned and faced her newly sharpening features. "What does---"

"Never mind that, beautiful," he exclaimed. "And nice ears. Good work today! Nice trial run. Now remember, do the exact same thing next time. Tonight, tomorrow, whenever. This device," he said, grabbing the clunky, pink smart phone from the table and shaking it at her, "is your shield. It's justice."

In one fluid movement she snatched the device entirely from his grip. She adopted a serious expression and shook the phone at him mockingly. "You no Superman. Go cook me food."

"I was thinking the same thing." They sat back down, relaxing comfortably into the cushions of the sofa. "Well?" she motioned impatiently after a time.

"Well, what? I'm afraid I simply don't understand what you mean."

"Cook food."

"Oh, about that. I meant to talk to you about that. Turns out I'll be unable to prepare your dinner tonight. I'm busy sitting. Just stand up and fulfill your womanly duties like a good girl."

"Excuse me!" she shot up with a start and a grin. "I just finish spy for you. Now I hungry. Now I *am* hungry," she corrected, "Feed me," she growled, moving close and baring teeth like a wolf about to pounce. He launched from the sofa, grabbing a shoulder and hip as he flew by and spun her so that they landed reasonably softly on the carpeted floor. They kissed passionately, their love howling into the night just like that wolf.

They disentangled, ungluing themselves from one another's embrace and went their separate ways still breathing heavily: she directly to the shower, Remy catching his breath, enjoying watching her go. Sensing she desired a bit of privacy, he decided not to join her and instead engaged himself in the kitchen. The refrigerator revealed nothing of particular interest, save for the loose beer or two rolling around in the crisper. He rarely felt hungry around her, her company the only sustenance he craved, the only need he felt. *But a cold beer wouldn't be so bad,* he thought, taking one in his grasp and subconsciously pivoting to the kitchen window to catch a glimpse of the school below. He stood there for some time, listening to the water in the pipes, grinning, grateful. *I thought I would just settle down with someone I shared some mutual interests with, someone that I respected and could share a bit of silence with. But this... her,* he opened his eyes and became one with the surroundings once more, *she is something else altogether.* Just as this thought was firing across his neural network, changing chemical properties of the brain or whatever it is thoughts do, a loud squeal bounced about the stark peeling walls signaling the cessation of the shower.

Returning to the fridge, he retrieved an onion, an eggplant, and a flat cube of tofu. He produced a pan, added a bit of oil and set it gingerly on corroded stovetop rungs, all the while keeping an ear and a portion of his brain on reserve for her interactions in the bathroom. Wanting to catch her in the doorway for a smooch and sensing she was soon to reenter the living area, he ignored the cutting board and glided toward his target, taking broad, quick, soft steps. Turning the corner and arriving at the door as it opened, he grabbed her tightly and kissed her, turning her about in the process so that he was in and she was out.

"I'm almost finished cooking," he said, slowly pushing the door closed. "Just work your magic in there and dinner should be done in no time at all. All the hard work is done already."

"That very quick," she spoke hesitatingly through a shrinking wedge of doorframe.

"Well, you know, I do what I can. Hurry up now, don't let it burn."

The sound of her cursing in Mandarin was a musical score to his ears the likes of which Vivaldi himself could not master. Truly content, in love and at ease, he bathed and basked in his adoration of her. The din of metal cookware banging and clacking in the kitchen reverberated throughout the flat as he thought of the situation at hand. *A successful field test of procuring audio evidence*, he began. *Didn't think she would do it when it came right down to it. She is amazing. She constantly amazes me.* The feint aroma of garlic came drifting in, mixing with the shower steam clouding the washroom. *If she did it once, she'll probably do it again*, he rationalized. *And eventually something meaningful will stick. Now who could I entrust such a recording to? Who do I know in this place that would transform a recording of a lecherous old man into righteous action?*

His mind whirled, *Chinese school leaders? Doubtful, odds are good they have relationships built in place that they don't want disturbed. Local media? Not a chance, completely under the thumb of a government that refuses to print or air anything remotely negative about itself. Local police. Probably not. Like the school leaders, relationships have been established, favors earned. Attorneys? Better, possible, and the farther from this good-old-boy network in Nanchang the better. Maybe Beijing or Shanghai attorneys. Expensive, though. An anonymous blanket email with an attachment of the audio recording to each member of the faculty of the school? Excellent. High probability of resignation due to shame.* Coming back to his senses again, twisting the tap sharply, the shower ended. He dried off whistling a happy tune and exited the bathroom, light-colored towel wrapped around his hips, steeling himself to the chill of the flat, flexing muscles that protruded slightly through a thin layer of fat, of average build, one who exercises and stays relatively trim but not one devoted to honing the body.

"Smells delicious, baby. Almost finished."

"Yes, my dinner almost finish. If you hungry, you cook your food," she called from the kitchen.

He sniffed the air and followed the aroma to its source in the kitchen where she tended to a stove, mixing ingredients on the highest possible setting. She turned about as he approached, whirled back to the meal, long silky black hair tracing the outline of her movements. Her lithe, trim body remained firm as she glided about the kitchen floor. He slowed his steps to match the rhythm of her movements and inserted himself directly behind her as she slid cubed tofu into a hissing wok. He placed his left hand around her waist to her flat stomach, kissing the back of her neck, nibbling a bit. His right hand searched for the stove gauge as she spun into him, eyes slightly less black than her hair, eyes void of shine, eyes that captured light as surely as a galactic black hole, eyes that engulfed him each time. He melted in place as he twisted the temperature down to the medium setting, fairly certain that his action went unnoticed. *So hard to tell with this one*, he thought, absorbed in her gaze.

"You like my dinner? You no have it. I eat all and nothing for you."

"But there is so much. If you eat all of this you will become big and fat and no one will love you."

She thought this over, turning back to the cooling meal, "You will still love me," she said, facing the meal she cooked, "but you would cheat with skinny girl."

"Whoa, babe! I surrender! I love you. You're gorgeous. I'm joking. Let's eat."

There was no further satirical back and forth as Remy tidied up the kitchen around her. They pecked at their dinner, saying little and comfortable together with that.

CHAPTER XVI

CHINA

"That's a hell of a story, Rem," the man said, eyes narrowing as he picked up a chilled, nearly full stein of beer and drained most of its contents. He slammed the glass down, the bottom banging against the table top, beads of perspiration coalescing with the small puddle the tabletop had accrued over the past hour and jetting them up and outward in a misty explosion. Remy, who had been leaning in as one does when sharing a private story, jumped back, bracing his bulk on the wooden bench that lay opposite the fellow. His hair was close-shaven and a squared jaw and high cheek bones gave him a rather boxy, militant look. A smidge shorter than Remy, but stocky and stout, sporting bulging biceps proudly through a very short-sleeved shirt.

"It's all true, I tell you. A true story, Mike," Remy smiled wanly. "I had to pull it out of her but it felt true when she finally let down that wall. People do things when they lie and she's either a master of lies, and I mean she must just excel at it, or she was telling the truth."

"You aren't being objective. You want her to not lie," he said around a belch. Mike eyed the nearby bartender who was immersed in conversation with a patron. Disappointed, he returned his attention more or less to Remy, eyes flitting about the room periodically as others entered into their vicinity.

"Of course, I don't want her to lie," Remy replied. "But that doesn't matter because I remove myself when I contemplate the situation."

"What the f&$* does that mean?" Mike's attention came around fully to Remy. "How do you think you do that? You're there but you aren't there?" He chuckled, pleasantness returning to his features.

"Exactly," Remy answered matter-of-factly. "When I observe or synthesize data or imagine outcomes, I lose myself entirely. I'm not where my body is. Like daydreaming.

Mike shrugged. Remy shrugged. They both looked around for a deliverer of more booze. Remy located the owner of the pub's wife's friend who served as the bartender-slash-waitress and called her out of conversation from across the bar with a loud shout. Mike turned and motioned for two more drinks, both men putting on their best sorry-to-disturb-you smiles. She bounded away. The men faced each other once more.

"Do you remember that time in Chengdu when I cracked my head open?" Mike questioned straight-faced and somber.

"Yeah, I definitely remember that. You split your crown wide open. Blood all over the tiles in your bathroom. You showed me the pics on your phone last year," Remy answered, flashes of memories popping as he spoke. "You took some stitches," he added. Mike's eyes continued to shift about. He was a solid man, not just physically, and Remy was taken aback by the worrisome ocular movements. Remy thought it wise to fall silent and let what needed to be spoken be said but the silence produced nothing. Continuing to recall, Remy added, "Around the time your e-bike's seat got sliced up. Someone took a knife to it, yeah?"

He became alert then, eyes coming to rest on Remy. He opened his mouth to speak but only the first syllable escaped before it was cut short by a shrill ringtone. His mouth clamped shut while his fingers forged their way into his pocket to answer his phone as a pudgy, caramel skinned man in his thirties appeared at their table producing a wide crocodile smile.

"Good evening, gentlemen," he spoke in a crisp, clear English accent.

I've seen him around, Remy thought. *Indian fellow. What's his name? Melvin?*

"Well, good evening, sir," Remy said, greeting the newcomer in an eloquent style of speaking, English accents having that effect on him. "What brings you out and about tonight?" he asked, holding one of those smiles you put on for photos and keeping it rocksteady.

"I need to get up," Mike announced, standing, sliding out from between the bench and table. He kept his eyes lowered which wasn't abnormal given the tightly scrunched seating, though upon reaching the head of the table where the Indian stood, normal eye contact that occurred when shuffling past someone was shirked. Remy filed this knowledge away for future reference. *That's a little out of place. Odd timing with the phone call and this guy's arrival. What were we discussing? Monica's sexual harassment and then Mike's bout of feinting last year... why did he change the subject to that?*

These thoughts ran through his mind as he danced the waltz of small talk: local bands, seasonal shifts in weather patterns, pub paraphernalia. A poster on the wall advertising tourism in Rio de Janeiro sparked a conversation about South American politics that shifted to local news. Remy and the man who might have been named Melvin bantered, trading economic opinions concerning the development of the city and Brazil as a whole until Mike returned. He looked better. Fresher. Surer of self. His footsteps came down hard and true on the cheap linoleum floor. He carried three perspiring mugs of beer which were promptly placed in the middle of the trio as he took his seat.

"No, thank you. Mike, is it?" Melvin asked politely.

The queer look that passed between the two men caused a tension that Remy quickly interrupted.

"Oh, come on. Drink with us. Imbibe. Relax. All the cool kids are doing it," he said playfully, spinning the glasses so that the handles jutted outward in line with each of the three men.

"Not tonight." Melvin replied, taking a step back from the table as Mike and Remy raised their steins, chinking them together with a look that said cheers before each downing around half of the contents. As they returned their glasses to the great condensation puddle atop the table, he faded away, deeper into the pub's nightlife.

"Enjoy the night," Remy called out.

"You, too, Remy," he replied over his shoulder.

"Oh, but what is his name?" Remy asked himself, drunkenly motioning to the man with his beer glass, the contents sloshing like waves in a stormy night at sea as he watched the man turn and melt into the crowd. *There is more to that fellow than meets the eye. Can't quite a put a finger on it, though.* He swiveled his head back to Mike.

"What were you just thinking about?" Mike asked, drinking deeply from his mug of beer as soon as the question was out. The seriousness of the past half hour having diffused significantly, both men in higher spirits and buzzed.

"Nothing much. The wise man knows he knows nothing, you know."

"Your wise men sound like idiots," Mike retorted. They drank more. "Where is your girl tonight, Rem?"

"Out with her friends. A girl's night out. She suggested that we do this, you know. Meet up for a drink. Said she'll meet up with us later," Remy put an empty mug down and reached for the full unclaimed one, doling half into Mike's and half into his own.

"Did she now? Well, let's not waste any time while you still have your freedom. Let's drink."

And so, they did, round after round. They wandered off, engaging in separate conversations, wandering back together again after a while. Tequila was ordered and shot down between salt licks and lime wedges. More tequila followed, a gift from the owner. Monica arrived well past midnight to find two rather inebriated men. There were overenthusiastic shouts of welcome and promptings of more tequila-shooting, of which she had but one. The hour growing late, he departed with her arm in arm, as much out of romance as in need for assistance to walk upright. He kissed her passionately, albeit a tad off-center, in a shadowy region outside of the pub, professing his love of her with a clumsy tongue.

"Do you have nice time tonight?" she asked, nothing but innocence in her questioning, knowing this to not be a question at all really. One of those rhetorical spiels but delivered so expertly that it appeared in every way a legitimate question. She was excellent at that sort of thing.

"Quite," he answered, arm and head resting outside of the open window of a speeding taxi, enjoying the feel as much as any dog enjoys an open window in a speeding vehicle.

"Meet anyone new?" she asked, fixated on his response.

He felt her focus but was unsure as to what it might represent. He responded simply, "Yes. Almost everyone is new to me here."

"Any people special?" she continued.

"Nope," he replied quickly, before his alcohol addled brain could remember details to the contrary.

She let the answer hang, weighing the response. She could be quiet at times, times when he would've appreciated a word or two, though all things considered, he did prefer a tense silence to mindless chatter. He mirrored the quiet as the taxi sped and swerved along the dark, empty route that led home. In his drunken stupor, he'd conveniently almost forgotten about the Indian fellow altogether.

CHAPTER XVII

CHINA

"So, who is the protagonist in our story?"

The class looked at each other ruefully. Juicy, the go-to star student, opened her mouth to speak and would have undoubtedly provided the correct answer had she not been silenced by Remy with a subtle gesture. Her face drooped slightly into a frown. He scanned the classroom, looking for students less involved in the discussion and therefore more apt to be trouble if left unattended.

"Peter!" Remy called enthusiastically as he walked down an aisle towards the back of the classroom. The young man shot upright, affixing sleepy eyes to the approaching teacher, slowly transitioning from daydream to reality. Remy assumed that Peter had missed the question entirely. Speaking more slowly, pausing a bit and adding information, he repeated himself, "In our story, *The Great Gatsby*, the one we've been reading as a class, who is the protagonist?" Still nothing resembling recognition. *Ah*, he thought, *the boy doesn't remember the word protagonist from last class.* "Characters, this story is full of characters, right?" Remy rotated slowly from the center of the seated students to take in the class, most of which were paying attention. Recognition flashed at last on Peter's tortured face.

"Who is our main character, Peter?"

"Nick. Nick Carra.., Carra..." he stammered, unable to procure the last syllable of the character's name from memory.

"Close enough. It's Carraway. Well done. That's a protagonist. He, or she, does much of the action in a story. When things happen, that character is usually involved, either directly or indirectly. The story revolves around that person. They interact with other characters, too. Characters such as....?

Juicy's hand shot up fervently. Observing the remaining thirty-one students in a cursory glance, noticing each one was now focused on the discussion, he turned to the star student and nodded the go-ahead. Juicy answered, "Like Daisy."

"Bingo!" Remy rejoined, writing *GG Characters* on the white board in blue ink, underlining it, switching to a red marker and adding the word Daisy slightly smaller below. *Daisy,* he thought as he wrote, *how is that young lady doing these days? I would've married her. Lived comfortably. Calm. We weren't very passionate for one another but we got along well enough. Relaxed.* Rotating back to the class, he fielded other character names from a variety of students, writing each on the board, circling Nick and driving the protagonist point home as understanding lit in their eyes one by one.

"Arguably, Mr. Gatsby is a protagonist, too. Multiple protagonists can exist. So let's change it up. What's an antagonist?" He hadn't taught them this term yet and he allowed time for the question to sink into the ears and minds of his charges, repeating, "antagonist" and writing it on the board opposite to Nick. He was greeted with blank stares.

"Pro. Think about that portion of the word. I'm pro-war." They turned to look at him with shocked expressions. A soft mumbling in Mandarin began bubbling up from the back corner. "Well, I'm not actually, but just pretend. What would that mean?"

"That you want war. That you like it," one of the students chimed in.

"Yes, yes exactly, which I'm not by the way. I'm anti-war. Peaceful." The majority were getting it, but a quarter of the class still struggled with the new term. "Let's practice this a bit more. Icarus, what are you pro for? What do you support?"

"The law. I am pro-law."

"Okay, that's a fine answer. Anything in particular?"

"Everything that is law."

"Alright." *Kind of odd*, Remy thought but rolling with the technically correct answer. "You," he called to a teenage girl seated directly in the center of the classroom, pointing to her as a pompous batsman signals where he'll hit the baseball. "Tabitha, right?" she nodded. "I like that name. Tabitha. Sounds classy," she continued nodding, smiling now, defenses lowered and warming to the idea of learning. "What are you anti? What are you against?"

She gave this some thought while those seated next to her translated a bit into Mandarin. She wasn't the highest performing student and needed a bit of assistance. He held out his outstretched fingers, counting down from five, a cue the students knew meant answer soon.

"Drugs. I'm anti-drugs."

"Splendid! That's a great answer. Any others?" fielding a barrage of answers, every single one of them legal in issue. "Anyone have anything more debatable?" Remy queried. "Something that isn't so black and white? Something more personal." Thirty-three faces looked at him quizzically. Remy explained the word personal, adding opinion, in the attempt to explain the word more accurately but only drawing more blank stares. He gave the example of abortion, some support it, others do not.

"But isn't *abortion*," a student began, slowing the new word down significantly in mid-question, "law?"

"Yes, yes, it is. But some are anti-abortion because they don't agree with the law. They think the law is wrong and want to change it." Clarity and shock spread through the room.

"But it's the law!" one of the more vocal students called out. Most of the students were quick to agree, even the most soft-spoken suddenly finding a voice.

Ah, that's it! Remy thought, coming to his own realization. *Law, the government, the status quo, the good, normality: they're all one big thing here.* He began hushing the now borderline frantic students by raising both hands high, splayed out, and then slowly lowering them. The students began to settle into an excited silence.

"In any event," he began, "we seem to have wandered off on a tangent. Let's get back to it. Pro. The protagonist is Nick Carraway. He's our hero. The story moves around him. We cheer for his successes. We mourn his losses. How many of you like the character Nick Carraway? Raise your hands." A sea of arms rose, some high and tight, some on crooked elbows resting on a desk, wrist barely held upright. "There you go. Definitely protagonist material." He pointed and repeated this question for the other characters coming at last to Tom Buchanan who received only a sparse pecking of hand raises.

"Tom is our antagonist. He isn't very likeable. He's rude, violent, abusive, uncaring, unfair. He opp---" the classroom speaker blared a few semi-melodic, distorted notes through a battle-hardened speaker mounted in the corner. A woman's voice, mechanical in its repetition, informed the school in Mandarin that the current class period was finished. "Don't forget your homework. The future of China rests in your hands," he ended somberly, only a few of the ace students getting the small joke, most out of their seats already and chatting amiably with one another. He answered a few loose questions from students who converged to the head of the class, then gathered papers together and left.

She was waiting for him in the hallway, situated westerly into the setting sun. He was overcome with the brilliance, squinting sharply at the silhouette cast before him, dazzled by the sun that shone brightly behind her. *She placed herself there on purpose, I bet,* he determined, admiring her further.

"You are free today after class?" she asked, approaching Remy slowly, keeping her distance and maintaining the eclipsing position. She stopped just short of arm's reach.

"Come. Walk with me," and he turned east and began to walk away.

"Wait," she called at his back. "I no have time now. I see you later."

"Sure thing, baby doll. Just drop by. I love it when you do."

"Shhhh!" she exclaimed jogging toward him. "Don't talk about us here. We need hide," she loudly hushed.

"I'm afraid I never was any good at hiding. Not really my thing. I'll see what I can do."

She mouthed the words "I love you" and he kissed the air. Back in the teacher's lounge he found Mike hovering over his desk, files in hand, all business. Teacher mode in full effect. They exchanged greetings.

"Why don't my students know what a protagonist is by now?"

"A *protaga* what?" Mike quipped. "You know kids, Remy. It takes a few times for things to sink in and that's if they're trying."

"Yeah, yeah, yeah. I know. I know. I have these high hopes and expectations that tend to crumble around my feet by mid-semester. I was hoping to be done with this book by now and we're only halfway through it. Guess I need to cancel *Jane Ey---*"

"Listen, I can't do this now. That bell will ring any minute. We'll talk later."

"Whatever, not that important anyway. Have fun in there. Smarten 'em up real good," adding a country accent to the last sentence. A shared chuckling faded into silence as the door shut, leaving Remy alone in the empty office.

Though a people-person by nature, he did enjoy solitude from time to time. He sat and reclined in his rather average office chair, at first staring into the ceiling as he contemplated the pros and cons of his last class, analyzing himself and the students and everything in between, finding both faults and strengths, planning to duplicate the latter and avoid the former, and then as the flood of thinking subsided, he closed tired eyes and drifted comfortably into a doze. Thoughts of Monica drifted by: her returning home and announcing that her parents would like to see him; a family dinner with him as the guest; a round table with cooked dishes scattered throughout and heaps of clumpy rice being doled out to those seated; Remy announcing his love and intention to devote his life to the daughter of a set of parents he had never seen before. *I wonder what her ring size is?* he wondered, bearing a wide grin. The quickest hand of the most average of wall clocks ticked the seconds by soothingly.

Sometime later, he opened his eyes and set himself to the task of editing student writing armed with a refreshed mind and a red pen. Halfway through the stack, a familiar humdrum electronic tune and an accompanying female voice signaled the end of another period. Moments later the office door opened with a rush, the sound of a milling hallway -- laughter mixed with the pleased shrieks of teenagers, locker hinges creaking, metal latches clanging shut, books thumping, pages crinkling -- filled the room. Two students followed Mike into the office as he continued an explanation involving friction and a ramp. Circling an incorrect verb tense, Remy looked up later at Mike who was busy at his desk with papers of his own and then returned to assessing. They worked like this silently, separately, Remy waiting until his vision grew bleary and a break was needed. He was rubbing his weary eyes when the door burst open. A man of

Mike's stature plus a Buddha belly, trotted in. A fellow teacher by the name of Randy.

"Hey!" Randy exclaimed, "Those kids are nuts!"

"All kids are crazy. Adults too, for that matter. Why? What happened?" Remy asked, glad for the intermission. Mike looked up and returned to his stack of papers.

"Okay, so you know how I'm teaching them drama, right?"

"Yeah. Learning English through acting. Dynamite idea. It's fun and they work on mastering listening and speaking skills. That's why I focus more on reading, by the way. Balance of power and whatnot."

"Right," Randy continued with a nod. "So, we went through a skit together in the beginning of the year. An introduction, a how-do-you-do sort of thing. Now that that is over, we're working on something new. They broke up into groups and they're writing their own skit."

"Sounds fun," Remy chimed in, smiling, nodding.

"Yeah, but one group wanted to do a skit on prostitution. A jaded lover shows up at a brothel seeking revenge and the freedom of one of the prostitutes."

"Holy Hindu cows! That would be a fantastic skit to watch. Not exactly parent-friendly though, is it?"

"No, sir. Not parent-friendly at all. I had to... what's that right a president has?" Randy paused, searching.

"Executive veto," Remy answered.

"That's it! I vetoed that one."

"Ah, that's a shame. I would've paid money to watch that one." Remy glanced sideways at a stack of unassessed papers on his desk. Randy pressed on.

"The second one involves a guy going to a job interview. He sits down with the employer. Answers some questions."

"Is it called *pretty much every year of my life*?"

"Smartass. The good part comes at the end. The guy gets the job and shows up to work the next day---"

"And proceeds to assemble cellular phone parts for half of the American minimum wage to supply the American market where the hardware is later exported and sold for an enormous profit?"

"I wish there was a word stronger than smartass."

"Remy. The word is Remy."

They chuckled together. Knowing he had stretched his comments to the breaking point, he fell silent as good humor returned to the conversation. Randy picked up again.

"The employer really likes the guy. The interview goes well. The guy leaves the interview feeling like a million bucks." A silent, dramatic pause. "He comes back the next day and the boss calls him into his office for orientation," Randy leaned in, ending in a loud whisper, "Where he's told that he has to kill someone. He's a hitman."

"Oh! A cleaner. The employer snuck him into a cleaning position!? That's gold! That's a story."

"I told you, smartass."

"That's not nuts. Those kids have style. Crazy and style are often confused with one another."

"Well, one of those students sketched a picture of me with goat horns kissing a teddy bear."

"That, that is nuts. No doubt about it. Certifiable."

"What's new with you, Mr. LeBeau? How're the classes?"

"Well enough, I suppose," He took some time and thought about it a bit more. "Oh yeah, I've been teaching them literature. Easing them into the more difficult stuff. Don't want to overburden them with a bunch of jargon right out of the box and lose their attention, you know?" An affirmative nod was given. "But I'm beating myself up because they don't know what a protagonist is yet. They should really have learned this by now. We went over it in class last week. Today, I introduced the term antagonist but since they haven't learned protagonist, it got off on a rocky start."

"Protago-whatzit? Antaga-who?"

"Really, Randy? I thought you would teach them this stuff in your acting class."

"I don't teach them procedure and structure. I just give them a chance to express themselves and have fun with English."

"Well, that's important, too. But I want to fill their brains with as much knowledge as I can. That's my mission in life. That's what I do."

"Sounds stressful."

"It is," Remy replied, brightening as he expressed the discomfort, "It does stress me out sometimes. You know what's good for that, don't you?"

"Beer?"

"Yep. That doesn't explain why you drink, though."

"Oh, that's an easy one. I'm an alcoholic. Ask me a tougher one, professor."

CHAPTER XVIII

CHINA

Remy was washing the dishes from a mediocre dinner he'd prepared when he heard the faint sound of the door opening.

"Monica Hu. Welcome," he yelled from the kitchen. No response. Cutting the tap, he took a deep breath and held it, listening. There was a dull, almost inaudible whisper of footsteps. A slight click signifying a step made in women's footwear. He loved to hear her. "I'm doing the dishes," he called, his voice reverberating through the flat. He waited for the sound of her approach but sensing no movement his way, resumed the chore of washing cookware.

A few minutes later, he entered the living room and found her slumped to one side, face buried in the crevice of sofa cushions. Long, silky, jet black hair splayed haphazardly across her form. She breathed deeply and often, chest rising and falling in a continual sway that shifted swaths of her hair back and forth like the rigging of a yacht.

"Are you injured?" he asked flatly, suddenly very sober and focused on her.

She whimpered, a sound that was most peculiar coming from her. It hurt him to see her hurting, but he detached himself from sympathy, mind set on fixing whatever it was that ailed her.

"Look at me," he stated flatly, speaking with authority.

She complied, slowly pivoting to face him. He repositioned her legs atop his lap and sat flush alongside her. Sliding hands under her back and hoisting her more upright, he pulled their two bodies together in an embrace. Speaking into her ear, "You worry me sometimes, ferret face." He kissed her ear and set her back down. She smiled wanly and melted into the couch cushions again.

"Talk to me," he continued from an upright position perpendicular to her collapsed body. "What happened?"

She turned away, the fleeting smile long since departed. With a face pressed firmly into the crevice of cushions, she mumbled loudly, "Go away, Remy. Leave me alone. You no should be with me."

"Wow, okay sunshine. One of those not-so fantastic days, I suppose. You shouldn't be menstruating just yet, though. You've another couple of weeks for that."

She jumped up, "How you know how I feel? And what *menstruating*?"

"Lady time. It's a time that only ladies have. Not a happy time for us men either, as the cramps tend to manifest themselves in bitter attitudes. Well, I suppose it does bring with it the knowledge that no babies are on the way. That part is rather good and all but ---"

"I no menstruating!"

"I know. I just covered that. Now I'm at the part where I have to guess why you're in such an unsavory mood. Boss or peers encouraging you to abandon our relationship? It will never work; we're too different; yada-yada-ya."

She smiled a cold smile from a faraway place. "You wrong," she said softly and then sank back into the soft, dark crevice of couch cushions. "Go away."

"You nestled into the very heart of our happy home and then tell me to leave? Not a chance, love. But I will play some cards online while you relax."

The four of spades that turned on the river gave Remy the flush that he was looking for. It being the later stages of an online tournament in which the betting had grown massive and weak hands often won the round, he went all-in and was promptly called by a player whose two pair became a full house with that same four. "Damn it," he cursed, crashing a clenched fist into the couch cushion, relieving the tension of play. He stood with a smile, analyzing his gameplay, reviewing weak points that weren't so weak and finding confidence in the development of his play. A plate of half-eaten pasta had been laid on the coffee table next to the remote control and a small battalion of bamboo coasters. Her glass of perspiring soda sat directly on the table, surrounded by unused coasters. Judging by the pool at the base, it had sat there for at least two hours. *Have I been playing that long?*

"One of these days love, I'm going to take your drink and pour it on your head. I'm sure we've discussed this before, remember? Humankind has developed tools since its conception and these tools aid us in our everyday lives. One of these tools is called a coaster. They're pretty easy to use. You just set them down like so," he paused, waiting for her attention, nudging her gently until she looked up groggily. "See? Just lay it flush against the tabletop and viola! Civilization!"

She groaned and burrowed into the sofa again. "Hey!" he called out, raising his voice in an attempt to dispel the negativity, "What's wrong with you? What happened?"

"Not now, Remy," she mumbled through cushions. "I no want do anything."

"Stop wallowing. Talk to me," he spoke firmly and with love.

"Stop, Remy! I told you go away!"

"You do not command me," he responded sharply, annoyed with her behavior. Regretting his response, he continued more softly, "But I suppose I've just been commanding you. Listen, let's not do this. Please. Just tell me what's going on. I need to try to fix this if I can."

She turned and looked to him pleadingly, her face scrunching up into something best described as pity. He wrapped himself around her gently, spooning her, balancing tentatively on a cushiony precipice. She turned around, laying her hand on his face. They looked into each other and kissed and became one again, hearts beating in time.

"I did it," she spoke into the quiet. "I record him again."

Remy shot up, grinning. "That's great! Excellent news! This is good," his excitement coming through in his voice. Looking down he saw her smile faintly, smiling as one trying not to bring others down. A sad smile. He tilted his head to the side at this oddity, confused. "You should be pleased. Why aren't you happy about this?" She replied with a slight shrug and turned over once more, returning to the solace of a couch cushion.

He managed to maneuver through a soft-spoken conversation, gathering details. Principal Tan had called her into his office early that morning and deployed his perverted arsenal, approaching her and resting his hand on her thigh. She asked him to stop and he continued. She said she was uncomfortable and asked him to stop again more forcefully to which he complied. Later in the morning, he apologized and during the course of the apology asked for her to sit on his lap. Remy chuckled uncomfortably at this but cut himself short as Monica's face soured. She'd refused and he had continued again, only this time she raised her voice to near-shouting in her efforts to derail his intent. She brought up the other lecherous occurrences and he had admitted to them on record, trying in vain to justify his actions. All of this recorded as clearly as the toll of a bell on a winter's day. Twenty-three minutes and forty-seven seconds. Very clear and very obviously the principal's voice, she insisted in her limited English.

Remy was positively ecstatic. "We have that little bastard! This is great, truly great." He jumped up and began pacing the floor, arms clasped behind his back, chin down, as he pondered the implications.

"So now we need to find a way to ---"

"What *we*? I do this. Me. Only me," at first exploding into the question and then petering out.

"You know that's not true. This is my fight, too," he replied. He swallowed a bit of disgust and continued. "We should secure a duplicate of this recording immediately. Then, we find a way to confront him. We'll give him one chance to stop." *This wicked little man is mine for the undoing if I choose it*, he thought loftily. *I could ruin him now. Take his family, his job, his reputation. Everything if I choose it.* He stopped pacing at the kitchen window. Taking a deep breath and sighing audibly, he gazed down at the school. He pulled his arms tightly to his side and bowed, a slow, deep bow done properly with an erect spine and eyes fixed on the recipient. *I win*, he thought, straightening. *You abused your employee, your assistant, my lover. You disrespected her. Me. Unknown others. You won't be doing that anymore.*

He turned about to find Monica's eyes upon him, taking in the scene, drinking in the sentiment. "You feel good now. Proud. Strong."

"Yes. Well done, good read. Yes, I do. But we need to see this through. Use the recording correctly. I was thinking the other day of creating an email account and sending a mass message to the school staff with the recording attached. If he fails to keep his pants on around you again, that is."

"That very mean thing," she said.

Remy laughed good-heartedly. "Oh, being nice to that little frog is not what I have in mind at all. But I will be fair, even to that sexual miscreant. First, the proper warning. Let's call a meeting with him tomorrow and ---"

"No, that no good idea," she said, cutting in, "You, I, Principal Tan?"

"Yes, of course, the three of us. His abusive, dishonorable actions involve all three of us. The three of us will sit down and have a chat tomorrow but we need a secure copy of that recording and hide it away somewhere safe tonight. Email me the recording."

"I no email you. If it go many people, that make his life," she looked up a word on her phone, "destroyed."

"I'm aware of that. That's been the whole point, love. Do you remember why we did all of this? Do you recall why all of this was necessary or have you already forgotten his hands on you today?!" his voice rising, angered at the memory of such disrespect to the woman he loved.

She ignored the questions and waited for him to relax. He slowed his breathing and sat down next to her, calmer. She spoke. "I play recording to him. He listen this morning in office."

"What!"

She waited again, weariness of the outbursts of emotion showing clearly on her face. A cool smile parted her lips. "He no problem now. It upset him." She paused and added, "He different now."

Two sides warred within his consciousness: one part comforted in a problem's rectification, the other remorseful that he hadn't carried it out himself. "Maybe."

"No maybe. I there, Rem. I know."

"Alright, let me think this over." He looked at her appreciatively. *More here than meets the eye. Much more.* "You'll tell me if his disrespectful behavior returns," no question in the tone.

"Yes."

And with that, he scooped her into his arms as a new groom carries his bride across the threshold, kissing her madly about the lips, mirthful cooing pushing back the evening's troubles into the deepest recesses of his mind. The old fool had kept his job, kept his face in the community, which Remy was not thrilled about, but the message had been delivered. He was not entirely pleased with the notion of Principal Tan left unpunished, however, imagining one or two other new hires who may have already been sexually harassed, molested more likely, or soon would be in the days to come but he decided to let it go. A crusade to impeach the man in a foreign land could likely end disastrously for him and he knew it. Content that Monica was safe, he slept soundly while she thrashed, tossing and turning throughout the night.

CHAPTER XIX

CHINA

Principal Tan officially left Jiangxi Attached Middle School of Nanchang, China that same week. *Transferred to another school,* some said, *because of a promotion. A demotion,* said others. *A lateral move,* suggested another. *Early retirement,* said another bunch. "Is that so?" Remy would reply to each conjecture, wearing a sly smile that seemed hugely out of place given the topic.

Days accrued into weeks and a season came and went. At first, he took comfort in gazing down at the dark, empty office window that had once shined so tauntingly, but as winter came and went, this practice faded with the bad memory. Those evening calls to the office ended just as she had predicted it would. Afterward, she filled that apartment, transforming it into a home, a thing he had not had in a very long time. They spent their non-working hours together cooking, cleaning, shopping, outings to restaurants and bars, listening to each other's tales of family and friends, of pasts both pleasant and painful. They related western and eastern news to each other, told jokes, laughed, loved. And then:

"Well, you're all dolled up. Are we going somewhere?"

"Thank you," she replied curtly, something of a nod and a smirk flashing as she breezed by him in the hallway of their happy home. She continued into the bathroom where she called over her shoulder, "But we going nowhere."

"Ouch," he muttered through a half-smile and raised eyebrows. Instead of mooning over this, he attempted to joke, raising his voice to be heard across the flat, "You cut to the quick! Really? Nowhere? I think we're definitely going somewhere, you and I. I thought for certain that I'd be meeting those elusive parents of yours any day now. At least a cousin. I beguile your family with my radiant charm. They fall in love with me, beg me to take your hand in marriage. Everyone wins. I've got it all planned out."

He strolled to the bathroom doorway to see her reaction. Her hands were busy fussing at a lock of hair warming in a curler. She glanced at him briskly.

"Well?" Remy stretched both the word and himself.

"What? You no ask question. You just say well." But something in the slightly higher-pitch of her voice told him something was amiss. *One of the rare few times something felt off,* he thought. He was content with this, feeling that she, like him, understood the uniqueness of their relationship, an oddity unduplicated and worth preserving. Something solidified between them, something incorporeal but very real. Through the reflection of a mirror, he held her gaze with serious eyes that stated plainly, "I'm not pleased to be excluded. I don't want mystery in my life. I want you."

She became more somber. Turning away, back to the curler and hair, she mumbled softly, "I know."

He shrugged and turned about, retreating toward a cyber-world of poker cards. She entered the home office sometime later looking perfect. "Goodbye, gorgeous woman who used to be mine," he cynically pined. "Have fun doing whatever it is you'll be doing."

"I won't be home tonight, Remy." The words hung, stinging. "My sister here and I no want her know that I living with you. She know, then her mother know, then my mother know." The words just lied there flatly.

"Well, we can't have that, now can we?" he spat rhetorically, trying to sound cool. Failing.

"No yet," she leaned over, bending low to kiss him before departing, Remy hungry for her before she was even gone. *But here it is again,* he thought as they detached, *Darting off in the middle of the night. Again.*

He stood and walked with her to the front door, holding it ajar while final compliments were issued. A final, farewell kiss, brisk and cursory, and then she turned about and walked down the outer hallway, high heels clicking into the distance. He stood in place, eyes fixed staring absently at the shutting door, through the door really, at a wild idea. He returned to the online poker game, clicked an icon to discard automatically and swiftly changed into dark outdoor attire. Stumbling as he hopped toward the door while pulling on shoes, he gathered himself, stood straight, and vanished from his abode, a ghost on legs. He ran quietly on the pads of his feet, around the most direct path from his flat to the neighboring street that divided work and home. He crouched and slowed his pace, adhering to shadows as he approached the outer perimeter of the apartment complex.

Fifty meters away he caught sight of her as she sashayed her way across the street. A triumphant feeling of success emerged and was quickly quelled. *I have no idea what I'm doing and this has only just begun. Stay focused,* he ordered himself. *Remain unseen. Observe.* She finished crossing the street and turned back to face the immense apartment complex. Remy faded further back into shadow, accidentally backing into the proximity of a small family out for an after-dinner stroll. He turned about to face them, hopefully shielding the act of slinking in shadows -- an act difficult to explain in any language -- and strolled directly through the family, smiling, nodding and waving in passing. Pleasantries exchanged, he gave the family some distance before turning about and creeping back into place, keeping out of sight of both the retreating family and stationary lover. Monica was focused on her phone, looking up periodically as headlights approached, looking down again as they continued on their way. She took a moment to study the fourth floor of the apartment, to the kitchen window of the flat they shared. *It's a good thing I left the light on. Looks like I'm still there now.*

He smiled despite the situation when a pair of headlights slowed to a stop alongside Monica. His legs were aching and two mosquitoes had been making quick work of his flesh. Ten minutes of squatting silently in shrubberies had brought a dozen itchy welts and little else.

A modern, two-door, silver car with a boxy design pulled up. She greeted the driver in Mandarin, her voice barely making its way across the street to his uncomfortable perch. The back end of the vehicle eclipsed his view of the driver as she opened the passenger door. They sped off, leaving Remy free to dispatch the mosquitos, no longer needing to remain silent and motionless. His frustration turned to ruining their bloodsucking bodies, sparking the tiniest smidgeon of happiness. *Don't know what I expected to find. Seemed normal enough. Tan is gone. Guess I should be more trusting.* He gave his head a shake and jogged the long way back to his flat, gradually accelerating, sprinting the last stretch, pouring his heart and soul into the dash.

CHAPTER XX

CHINA

"Mr. LeBeau?" she queried, raising her hand. Remy brought up his index finger, signaling awareness of her question while requesting patience. Concluding an explanation with one of the go-getters in the front row, he strolled a wide circle around the classroom, making eye contact here and there to encourage student engagement of the assignment.

He returned back to her desk. "Yes, Athena. What's your question?"

She looked up grinning a teenage grin. "I don't know the *--ing* words."

"Sure you do. You use them all the time. Present continuous. What are you *doing* right now?" applying emphasis on the verb, raising eyebrows.

"I'm in class."

"But what are you doing?"

Her forehead furrowed while she gave the situation thought. She answered in a way that sounded like a question, "I'm asking you a question."

"Ah ha! That's it!" Neighboring students slightly jolted at the exclamation. "See? You know what you're doing."

"But I still don't understand."

"Oh, you aren't *understanding*," he agreed, emphasizing the verb once again. He looked down at her, seeing in her eyes that she just didn't get it yet. He crouched, lowering himself to her eye level. She nodded.

"And now you are *nodding*." He added, beginning to nod with her in unison, rhythmically. She snickered, causing the neighboring students to break into chuckles. Remy, too. "Now we are *laughing*, right?"

She still looked perplexed, and Remy waited, knowing the power of giving his charges time to gather themselves. A flicker in her eye. A flash of something. A confident smile pushed back full cheeks slightly pockmarked with oily clumps. "Oh!" she exclaimed quietly, sureness intermingling with realization, "I'm doing it now!"

"That's it, kiddo. Now, now, now. You get it? That's the *-ing* form of a verb. It shows that the action is happening right now. Puts emphasis on the current nature of the action."

She nodded her understanding. Remy synchronized his own nodding with hers again, making a joke of it, eliciting more chuckles. He strolled away from the mirthful outbreak, a duck in water, a man in his element. Checking the time on his mobile phone, he reminded the class of their homework, his words drifting off into the sound of chimes that marked the end of class. He chatted amiably with a few students, gathered his things and returned to the shared office that made up the foreign teaching department.

It wasn't long before the liaison between the directors of the school and the foreign teachers opened the door, audibly stating, "Knock, knock." Remy looked up from his desktop computer which was loading slowly. "Are you busy, Remy?"

"Not so much. Papers to grade, assignments to design. Same old, same old. What's up?"

"Mr. Zhang would like to see you," she announced, keeping the door propped open with one arm that was beginning to tremble slightly under the strain. She switched arms, maintaining her position.

"I guess you mean now," he said, rising from his desk as the operating system of the desktop computer slowly came to life, icons flickering into existence on the monitor, the hum of a fan softly spinning. "Lead the way," he said, stepping out. The liaison maintained a steady lead, walking briskly. He mimicked her gait to the best of his abilities and found himself marching down the hallway arms firmly planted along his sides. *Very militant.*

"Do you know why I've been summoned this fine afternoon?" he queried using his most professional tone of voice, preparing for the upcoming encounter. She glanced back halfheartedly, shrugging. Director Zhang, the vice principal, the direct overseer of the foreign department and one the most scrupulous of former Principal Tan's right-hand men. A little over two months had passed since the incident had come to a head. Remy had expected a reaction much earlier but none had come. *What's the expression? Revenge is a dish best served cold.*

The assistant stiffened, knocked on the door as she pushed it open and began speaking very formally in Mandarin as she entered the room. *Announcing my arrival, I'm sure. Funny, this is the first time I've been here. Halfway through the school year and this is the first time I've been in the boss's office.* Sensing the formality's conclusion, Remy brushed by the assistant and motioned to the chair lying opposite Mr. Zhang's desk. Zhang nodded somberly and he took a seat, a soft click of the door latching shut as the assistant left the only noise in the room.

Remy crossed his hands and took in the scene. Certificates and degrees lined one wall, a bookshelf along the other. The wall behind the desk was composed of two wide windows, closed and curtained. Judging by the fabric folds and dust patterns, those windows were rarely opened and certainly hadn't been opened recently. The desk was a massive thing, both deep and wide, its edges running so close to either wall that he marveled how this man could access his seat. *He works hard at isolating himself*, he inferred. *That explains why I haven't been here before.* Associating the man's isolation with timidity, Remy relaxed, but when Zhang spoke, he realized his folly.

"Stop seeing her," the vice-principal stated flatly, their eyes meeting in the cool, dark office, the only light leaking in from the edges of curtains drawn shut.

"Excuse me?" Remy wasn't quite sure he'd actually heard what he'd heard, the surreal having replaced reality in an unfortunately growing trend.

There was no immediate response. Their eyes remained transfixed on one another, Remy's go-to half-smile emerging while he absorbed the gravity of the situation, steeling himself. He had always interacted with this man via an interpreter and was expecting a broken conversation full of misunderstanding. Zhang's message came through clearly: *This is not a discussion. This is a command. And no, questions are not welcome.*

"You are kind man," he said in English far better than what Remy had been expecting. It took a moment for Remy to piece together the cryptic comment.

"Christmas," he remembered aloud. He'd purchased the man a somewhat expensive pen having noticed that he carried a cheap, poorly made one. Remy even added a self-made card, a doodle of a Christmas tree and a snowman in a wintry realm. The words continued to hang, both men comfortable with long bouts of silence, neither fidgeting. "I remember," Remy stated when the time was right. Looking for the pen, he found it right next to Zhang's right hand atop a stack of papers, indubitably well used. Remy smiled nervously. "Think nothing of it. Merry Christmas," he added though the holiday had passed a month ago.

Zhang looked at him a long time, holding him still with sobering eyes. "Leave her," he repeated, letting the words hang. Remy's demeanor shifted suddenly, in preparation of defending both his own freedom and the woman he loved. His eyes squinted, cowboy fashion, as he leaned back and away from the desk, all warmth disintegrating.

"Now listen here. I will date and love whomever I please. You're the vice principal. You rule supreme here in this school. I get that. I abide by that. Tell me what to do and I'll do it, better than most. But you can't interfere with my love life." The words rushing out free and untethered, feeling he was doing his part to instill justice, putting things straight. Zhang listened and waited and held Remy still with those piercing eyes again. There was another pause, a long one, while Remy calmed.

"Leave her," he repeated more softly. Not commandingly, no harshness to the tone, no dominance, no superior alpha-male bullshit. Something like compassion flitted about facial features Remy didn't know much about. Confused and understanding the point of the meeting, he thanked the man for his time, shifting the mood abruptly to a more cheerful note. He stood and shook hands, all the while Zhang keeping those sobering eyes trained upon him as he exited.

"Leave her? Who does that man think he is, telling me what I should do with my romantic endeavors? A God complex, that's what he suffers from," he spoke sharply to himself, speaking words aloud that didn't ring true. *Jealousy? Is Zhang another Tan-to-be? Has he been biding his time, waiting to make his move on Monica, only to find out that she's taken with me? Possible, I guess.* But the notion just didn't resonate as truth. Puzzled, disoriented, Remy plodded downstairs, lost in thought.

CHAPTER XXI

USA

Three years later.

Little rest overnight, coughing up cloudy compounds. Another infection of the lung. Free-clinic student-doctors had prescribed generic antibiotics. A few expired tablets remained, too few in number to amount to a full dosage. Remy had little desire to take them. *Have to end this mess with some class and dignity.* Having perused the internet, he'd found hemlock on eBay. Two ninety-nine for half a gram. One-eighth of a gram a lethal dose.

First, a chill in the extremities, then numbness pressing inward, eventually reaching the chest, bringing about suffocation as the lungs fail to inflate and deflate. A method favored on a do-it-yourself website designed to instruct those who wish to perish. Socrates went that way. Chose to drink it while imprisoned rather than face exile from Athens, punished for speaking against those in power.

Classy. A classy way to go. No denying that. No mess, no fuss. Some dignity at the end of it. Not hanging like a piñata for someone to find. No bloody clean up. A considerate way to go. He had six dollars in his wallet, no job, and no source of income on the horizon. Eight times the lethal dose would definitely do the trick. While he had access to the hot water required to make hemlock herb tea, he lacked a steady, secure address to ship it to as he was living in yet another homeless shelter. All incoming packages required to be opened with an employee present. Would be hard for an honest man to explain the hemlock.

He finished composing a letter that didn't explain much and settled into a sea of bunkbeds to cough restlessly throughout the night tightly surrounded by men legitimately concerned of disease spreading.

CHAPTER XXII

CHINA

"I said, you should listen to him."

Remy found it difficult to believe what he'd heard. Twice. Mike often spoke openly and with passion about the over-extent of Chinese authority in pretty much every facet imaginable. The thought of him supporting this clear breach of a business relationship was baffling.

"It's pretty much ingrained in me to expect nothing but I must say I'm caught off-guard. Thought I would find a sympathetic ear here."

Mike shrugged and pressed on, "You want to talk to me, I'm talking."

"Well then, tell me why. Why should I follow my boss's commandment involving my private love-life? She doesn't interrupt my performance teaching. She seldom pops into the office and never cuts into my teaching hours. I feel great being with her. We don't argue. She's magnificent in so many ways. Why do you want me to give that up? How can you want to take that away from me?"

He shrugged again and resumed the video game. The conversation turned to lighter fare and they decided to do a bit of light grocery shopping for beer and snacks.

Remy slowed his motorbike to a stop for a green light at an intersection, contemplating a safe passage through a flood of oncoming motorists that were clearly displaying no regard for the traffic signal. He didn't curse the drivers inwardly or outwardly, didn't sigh in disappointment of the selfish decisions the general public made to take often and only give when necessary. At times, he too would run red lights along with the herd, justifying the disobedience as retribution for moments such as the one he was in, stopped and staring at a green light, unable to proceed. Fighting injustice with injustice, fire with fire. He felt a bit of himself slipping away and growing numb, and with the erosion of spirit, came a diminishing fury at waiting to move forward at a green light. With detached acceptance he found a break in the flow of traffic and cut a path.

Mike had already arrived. Remy parked and attached a massive lock to the tire. Five minutes had proven more than enough time for a thief to begin the process of grand theft auto. Remy had experienced such an attempted robbery twice in China: once with Mike during lunch, the two men jumping up and sprinting down the road after a thief until congested traffic caused him to abandon the motorbike and run off, and a second time when Remy exited a convenient store to find a thief twisting a screwdriver into the starter switch of his bike. The thief had begun to saunter off, Remy following right behind, temper raging, announcing the ne'er-do-well as a thief in loud Mandarin, pointing, insulting profusely in English, and finally inserting his nose into the other man's face to provoke a reaction, of which there was a half-hearted brandishing of the screwdriver as a piercing weapon. Remy had found that humorous at which point the thief basically fled the scene. Opinionated and free with his words, he'd been attacked before. Having experienced a scrap or two, he hadn't found the makeshift shank especially frightening.

Mike waited as he always did, straight-faced but not grim, more blank than melancholy. "I need to pull some money out of the ATM first," Mike said as Remy approached. He set off for the wide automated doors of a building housing both a bank and a grocery store, stopped halfway, and turned back. They stopped near the entryway in front of a wide automatic door that slid open and closed as scores of Chinese passed around and between them. "Turn your phone off."

"That's a weird thing to say. I'm not on the phone. Look," Remy displayed his open hands, "no phone. No Bluetooth device in the ear. Just me. Incredibly handsome, intelligent me."

"I mean it. Turn it off. Reach into your pocket and shut off the power to your phone."

"Mike, what the f&%* are you going on about, man?" Remy grinned widely. "Is Big Brother watching you, Mike? Do you have tinfoil sheets lining the interior of that motorcycle helmet of yours? You can never be too sure, you know. Should I wrap my phone in aluminum? Would that help reflect any hostile transmissions?"

"Are you going to turn it off?" Speaking in a tone of finality to which Remy complied. Content that the phone had indeed been shut down, Mike turned to him with a grave face.

"I would never give my PIN number to my girlfriend, you know? Like if she asked me for it, to buy groceries or buy something online, I would never give her that number. You know what I mean?"

"That sounds awful, Mike. You've been with her for a year now. You sleep right next to her. You don't trust, Megan? You kiss and laugh and look every bit the happy couple."

"Yeah, Remy. The happy couple." For a moment there was something deeper and sad that played about Mike's face, and then it was gone, replaced with resolution. A soldier's determination. "I would never give her that PIN number, Remy. It's a bad idea. Don't do it."

"Are you telling me not to give Megan my PIN number? This is getting even odder. Why would I give your girlfriend my PIN number? This is about you my friend, not me. You have some serious trust issues with a woman who probably loves you dearly."

Mike smiled. "It's about me," he quietly chuckled. "Turn your phone back on, Rem."

"Oh, is it okay now? Have the little green men left the area?" Remy asked as he retrieved the phone from his pocket.

Mike turned back with a smile that shielded something unsettling underneath. "Why do you bring your phone with you? Why not leave it at home?"

"It's a mobile phone, Mike. Mobile. Why does anyone bring their phone with them? Why do you bring yours with you? It's just what people do."

"I don't have my phone with me today. Must've left it at home." He smiled that smile again but Remy didn't notice, his attention focused on his mobile's activation screen as app icons flashed into existence against a personalized background image.

"You know, I used to just keep the cellphone at home," Remy expounded as the screen rebooted. "I never really use it when I'm out and about. The roads are too dangerous to check a map and ride a bike at the same time. And man, I hate it when you meet people and they focus on QQ or Facebook instead of actually engaging in conversation and activities with the group. Bringing it with me seemed pointless since I never really used it outside of the house. I used to just keep it at home. The mobile phone was a home phone."

"What happened to that idea?"

"Moni happened to that idea. She began getting upset when I didn't reply right away or pick up the phone when she called. So, now I carry it with me. Making the wifey happy."

"You want to marry her?"

"Maybe. I'm not getting any younger."

"And you call her 'Moni'?" pronouncing the shortened name as *money*.

"Yep. Like all the money in the world."

"That's funny, Rem." But there was no humor in the flat tone. No smile on his face.

CHAPTER XXIII

USA

They began grouping together around a locked chain-link gate around one p.m. Some of them hadn't left the vicinity since they were ushered out unceremoniously into the cold pre-dawn morning at six o'clock in the a.m. Others had waited overnight. Only the men in closest proximity to the gate as it opened would be guaranteed a night's lodging and there was always contention in the milling crowd to be positioned as closely as possible. There existed a finite number of vacant beds and once filled the only alternative was a cold night's unrest on the sidewalks nearby.

Around two p.m., the gate was unlocked and the men flooded in, sometimes pushing through the elderly, the physically disabled, the psychologically battered, the intellectually challenged, in an effort to occupy seats on stone benches closest to the entry door. The first men to be seated were the first to be processed, the first to enter, and the first to begin showering. Only one hour of hot water would be available. Intake took two hours. They bathed together in hurried groups of four, side-by-side so tightly that elbows touched as shared bars of soap were lathered over various bodies: black, white, young and old. Each man's shower water splashed upon each other man, the shared run-off pooling at their feet around insufficient drains. No walls or curtains to shield their nudity. Ten men adorned in underwear alone waited impatiently in a queue for their chance to bathe in a line so close to urinals that splash-over was a common occurrence. "Hurry up in there!" called one of the more seasoned volunteers in charge of issuing towels. "Five-minute showers! Five minutes is all you get." The narrow chamber was steamy and flooded, filled with the stench of feces and the gas of some one hundred men who had been waiting since they had departed the facility at six for the chance to use the toilets contained in the same corroded room as the shower stalls.

Each man was encouraged to volunteer some of his time cleaning the facility and/or preparing and serving the nightly meals. Failure to volunteer would earn one the title *freeloader* though there was nothing free about the homeless shelter. Each destitute man was forced to come up with forty-two dollars each week in order to utilize such restricted, decrepit services. Failure to pay the forty-two dollars, by money order only, would result in removal from the shelter for a minimum of three months.

One suitcase per man was allowed and housed on shelves in a rundown, dingy storage room. Access to that suitcase was restricted to one thirty-minute window around five in the morning, and a couple of hours in the afternoon when the men returned. In the pre-dawn morning, the men changed clothes in the open air outside of the dilapidated storage room. They sat on stone benches in a small courtyard and stripped down to socks in need of both darning and washing and applied layers of clothing to stave off cold temperatures. By noon, the layers would prove uncomfortably hot, but by then, it would be time to return to the shelter and group together in clumps and wait uncomfortably for the gate to open once more.

They would exit the shelter each morning after a meager breakfast of expired donations into the dark and cold at six a.m. with nowhere to go. The public library downtown would open three hours later at nine. Starbucks would open at seven but the impoverished knew not to arrive exactly at or even near that seven mark. A destitute man is rarely welcomed into a place of business so melding with paying customers, blending in with the crowd, was imperative. Many turned to the public transportation system, riding in buses, no destination in mind, just making use of a heated seat until indoor spots became available. Bus drivers were charged with the task of removing passengers who completed one full trip along the bus route and failed to disembark. In accordance with policy, the driver would stop the bus and force the occupant out, seemingly anywhere along the route, wherever the driver made the connection that the occupant was not interested in actually traveling to a destination. The bus would remain stopped until the occupant left, other passengers often pressuring the freeloader off, though many of these individuals were in the exact same position and only pressured the other so as to avoid the same fate. Some drivers risked their jobs and didn't engage in this activity. Some were more inclined to fulfill their duties. No one was very happy with the situation and joy was in short supply in those early morning hours.

Remy, clad only in briefs, waited in line alongside a crumbling wall in the toilet/shower area, a stained towel and clean clothes in one hand, soap and shampoo in the other. He hugged a wall filled with unwashed clothes hanging on hooks but still felt the warm misting of another man's urine back-splashing from the urinal a couple feet away. The floor so flooded that the sandals he wore were unable to keep his feet dry. Many men went barefoot, sloshing through waters teeming with things best unthought of. Many of these men's feet showed all the signs of infection and a wide array of diseases. In and amongst, Remy smiled and remembered a poem from Shel Silverstein.

"I am reminded of a poem," he began. No one responded. "Oh, come on, you lot. You're going to love it." A fellow he had spoken to while grouped around the gate glanced up while lathering. A veteran. Army.

"Go on then," the veteran said, at ease with public nudity. "How does it go?"

There are too many kids in this tub.
There are too many kids in this tub.
I just washed a behind.
I'm sure it wasn't mine.
There are too many kids in this tub.

The vet started to chuckle, then a full-fledged laugh, which bounced around the cramped tiled walls oddly. The mirth, like the massive bathing/toilet puddle, infectious.

Someone else, "What was that? Say it again." Remy complied and the men's spirits were lightened for a time. One man who had finished rinsing, brushed through the line, shouldering his way through to get to his clean clothes which hung gingerly from a loose hook. Remy stripped out of briefs and entered in his wake on the far side of the showering area. It was a good position, only one naked man on his side, the other side a crumbling wall. The shower head streamed cool water upon his naked form, almost completely cold.

"Cold showers in winter. Better than no shower, I guess," Remy thought aloud to no one in particular.

"Hey! Hurry up in there!" came a familiar call. "And someone flush that toilet."

There was an hour or two wait before dinner was served. Reheated, unsold pizza from an all-you-can-eat chain. Neither vegetable nor fruit accompanied that and most meals. Sugar, meat, and carbohydrates the prevalent components of each meal. Three slices were allotted to each man. The pizza dry, the crust inedible, impossible to chew and tear with human teeth. With stomachs filled, the men were forced into a single-file line where they traded their bed ticket for a seat in the chapel. Attending chapel was not optional. Hats and mobile phones were forbidden, as was talking or sleeping during the services which occurred each and every night from seven to eight p.m. Guest preachers delivered their sermons to a crowd of mostly uninterested men who had long since given up hope for better days and a compassionate God that meant them well.

Most stared away at nothing, planning out the following day though they had few options. Daily-pay labor at the rate of $8.50/hour, often back-breaking work of heavy lifting, pushing, pulling, dragging, digging. Or recuperating after such a day's labor by riding buses to nowhere until the time came to either drift into a café unnoticed or into a public library or sometimes exhaustion and pain from the previous day being enough to lead a man to just lay down in the street outside the shelter, a position from which he would likely be guaranteed a bed and a shower with hot water later.

Most did not give the sermon much, if any, thought, it being difficult to imagine a benevolent, loving God in such an environment. Some had abandoned themselves to alcohol, weed, and heavier drugs, spending most of their meager earnings on intoxicating substances. This was especially true during the first half of each month as SSI checks and food stamp funds were issued by the state. During this time the shelters were lightly occupied, many men compiling their funds to rent cheap motel rooms where prostitution and drug use ran rampant from the first to the fifteenth or so, but then the government funding would dry up, leading to a crash of sobriety and a return to the shelters. In the latter half of each month, the showers were often cold as these regulars returned and filled the premises until the government checks arrived the following month, stretching minimal resources even farther from the point of decency. The newly added men entered in crashing from highs, hungover, going through withdraw, and even broker than the average poor who inhabited the shelters.

In a makeshift chapel composed of a pulpit, piano, two hundred folding chairs, two hundred men, two hundred bibles and not much else, the preacher-of-the-day would conduct his sermon. The preachers would make their rounds, preaching one night in prison, another night in one of the three shelters in the city, another at a small, thinly populated church elsewhere in the city that served as a headquarters. The prison and shelter sermons were practically identical and repeated with each rotation, usually two weeks or so apart. Life in a prison and in a shelter practically identical: each man's name eliminated, his identity reduced to a number sequence, privacy all but eradicated completely.

In the homeless shelter, eighty men slept on forty bunkbeds spaced two and a half feet apart. Prisons, by comparison, housed a single cot in each cell, maybe a bunkbed in crowded situations. Prisons also offered three hot meals, whereas the shelter offered only dinner and a meager and inconsistent breakfast. The showers in prison were kept clean and the water was hot, or so it had been explained to Remy by other shelter locals. There was no need to walk through cold, dark streets in prison, aimlessly wandering until something opened up. Televisions in cells. Paintbrushes and canvases. Books. Access to a doctor and dentist.

Hearing all of this, Remy was tempted to begin a life of crime to avoid his miserable living conditions. The proceeds from the would-be crime would've added to an achingly low coffer. Getting caught and arrested would have amounted to incarceration and the better life that entailed. A win-win situation. But he continued to obey the law instead, forgoing the logical win-win criminal activity, putting the greater good ahead of himself, and maintaining a life of intense poverty.

"I don't know about you all, but I know I wasn't descended from no monkey men," the preacher exclaimed, chubby, red-faced, and a little winded, worked up by an abnormally high number of attentive listeners. Half of the congregation tittered. "That's a really obtuse way of looking at the concept of evolution," Remy mumbled softly to himself. His neighbor, reeking of soiled clothing clinging to an unwashed body, turned a glassy-eyed gaze upon him. Remy eyed the man back, "It's a little more complicated than 'monkey men'." The man showed no recognition and returned to staring blankly at the flooring ahead.

"We live in a world of sin. Don't you see it? People live without morals. Indecency is normal."

Remy returned his focus to the outlandish preacher, concurring with the last statement. There was much evil and it seemed to be winning. The selfish were solidifying their rule with each passing day. Sacrifice for the greater good had become a laughable concept. The concept of good, of right, had faded away into subjectivity. The preacher continued.

"And while we're at it, the Lord made Adam and Eve, not Adam and Steve." He concluded with a self-serving smirk, pleased with his ability to interweave ethics and humor.

"Wow. Really? That old cliché? That's what you find troubling with the world? In the entire world, that's what really grabs your attention? Yikes, look around, sir. Open your eyes."

A quarter of the congregation shifted focus to Remy who had not noticed that his thoughts were vocalized at a normal speaking volume. They looked to him not to shush him, not angered by the interruption. Suggestible, mildly approving eye contact all around. He was a bit taken aback at the newfound attention, his intent not being to interrupt, having had no intent at all. He forged on. "I'm just saying, there are worse things happening in the world now. Look to Syria. The Congo. North Korea. Look at us." The crowd didn't know much about those places and soon shifted their attention back to the preacher who continued unaware of the goings-on in the back corner of the chapel.

"You drink. You smoke. You lie down with women you shouldn't be caught dead with. You gamble. You spend your money on unclean things and then you wonder why you don't have anything or anybody. You need someone else to come and put shoes on your feet, to give you clothes, give you food and a place to sleep because you just won't work for it. You'd rather live this way than work and build something for yourself. Bad things have happened to you, that's true. But you've brought this burden upon yourself. You're reaping what you've sown and if you don't change your ways, you'll die in a place just like this. Maybe in this exact room."

Remy didn't like the sound of that. He'd been stuck living in shelters for a couple of years already and the thought that there was no escape, no betterment despite his best and most persistent efforts had indeed crossed his mind long before the jolly accusatory preacher began pointing fingers. No escape from homeless life: shifting from shelter to shelter, walking street after street, waiting for buses while the summer sun scorched his skin and the winter winds blew another influenza into him. Death a release from suffering and not to be avoided. Suicide not an alien concept.

Oh, Remy had thought much about just how bad it would be to continue living in such a way into his forties and beyond, his body growing less and less obedient, bones aching at the joints, muscles sagging behind looser and looser skin. Remy had longed for death for quite some time. This mindset had led him down paths seldom ventured, opposing those best avoided, not picking fights but certainly not backing down if injustice encroached into his territory. His desire for a cessation of life's suffering had only increased as the months ticked away. He had toyed with the idea of committing a violent crime just so a police officer would be forced to shoot him down. But he wouldn't burden the innocent with a crime, nor a would-be officer with an obligation to end his painful, hopeless life. Yes, Remy knew quite well that he may very well die in a shelter, homeless and alone. And he loathed it.

He was furious with the preacher's trespass, a man who had no idea what he had lost, the struggle, what he had overcome, what he had sacrificed. To think that he deserved such treatment, that any man deserved such inhumanity, let alone himself, triggered what happened next.

Remy shot his hand into the air and held it high, unabashed. The preacher saw this and continued with broad-stroke accusations that demeaned and captivated the audience. Worked into a frenzy of finger-pointing, the preacher ignored the hand, hoping that its owner would lose interest and leave him to his joy: instructing others how they should live their own lives. But a minute later, the hand was still there, stiff and unyielding. Half of the audience had shifted their focus to the man. Losing the attention of the crowd, the preacher grudgingly addressed the query. He adorned a wide, false smile and set his sights toward the back of the chapel where men slept on floors overnight if the bunkbeds were overbooked.

"Yes. In the back there. Do you have a question for me?"

"Yes. I'm a little confused. Are you saying that only good comes to the good and that bad things only happen to bad people? That there is no injustice in the world?" Remy was ready to sacrifice his bunk for the night, or month, or forever. He wouldn't let the issue go. Couldn't.

"Well, er…"

"Because I don't drink. I don't smoke. Not cigarettes. Not weed. Not Cuban cigars. I didn't gamble away my savings. I don't watch pornography. I have no lover, indecent or otherwise. I'm neither a drug addict nor an alcoholic as are quite a few of these men."

"Right. I understand that but…"

"I apply to at least ten jobs a week. More like twenty or thirty, the more that I think about it. Filling out forms that redundantly state what's already on my resume to potential employers who are quick to prove just how little they care about my time by asking me to re-produce my work history on applications when I've already outlined it on my resume. I work daily labor, from seven a.m. to five p.m. for a little over fifty dollars a day, if I'm chosen to work that day. It's in-consistent work, incredibly consuming, often dangerous, and pays very little. A couple of days ago, I loaded desks and tables into a new school from a tractor trailer up a flight of stairs to the second floor. I worked until there was no energy left to give and barely given access to drinking water. I rolled my ankle in the process, but I was immedi-ately told not to notify anyone because I would be blacklisted from the pool of workers who are actually chosen to go out each morning. Because many men aren't even given that opportunity, if you want to call it that, to work as I did last Monday."

"Well, you're working. That's a good---"

"I'm still aching from that and it was days ago. So, I come in and sit down and give you my attention and you tell me that I deserve this? I don't deserve this. No one does."

"Not all of these men are working like you are."

"Are you saying that bad things only happen to bad people or not?"

"I'm not. The Bible is full of stories of good men enduring hard times. The rain falls on the just and the unjust alike."

"Yes. Yes, it does," Remy agreed. "I'm so tired of the rain, sir. I'm so tired." Suddenly, Remy's eyes clouded with tears. Acceptance, res-ignation of his fate, of his cursed future, pooled into droplets that threatened to leak from his squinting eyes. "I just want it to stop now," he said to no one in particular, though two hundred men lis-tened attentively.

The preacher filled in the gap seamlessly, anxious for his chance to regain control. "Jonah was a man who shirked what God wanted him to do, serving his own desires instead. And do you know where that got him?"

From the second row, "Inside a fish." Smiles all around, Remy quickly forgotten.

"That's right. Swallowed up whole," the preacher agreed, pleased to turn the proceedings back along the proper course. "Of course, that was thousands of years ago. Fish were bigger, then. The Bible tells us that the Earth was created six thousand years ago. Jonah was swallowed up thousands of years after that."

Remy ignored the absurdity of the chronology. *Swallowed up whole. That feels right. That's exactly what happened to me. I was swallowed alive.* Eyes drying, he thought to reengage, though once again he didn't notice that his thoughts were being vocalized, "The Earth is not six thousand years old. That's not subjective. It's not an opinion. It's been proven to be much, much older than that. Carbon dating. Google 'carbon dating' somebody. Someone Google that right now. And how is this man saying that fish have changed over the years but that evolution is not real? Does that make any sense to anyone?" Realizing towards the end that he was indeed speaking aloud.

But no one was paying any attention to him. They didn't know what carbon dating was but they did understand big fish, so the makeshift congregation's attention didn't waver much as the preacher continued delivering his sermon.

"Swallowed up whole," Remy muttered.

CHAPTER XXIV

USA

Monica grew more distant. Tan was long gone but the solitary evening outings remerged, especially on the weekends. They'd grown quite close after expelling Tan, but as a cat that has grown tired of a petting, she began sauntering off on her own. The distance had been growing throughout the spring and with summer emerging and a new job on the horizon in the southern city of Guangzhou, Remy wondered where they stood.

Most nights she produced tales involving visiting cousins or friends that for a variety of reasons had never been introduced to Remy. He had followed her again a few times after she left the flat all dolled up on her own and began spotting a recurring vehicle -- black, two-door, sporty -- that came to retrieve her. She would slip in dressed well and the vehicle would roar off, leaving Remy alone in the shadows to wonder and brood. When questioned later, she told him a taxi had picked her up from the apartment complex. Remy nodded sagely, concealing the fact that he knew this to be untrue.

He delayed telling her that vice-principal Zhang had commanded him to stop seeing her, searching for clues before opening up and putting all of his cards on the table. When he did impart the occurrence, a month later, she took the news with obvious surprise, slack-jawed and wide-eyed.

"Why would he say that, you think, Moni?"

"I, I not know. I not understand what you say," she answered after recovering from the surprise.

"Are we back to that again? Come on. We know each other well. Be honest."

But she deflected instead and left their home shortly afterward, called away to some school function. *Maybe Zhang really has taken Tan's place,* Remy thought, alone again on a Thursday evening. He wanted desperately to get back to that Monica he had shared his life with over the winter, a season in which they were inseparable, every bit the happy couple. But by mid-spring, the once infrequent absences had become fairly routine.

He stayed awake that Thursday until she returned around two a.m. They had spoken seriously then, Remy demanding concrete answers that she refused to give. She parried and dodged behind a veil of English misunderstanding, no matter how many times Remy repeated statements, no matter how much time he gave her to think about and look up words, no matter how simplified the wording.

"What is *late* mean?" she had asked, attempting to deflect another question.

"Enough, Monica. You just look like a fool now. You used the word *late* just five minutes ago when speaking with me. Tell me what you're doing out so late so often. Why won't you introduce me to any of these friends and family members of yours?"

She looked away, tense, muscles taut.

"I love you, ferret face. I do. Now talk to me."

She turned to look to Remy, her façade crumbling, teary eyes underneath.

"I, I break up. Break up with you. I leave you. I tell you before, leave me. Go away, Remy," she was sad and resolute, something akin to pity playing about her fine features, though that didn't make much sense to him. "I take my thing and I go. I go back to room at school."

He insisted she stay but when she didn't, he helped move most of her things back to the school dorm, rolling a suitcase while trying to convince her to remain, to turn around and work it all out, to open up and come clean. She was precious to him and, distrusted or not, his life was empty without her. She wouldn't make eye contact with him that night as they walked together toward the school grounds, her phone ringing incessantly. She just stared off in the distance, neither addressing Remy nor the incessant mobile.

"Just turn off the phone," Remy iterated. "We're talking."

She looked at him then with a knowing smile, "It no matter. On. Off."

Remy's hackles rose. He did not continue to persuade her after that. They walked in awkward silence until she took her belongings into her flat and closed the door without a goodbye. Every fiber of his being had been poured into understanding her deceit and the cause of their division, but he had failed. The wall remained upright and strong and he was no closer to knowing what had caused it than he had been the beginning of the school year. He walked home confused, immersed in loss.

Life was miserable without her and when she returned later in the week, with severely bruised knees and not wanting to be touched, refusing to talk about it -- timidity obscured by posturing, something deeply wounded lying underneath the stolid surface -- he still rejoiced that at least she was sharing her life with him once again. She had withdrawn even further and he was determined to find out why and how to heal the damage, how to bring things back to those glorious winter days, when they made fun of each other in a grocery store and loved deeply and true.

CHAPTER XXV

CHINA

The school year was coming to a close. Remy eagerly began transitioning into a new scholastic environment in Guangzhou which offered higher pay and less required hours. The new employer would pay for the move, including the cost of shipping Remy's household goods along with his German shepherd, William, via air delivery. He fielded a phone call from the new employer during the last week of schooling requesting that proof of payment of shipping costs be procured and sent to them immediately. There was a strange urgency from the assistant of the new school that some sort of a receipt would be needed that very same day.

"Don't you think this can all wait a day or two? I don't need the money to be refunded immediately or anything."

The assistant maintained the imperative nature of the receipt, a sentiment strangely echoed by Monica, insisted on in fact, pressing Remy to rush to his bank's ATM after classes had let out to take care of the urgency. They arrived at the bank shortly after it had closed. Iron shutters were lowered and locked in place, preventing access to the bank inside. Five ATMS were set into the back wall of a lobby shared by a grocery store.

"You need type your PIN."

There was an awkward overconfidence in her tone that contrasted her subtle nature. Her eyes masked well-concealed turmoil. Curiosity, love, and hope culminated into Remy's next move, a move that would set his life in a vastly different direction forevermore. Taking a deep breath, he thought of the past year they had spent with one another, of the love that had grown, the surrender to one another. They had shared a life together and grown to know each other's intricacies well. Remy knew that she was wrestling with herself. It was written on her face and posture and tone and speed of voice. *She will do the right thing,* he decided. *She will resist whatever external forces must be working to provoke her into this action, whatever it may be.* They stood two meters apart sizing each other up in the exact same lobby in which Mike had instructed a more dubious Remy to turn off his mobile phone.

"It's up to you now, Moni. This is your choice."

It should've been an absurd response to her command of him to input his PIN so she could wire a small payment to the air transport company and produce a receipt of the transaction, but it was proper and it gave her pause. He saw the impact the statement he had made and grinned, knowing he had found a core that was good and true. She reeled back as a prize fighter suddenly struck senseless, as a thief once concealed in shadow stands exposed. He entered his PIN and stepped back two steps, allowing her all the room she would need to act.

And act she did. She entered in an amount of 49,950 yuan -- 50,000 being the maximum amount allowed in a bank transfer made via ATMs in China -- and then struck the *confirm* button on the keypad rapidly over and over, each strike of the button signaling the completion of the transfer, each strike of the button driving Remy's smirk farther and farther away. He crumbled to the floor of the lobby, suddenly winded and legless. His hands clutched at his scalp, pulling hair sharply. "What has she done?" he asked himself, choking on the words, forgetting how to breathe and speak, completely overwhelmed. Several orienting breaths later, he looked up from a crouched position. "What have you done, Moni?" She didn't reply. Her eyes were miles away. A coldness long-hidden had come to the fore. She turned back and faced him wearing a smile that was severely out of place.

"Done what?"

"It's all gone now, Moni. You actually did it. You just sent my money away. You stole," he replied dully. Feeling the last sentence had failed to capture the enormity of the situation, he tried again. "You stole from me." It was difficult for him to string thoughts together. He tried to stand but his body wasn't responsive. He was barely able to remain crouched, his body failing on multiple levels: balance, strength, breathing. Wobbling, he gave the hair clutched in his tight fists a final sharp tug. He looked down at strands and tufts of hair, the pain clearing his head. He stood and looked about, spying Monica at the ATM terminal once more.

"What are you doing?" he called out, though he knew what was being done. She was at the keyboard again and had begun the process of resetting the transfer section of the ATM to establish another transfer to properly clean out the remnants of his life's savings. He found his legs and moved swiftly, catching her left hand in mid-type. Without looking, she shifted and brought up her right to continue the transfer. Remy batted away the new probing fingers and adopted a martial stance, feet firmly planted, hips and shoulders aligned. Their eyes locked. She looked tired and worn and ashamed.

If her goal was to take my money, she should be glowing with an inner smugness of a job well done. Oh, she has something good in her. I know it. But why is this happening?

Monica rushed forward suddenly, focused on completing a sequence of numbers on the ATM keypad. Remy deflected her advance at the finger, sliding his hand across her skin, down the wrist, the elbow, moving through to her shoulder. She was thrown backward, off balance. "Don't make me do this," he spoke softly. She looked to him with defeated eyes and shuffled forward intent on seeing the hated event through to completion. He took a step forward, pivoted, and interjected his backside into her approaching path. Facing the ATM, he ejected his bank card and pocketed it in a single, fluid motion. With the situation as controlled as possible, he pivoted back to find cold, hard, steely eyes staring him down.

Or maybe I'm wrong. She's all over the place.

"There must be misunderstanding," she said, the voice tender, the eyes not. "Movers know what to do." And with that she was on the phone, smiling and all a buzz with some unknown person on the other line. It was as if two people lived within her, appearing and disappearing with the frequency of strobe light flashes. Perhaps just one person, the other a demon. She looked over to Remy from across the lobby wearing a pleasant smile.

"They say they just need better connect. I send little money and then can return money here."

"What are you talking about? Are you crazy? You really might be," answering his own query. He took a good look into her dark eyes and felt adrift at sea without a paddle and no land in sight. "These are thieves. I was robbed. You're a part of it. What're you thinking? Don't jeopardize your own money." The words fell out, observations, simple sentences the best he could muster, on the verge of babbling. She unsheathed her own bank card and inserted into the same ATM. *It would be improper to force someone to stop using their own card,* Remy thought, feeling something was wrong with the situation but uncertain what exactly. Wanting to stop her but obligated to not physically intervene, she transferred one thousand yuan away into the banking ethos, the equivalent of one-hundred and thirty U.S. dollars.

"Oh, no," she exclaimed calmly. "They take my money." And then Remy understood.

"Nice touch, kid. You're just an innocent victim like me now, right? Wow. We're going to the police now. Get your bag." He motioned to her purse next to the ATM.

"We no call police. That not how thing do in China."

"Then what do you propose I do? Just lick my wounds and feel sad?"

She nodded, creepily smug. "All you can do."

And with that Remy laughed in a manner similar to her smile, creepily out of place: deep, true, and long. He gave a final smirk and then began screaming and waving his arms about, gesticulating wildly, yelling about lost money and a thief right there, "A thief, a thief has robbed me!" Grabbing the shoulders of those that passed by, grabbing Monica's shoulders and hauling her back to his side as she tried to escape during the turmoil. A crowd quickly formed around them. Of the twenty or so people that made a ring around Monica and Remy, an English speaker emerged, a man in his thirties.

"What wrong? Why screaming? What happen?"

"I've been robbed. At this bank I was robbed. A thief. Stole money. My money is gone," Remy answered in a form of English he knew to be more easily understood, simple and concise.

"Phone police. You need phone police," he stated earnestly. "I call them now. Wait here." The man slid a phone from his pocket and dialed the emergency line.

"Thank you," Remy replied, turning and facing Monica with a wry smile and a cold sense of accomplishment.

CHAPTER XXVI

CHINA

Remy wasn't certain how they'd arrived at the police station. The good Samaritan may have driven the two of them there. If he had had to bet on the matter, Remy's money would have been on that, but perfect recollection of the journey to the police station simply didn't exist. Having the majority of his savings emptied out into an unknown thief's pocket via the woman he dearly loved had taken the wind out of his sails. Defending the remainder of his savings while taking care not to harm his lover-turned-foe, forging a crowd pliant to his needs, him a stranger in a strange land with a weak grasp of the language, while simultaneously preventing Monica's escape, had all taken its toll. He was wide awake but unconscious during the ride to the police headquarters, a thing of primality, all instinct, dangerously exhausted. In a sense, he woke up as the vehicle came to a stop at the station. He exited and walked inside the large building where he eased into the task of reporting the events that had transpired. He accepted a paper cup of tepid water gratefully from the lobby assistant and began to tell the tale to an officer.

While he sipped on water that he would have preferred to have eagerly gulped down, he explained some of details that had led to the bank theft. He took care to use precise but simple English as he explained the new employer's request to send proof of payment of shipping costs, of the air transport company that Monica had lined up, of her actions involving the automated teller in the lobby. As he explained the events that had led up to the theft, he appraised the staff of the police station -- only three people, two officers and one assistant -- finding them justice-focused and good-natured, while keeping an eye on Monica, who had a defiant look in her eye and little to say. While he spoke, he took in the environment with a dubious mind. He attempted to ascertain possible contents of pockets based on bulges, analyzed the staff's posture, gait, and stance to determine who would be a threat if he were to be attacked. He took note of the exits, the structural integrity of the window frames, the material of the door, who held handcuffs and where keys might be located, vital points if push came to shove, various impromptu weapons if the need arose. The impossible had just happened and he was tense and focused on not being surprised again.

"Hindsight is twenty-twenty, they say," he said.

"Yes. Right. Wait. I do not understand. English not very good," the police officer replied, taking the incident seriously and trying to understand each word clearly. *He is a good man, this officer,* Remy surmised. *There's much that one observes through the senses, but some things are felt, known through the heart and spirit.* There was nothing empirical in his belief that the officer was a good man, that he had devoted his life to solving crimes and bettering his community solely because it was the right thing to do. Remy didn't understand how he knew to trust him, but he did.

The officer recording the events ceased typing. He looked up with honest eyes above sealed downcast lips, tired eyes that showed the strain of trying to understand a language he hadn't studied in years.

"You said fifty hundred yuan taken? No. Fifty million," the officer concluded with finality.

"Well, I wasn't that rich, sir. She did take most of my savings but my savings wasn't that extensive. This woman stole fifty thousand yuan. About nine thousand dollars. All the savings one can muster on a teacher's salary. We teachers don't earn much money. Just like you, Moni, right? You're just a teacher."

Remy looked to Monica and smiled without feeling. She returned the gesture. "Yes," she said. "That true." Having shifted his attention from the new environment of the police station back to her, he suddenly realized that she was oddly comfortable, unconcerned even as she shifted her attention back to her lap where she had been typing stealthily on her mobile phone.

"I need make call," Monica said as her phone rang. She greeted the receiver of the phone call in Mandarin, stood and exited the police precinct. No one stopped her. The officer translated something in his head and continued typing away on his keyboard. She walked right out of the glass doors into the courtyard between the police station and the parking lot, cool and calm, coming to a stop just outside of the window of the room in which Remy was making his statement. She smiled as she chatted away on her phone.

"Are you letting her escape?" Remy asked, trying not to stare at the spectacle. "She's just walking away from all of this? She robbed me."

"I know where she live and work," he replied soberly. "She cannot run."

The officer spoke with such determinism that, when combined with Remy's discernment of the man's altruistic motivations, he felt content to let her roam free, boastfully happy though she seemed to be. And content or not, there was little else Remy could do at the moment. Against great odds, he had brought one of the criminal's involved in the theft directly to the police station. And while he had heard a great deal of troubling information involving the Chinese police force, from being overly heavy-handed in doling out punishment to completely indifferent of criminal activity, Remy was assured that justice would prevail in the end.

The officer recording the incident means to solve this thing, he mused, staring through the window at Monica while she spoke on the phone outside. *It's an easy case to solve. There are cameras in the corners of the ceiling in the ATM section of the lobby. A camera inside each ATM unit itself, I'm sure. Someone must have picked up the money on the other end. There must be a name registered to that transaction on the receiver's end. There's a website created under the guise of Air Express Relocation Services with the sole intent of stealing money. Someone must have registered an IP address to create that website, leaving more names and clues to follow up on. There was a phone number called, a false customer support that guided her to wire her own paltry sum, a decent ploy on its own, but the number itself even more evidence to act on. Surrounded by all of these clues, a myriad of footprints and fingerprints, surely even an inept officer will find a culprit or two swiftly.*

Yes, hope was burgeoning into optimism when he felt someone approach. Before he heard the footsteps, before the door swung open, he felt him. The figure at the door didn't enter the room with any sense of urgency. A giant among Chinese standards, a half-head taller than Remy and wider, much wider, swollen with muscle. He walked in, wearing a short-sleeved flashy button-up dress shirt, untucked over pressed slacks. On his upper lip, a mustache of impressive girth, thick and well-groomed. He entered the room slowly and purposefully, moving as a panther glides through the jungle.

Powerful and trained, Remy thought, taking care to note the man's arm reach and remain outside of the radius. *He will not be easily overcome, this one. Flight, if need be, is best.* He turned his attention to the window frame in order to calculate the pressure needed to force open a rusted portion he had spied earlier to the left. Instead, his attention was pulled sharply back to Monica Hu. The phone was gone. She just stood there, staring toward the highly reflective tinted glass of a room she couldn't possibly see the contents of. No smirks or smiles, smug or otherwise. She wore the face of an unhappy mannequin. It was a face he had never seen anyone wear before, so empty of emotion, so vacuous, that his first thought was that there was a different and rather frightening person outside where she had just been. His second thought, returning to the panther-man and the likely need to escape soon, settled on the use of the chair beneath him as a projectile to break the glass from the weakened frame in order to leap out and dash away. *Where to run, though,* he thought, *in a city of five million Chinese and about twenty-five foreigners? I'll be caught quickly but I'll draw a crowd in the process. Someone in that crowd must be able to get word back to an embassy, or a consulate, or other police.* It wasn't a great plan, but it had the distinct advantage of being the only one. *Whoever this panther-man is, I don't want to be alone with him.*

Remy returned to his surroundings. Much had changed in ten seconds. The newcomer was seated where the good cop once was. The receptionist barely caught Remy's eye, giving the briefest of nods in his general direction as she exited the room. The officer taking down the report, a man to be trusted, a man whose heart was in the right place, was awkwardly trying to return to the computer he'd been using to compose the official statement. The burly arrival waved his hands dismissively, halting the officer's progress and eliciting an apologetic slump to his posture.

"What's going on here?" Remy asked, speaking boldly, hoping this would energize the good officer into action. Resignation played out clearly on his face.

"I'm sorry. I should go."

"No, you shouldn't. There's plenty to be done. You could finish taking down my statement for one. And who is this guy?"

The new officer rose and moseyed up. Reaching forward he took Remy's hand in a shake that threatened to dislodge finger bones, his grip vicelike.

"Enough," Remy half-shouted, positioning his hips in a martial stance, pulling sharply up and to the side, retrieving his hand. The officer compensated, repositioning his own body in a manner best aligned to counter any additional actions. The officer with the good heart took this in with sad eyes. He was no warrior. He wanted to do more, knew that leaving was wrong, but leaving was most assuredly what he did.

"You're leaving me alone in here with this man? Are you serious? I was just robbed! Who even is this guy?"

"He helps you now." The original officer was almost gone now, half hidden by the closing door.

"This guy?"

He looked back, a little shine to his eye. "I'm sorry," he said, as he exited.

The tall, muscular, mustached man turned to Remy, smiling wide.

"Sit."

Instead, Remy turned his back on the man and walked across the room to the window. An inspection of the window frame yielded noticeable rust corrosion in the corners, providing the best opportunity for potential escape. Not a trace of Monica in the courtyard or parking lot. He listened intently to his surroundings, hopeful, but there was only the newly arrived "officer" in the vicinity. Wherever the receptionist and the good cop had gone, they were beyond earshot. Adrenal glands issued copious amounts of fight-or-flight. Blood vessels rushed the stuff throughout his body as his heart pounded a strong, steady rhythm. *If this man attacks, it is the eyes*

I must target. He looked back to the chair he had been occupying, wondering if breaking the thing down so as to use the legs as fighting sticks would be worth the trouble.

As he decided against this path, the sun suddenly emerged from behind a veil of darkened clouds, its bright rays cutting downward and illuminating the world below. Through the tint, the shadows of the room stretched and paled, dissolving in the new glow. The sky which had been full of dark, low clouds that had been threatening rain all day, was clearing nicely, the sun cutting through and dispersing the gloom. Remy suddenly felt renewed, as if a weight had been lifted. *If I am to die here, robbed and outnumbered, a lover turned bitter enemy in a foreign land, it will not be with a heavy heart.* He turned and approached his potential assailant with a wide smile of his own.

"Nice mustache. You look a bit like an Asian Magnum P.I. with that thing on your lip. But I don't think you're a P.I. Or rather an I, private or otherwise. Curiouser and curiouser."

The bravado was palpable.

CHAPTER XXVII

USA

Remy stared at the flag trying to make sense of the thing. He had no idea how long he'd been there, motionless, arms crossed with neither hand tucked in, leaning against the wooden edge of the wall. Perhaps twenty seconds had passed. Perhaps it had been five minutes. There was no way of knowing. His eyes had long since stopped focusing on the flag itself, the rows of white stars lined vertically on a blue background: six, then, five, then six, five, and so on until fifty; the horizontal red and white stripes beginning and ending with red. The flag wavered slightly in a makeshift breeze generated as the air conditioner kicked on. He held his gaze through the banner as it gently fluttered in the manmade breeze. All vision had become peripheral, all sound distant white noise as his mind pulled farther and farther away from reality, toward both the future and the past.

Daydreaming. It was a trick he had picked up years ago in the crowded subways of downtown Tokyo. The stations themselves were cramped enough, but it was inside the trains, in which passengers were literally pushed inside by an official people-pusher employed by the various trainlines crisscrossing the underground of Tokyo proper, where one learned what cramped truly meant.

Crowded to the point where a stranger's nose would intermittently bump into his cheek as the train slowed to stops at stations. Arms pinned, wrists locked into place at the hips by the force of some fifty people pressing upon him as he drifted down the subway lines, billboards streaking by, one after the other, some of the more clever set up as pictures in a flipbook, designed so that as the train zipped through the tunnels an animated effect was delivered to those passengers lucky enough to see out of a window. But most of them weren't paying any attention to their immediate surroundings. The feeling of humanity pinned in one place. The aromas of so many bodies so close. The heat it all generated. A sea of upright bodies filled each car on every train. Many found it best to ignore one's surroundings altogether.

"Find happy place and go there," an older Japanese gentleman practicing his English with Remy had once told him.

"Sounds like you're advising me to go insane."

"I am teaching you how to not be insane. I am helping you."

"*If you're helping me,*" Remy said, switching to Japanese, "*than sell me an inexpensive car.*"

They had shared a laugh at this and then spoke of lighter things, small talk. The weather, work, music, the greatness of jazz. The stops came and went, the great sea of pinned people bobbing and leaning in great unison, unable to fall over as there was no room for such a thing. The doors would open and bring in a wash of much cleaner air. The crowd would shuffle this way and that, somehow managing to allow both the exiting and entering of passengers. Open, shuffle, close, accelerate, decelerate, stop, open, shuffle, close, accelerate, decelerate, stop, open, shuffle, close and so it went until on one of those instances the gentleman exited with a bow. Remy reciprocated with a deeper bow.

"Remember your happy place. Do not forget."

"*I will remember, esteemed sir,*" Remy replied in Japanese. And they parted ways, never to meet again.

He had remembered the lesson well. While waiting in a line for an hour for free food probably better left unconsumed on those impoverished streets of Los Angeles, he daydreamed. And along those similar streets in Portland. And in Orlando. Homeless for three long years.

Remy stood leaning against a wall of a pub at nine-thirty in the evening, his ability to find his happy place greatly diminished, thinking of a more important time in his life: the highs and mostly lows of attempting to solve the very crime to which he was victim. A novice in every sense of the word, outnumbered, flanked on every turn, woefully lacking in resources, contacts, and fluency of language. It had been a longshot at best but he often wondered if he had left the better part of himself back in that rabbit hole, a place where Alice-like oddities had become something akin to normalcy.

"I'm still in a hole. No rabbits here, though. Just one of those normal holes. A pit, I suppose. A financial pit." He spoke to no one in particular. It was very busy at the moment at the pub where he worked and that meant that most of the staff had lost their minds, dashing this way and that, furious at how they were being treated by customers and reflecting that fury on any gentle soul that crossed their paths. That was usually Remy. He took the blunt of this vile behavior with detached acceptance. It was a role he had grown accustomed to. He was currently being punished for gently explaining to a rude customer that perhaps it would be best if he didn't return to the pub if he found the place so displeasing. Remy had been given only two tables to tend to until he "showed improvement in customer relations". So, while the rest of the serving staff ran about, he leaned against a wall, relaxed and remembered the past: a mysterious lover, a theft, crime on a governmental level, and something else altogether. Something without a name that still ached.

"And now I serve tables at a pub," he muttered, spitting the words out. "How does one acclimate to that exactly?"

"How's it going, Rem? Did the flag move?" Mike, a completely unconnected Mike to those prior days, asked with a grin as he hurried by. He was one of the few servers that kept his composure when the place became packed full of hungry, thirsty people clambering to be served next. He was also one of the few people Remy enjoyed working with. Mike was serving nineteen customers at the moment. Nineteen meals and sides and sauces and appetizers and drinks and refills and preferred cooking temperatures, and preferred air temperatures of the establishment. Some wanted the drinks with no ice, or a little ice, or all ice. Customers pushing and pulling at the servers like saltwater taffy. Mike was one of the few who remained cool, calm, and collected.

"Yeah, when the AC unit kicks on it flutters a little. I feel a tinge of patriotism then."

Mike smirked at this and began typing away at a keypad, inputting a table's order. Remy continued, "Being punished is boring."

Mike cracked up a bit but didn't lose stride in typing. Tapping order buttons, *bacon cheeseburger, no pink, mashed potatoes, loaded, on side: butter,* not looking up, "Yeah, Rem, but what does it all mean?" It was an open-ended question meant to elicit any kind of answer. A glib remark made to keep the speaker speaking, a tool used to continue a conversation, an old hat that Mike wore well.

"It's not what it means so much as what it meant."

"What did it mean?"

Remy returned focus to the flag, yearning for a positive memory to latch onto.

"Something more."

CHAPTER XXVIII

CHINA

"Tom Selleck. That's the actor's name. That's who you look like. Tom Selleck if he were an Asian fellow."

"Did this Tom steal your money? A..., Mr. Selleck?"

"Ooh, no good, my friend. No good, at all." Remy approached as if to punch his arm good-naturedly. Meeting the man's eyes along the way, he thought better of his decision and began pacing the room instead. "You know full well, there is no thief named Tom. Or maybe there is somewhere in all of this. Someone needed to create a false website, a falsified phone number, the bank account where my money ended up. There may actually be someone named Tom in all of that." he stopped, turned, and smiled pleasantly to his opponent. "But you'll never locate him. Heck, maybe you're the thief named Tom. Not like I would know. Can I call you, Tom?"

"No."

"Alright, Tom. Alright. No need for the attitude."

Remy was feeling much better. If the man had been planning to attack him it would've already happened. Still, there was something about him to beware and so he kept his distance, smiling through the pain of loss of love and finances and justice.

No longer concerned with an imminent physical altercation, he sat down and went through the motions of continuing the official statement. Tom made no move to record any of it.

"Don't you think you should be typing some of this up?"

"I will remember it."

"What's my last name, Tom?"

"Rem."

"No. That's my first name shortened. What's my last name? My family name. Do you have the wits in your head to provide me with that?"

Tom rose swiftly, Remy's training forcing him to his own feet before he realized that he was standing. Tom made no move to come around the desk. Frozen, the two combatants eyed each other up. Tom angered and tense. Remy wearing a playful smirk.

"Oooh. You want it, don't you? I understand. I definitely understand that feeling. It would be a thing of beauty, don't you think? You've got me on weight, more muscle, too, but I'm probably quicker. We both seem well-trained. Your kung-fu versus my ninjutsu, an east meets other east sort of thing. China versus Japan. I want to say this already happened seventy years ago. The results were not in your favor, Tom."

Remy was indeed writing checks he may have very well been unable to cash, so to speak. He had taken the reprieve from fear a little too far. But his motives were cannier than they appeared. Remy's sharp words illustrated a technique dubbed "startling the snake from the underbrush" in the *Book of Five Rings* by Miyamoto Musashi, the idea being that whoever strikes first is at a disadvantage. This is why mixed martial artists dance around one another before throwing a kick or punch, and even then, the first strike is light, airy, not meant to land really, but to gauge how the opponent responds to attack. Proper swordplay, too, follows this rule. As any soldier worth his or her weight in salt will tell you, a well-aimed, informed strike is better than ten hurried ones. When one strikes, well-aimed or not, one lowers the defenses, leaving an opening for a counterattack. Unlike chess, moving first in battle is a massive disadvantage. Thus, Remy attempted to startle the snake from the underbrush by reminding Tom of China's failings in World War II, the idea being that he would grapple him, or at least throw a punch, either of which Remy had prepared to counter.

The fury dissipated, however, and humanity reasserted itself on Tom's face, leaving Remy flummoxed.

"Nanjing, Tom. Haven't you heard of that place? Do you know *that* last name? Nanjing? Or did you forget it like you've forgotten the details I've given of the crime you haven't been recording?"

The grin Tom wore showed a great truth: *I know you want me to strike you and I will not.*

"Well, f^\$*, Tom. What am I supposed to do? I'm all alone on the other side of the f&%*ing planet. Love lost. Obliterated. More than that. Love turned enemy. Most of my savings is gone. In the midst of great turmoil filled with various characters only a fraction of which I'm actually able to actually perceive, many of which acting against me. This new job in Guangzhou is probably connected to the crime and I can't even find solace in a police station, Tom. I was robbed and within the same hour, I'm put into this insanity: a kill-or-be-killed deathmatch against a tall, muscular martial artist, who could be anyone except a police detective. Definitely not an officer of the law. You aren't a cop, Tom, but you just shooed one away like he was a cat on a countertop. It's a little much, Tom."

He appeared amused by Remy's outpouring of emotion. "It's okay. I am here to help you," his smile threatening to turn into laughter. Remy approached in two swift steps, within striking range sooner than Tom had expected. No laughter now. No smile, either. Just two men nose to nose.

"It's LeBeau, Tom. My family name is LeBeau."

Tom didn't respond. He remained motionless, tense, muscles poised to pounce.

"You're not going to jot down any of my statement, are you?"

No response. Just a man on the cusp of attack.

"Triad. That's what you are. A triad thug. A mafia goon. I had no idea you lot had this kind of pull. You just walked in and relieved an honest cop from his post."

The man relaxed at this. No smile though he warmed hearing it, reveling in the fact.

"I won't rest until I have my money back, you know. I will not let this go."

"You will not rest." he said matter-of-factly.

"I don't like your eyes, Tom. Be careful with those things."

Remy took a step back and sat down in the chair opposite the desk.

"Come. Let's finish the statement you won't record."

He spent the next half hour making a formal statement regarding the bank theft. Tom made no motion to record any of it, though oddly enough, he did seem to pay attention. *Wondering how much I actually know, no doubt,* Remy realized toward the end at which point he began to be less clear in his descriptions, answering the occasional question vaguely and sometimes misleadingly.

Having concluded, he internally recapped the past hour. His entrance into the precinct. Monica's phone call that had undoubtedly summoned trouble. A good cop banished. The refusal to record his statement. He replayed these moments, analyzing the details for possible mistakes in observation or judgement, hoping that reality was something other than what it was.

"I don't like you, Tom. And I don't fear you either." A pause. "Enemy." Remy poked his own chest.

"Enemy," Tom repeated.

"You know I would mess up your face if it came right down to it," Remy said pleasantly.

Tom's pleasant demeanor turned sour once more. He leapt up and moved swiftly toward Remy who was finding his feet more slowly the second time. His opponent was positioned quite close by the time Remy found firm footing. A quick, tense moment elapsed and then Tom offered his hand to be shook. Remy bowed instead, keeping his eyes locked on his opponent.

"What have I become a part of now? What is all this?" Remy queried himself as he exited the station. No one was around. No one manning the doors. No receptionist behind the lobby desk. No sounds anywhere in the building. Just a presence in the room he had just left of a man best kept out of arm's reach.

The next morning, it was Tom who awaited Remy at the police station. The original good-cop, who had lined up the meeting that Remy had been careful not to vocalize during the official statement, was nowhere to be found.

"Are you ready to go to bank?"

"Yes, Jeeves. I'm ready."

"Who is Jeeves?"

"That's you my good man. And I do mean good. Honest and true, that's my Tom. Lead on."

They arrived at a non-descript car, definitely not a police vehicle. Half expecting to be driven to a desolate location and beaten savagely and/or killed, resigned to whatever may occur next and determined to show no fear, Remy sat comfortably in the backseat, arms splayed wide along the top of the seats.

"I thought your car would be nicer, Tom. You sold your soul to the devil and you can only afford this? Surely human decency is worth more than this old four-cylinder."

"Not my car," he said with a smug smirk. The statement rang true and Remy took a moment to reconsider. A feeling that he was in the backseat of the honest-cop's car crept in unannounced. The interior, old and frayed, but clean and well-cared for. The engine seemed reliable and little else. A practical car for a man living on the low wages of legitimate law enforcement in mainland China. All the pieces fit.

Remy sighed and stoically resigned himself to another bad day, "Fine. The bank, then. Let's go."

CHAPTER XXIX

USA

The lady ahead of Remy in the supermarket checkout line was on the verge of succumbing to a panic attack while she waited impatiently for produce and products to be tallied.

His attention turned to the tabloid magazines that populated the checkout stand. Covers bore faces he didn't recognize and names he didn't know. Acclimation to the homeland more than daunting. Impossible.

"How are you doing today, sir? Find everything alright?"

The cashier, a pudgy, cheery-eyed man in his early fifties beamed a smile through a bushy mustache that simply would not quit.

"Yep. Found everything I needed." Remy had little idea what he had just brought to the register. He glanced down as a pound of sliced honey ham chirped across a laser grid. "Just some sandwich stuff."

"Oh, sandwiches are fine. Fine indeed, sir. I love a good sandwich. I come from New York, so... you know." Flashing that mustached smile again.

Remy did not, in fact, know how hailing from New York tied into sandwiches. He thought sandwiches were made pretty effectively throughout the world, but instead of voicing this thought he replied, "Yep." But knowing that if you let an ex-New Yorker go on about New York, they will in fact go on, he felt pressed to alter the course of the dialogue, and so he continued. "That Earl of Sandwich. Changed the whole world with that idea of his. Probably his cook that deserves the credit, though. I doubt an earl would prepare his own meals."

The cashier paused in mid-swiping stride. "Yeah, that makes sense."

"I tell you what doesn't make sense. Where is this city named Sandwich? I've looked at some maps in my day, seen a little of the world, and I've never met anyone that hailed from Sandwich. I mean, is that a province or a township somewhere? I've come to doubt the whole tale."

"You know, you put some avocado on a sandwich and you've got yourself something good," the grocer replied, focused on a point of his own.

"I know that's true," Remy obliged, shifting with the conversation smoothly. "Avocados are amazing. Lettuce, tomato, and avocado. That's how I make 'em."

"Well, your total is $31.43." It was with a fair amount of humility that Remy removed a government assistance food program card from his wallet and punched in his PIN. He was earning just enough money serving tables that this benefit would not renew the following month. Upon earning $1600 a month, all assistance from the government was set to cease. Once the balance of the card hit zero, he was on his own. Sixteen hundred didn't feel like enough to be on one's own just yet, but he had little choice. He would not lie, and so, he rode along these mandated channels of government approved hardships head held high, waiting for the axe to fall.

He carried four bags of groceries out of the store and deposited them into the trunk of a silver, four-door Honda. The key twisted and the engine started right up. He negotiated streets that contained drivers he wished had been properly trained in the art of driving and arrived later at the gated apartment complex in the low-income part of town that he called home. He flashed a card and a machine beeped its approval. A sliding gate clanked and clicked and eventually opened enough to allow the car through. He reversed into a nearby parking spot, clambered up a flight of stairs to an apartment door and into a home shared with another destitute whom he had shared a shelter with just one month prior.

The appliances were quite new: automatic ice-maker in the freezer, dishwasher with heated drying cycle, glass stove-top with an electric heating element, an oven with a digital interface. It was the lap of luxury as far as Remy was concerned, though the furnishings were dated and worn, bargain deals obtained through second-hand sources. The bookshelf stood upright and was mostly straight once a bit of wood was wedged along the backside. The sofa needed more support, but this too was remedied with a plank of wood under the cushions. The once-wobbly dining room table was held resolutely in place with a full sheet of paper folded upon itself several times and tucked underneath a leg. A light-blue tablecloth concealed numerous blemishes.

The blinds were open. Sunshine lit the home and Remy thought, *This is good. This seemed so far away just a few months ago and here it is. A home. My very own four walls and a roof. I no longer dash this way and that to get to the bus stop on time only to wait a half-hour for a crowded bus to actually arrive. I have a reliable car with decent gas mileage. I am blessed and grateful and miserable and so very bored. The weight of this boredom just sits on my shoulders and crushes me down. I could do, and have done, so much. So much. And here I sit and waste away doing absolutely nothing meaningful.*

"After China," he spoke to an empty home, opening the refrigerator door, "the world lost its flavor."

CHAPTER XXX

CHINA

Who knows how deep this rabbit hole goes? I'm likely in the back-seat of a police officer's private vehicle being driven by a triad thug to a major banking institution that will undoubtedly be of no help in solving this crime. He resituated himself so as to take in Tom's face in the rearview mirror. *Smug. That thug is smug. Which means all his ducks are in a row and the bank will not assist.*

Remy gazed out from the backseat window. Pedestrians and riders of various two-wheeled vehicles and several motorists in Chinese cars that mimicked popular car model frames raced by as the car sped onward. *This is what Monica is a part of. This is what those hints and clues I have procured in my observations of her have led to. It is vaster than I imagined. Far more players involved and these players wield authority I had not considered possible.* The car slowed, turned, and parked.

Just Mike and I now. The only one left to rely on now that Moni has made her decision to--- It was then that he remembered the odd conversation over a shut-down cellular phone a few weeks prior at the same place where the crime had occurred. Remy froze, door ajar, staring straight ahead at nothing, or rather, directly into the past. *Wow. Mike. Really? Him, too? Then why...What was the phone...What is happening?* His mind whirled as he processed the connection.

"We are here."

"Yeah, yeah, yeah. I'm sure we'll get to the bottom of this caper now." Remy stood, putting aside all that was lost, smiling, putting on a mask of confidence. "Don't know what I would do without you, Tom. Probably have a much better chance of solving this case though, that's for sure. Someone needs to do it and it certainly won't be you. Guess that makes me a detective now. Well, truth be told, I've been detecting for quite some time now, I suppose."

"Spying." And the smile and smugness dissolved a bit, the real Tom sneaking through the mist.

Remy stopped in place and turned to the man. "Are we being real right now? Look, I can't help it. If I sense something is out of place, I'm not going to turn a blind eye to it. I'm not going to apologize for being curious. I don't feel apologetic for protecting myself, my loved one, and my property either."

"Protect?" Tom asked, showing that he didn't understand the word in English but truly, in double-speak, saying: *You think you succeeded at protection?* Smugness in the undercurrent, as his true self faded behind a mask once again.

"Oh, I do hate you. You and your tiny masters, wherever they may be hiding."

Tom's smile faltered and he stiffened as the insult to his masters fell upon him. No Chinese dared speak such words. Not police, not judges, not even the oligarchy that the rest of the world looked to as political figureheads of the Communist Party, leaders in name alone. Occasionally, there was timid griping among close friends, which was allowed if it done seldom and quietly enough, but to brazenly speak it outright to an enforcer in public was inconceivable.

There is a wild gleam in his eye. A murderous one, Remy thought, wondering what was going on in his opponent's mind. "If you and your brood had any courage at all you would approach me in the light, truthfully. Man to man."

Truthfully? Courage? In the light? This struck Tom as a foolishly simple way to conduct business, a man trained from youth to replace his father in a position unspoken. He wasn't ridiculed by such wording or shamed into action as Remy had hoped. It just wasn't how things were done. Straightforwardness was akin to folly and just wasn't an intelligent way to reach one's goals. Remy was targeting the man's honor and as such was firing away into the ether. This realization coupled with the memory of the Moni's emotionless, void face at the police station culminated unsettlingly. *These are hardened, unfeeling individuals,* he realized. *They don't just threaten and coerce. They walk a dark path. Evil exists and it is here.*

A feeling like cold water swept over him, freezing his mind and body, both of which screamed at him, *Go no further!* He shook off such cowardice internally and acted. "Enemy." Remy croaked, his voice cracking. He cleared his throat and tried again. "Enemy," he repeated, sounding more like himself the second time, poking into his own chest. "I'll always oppose you."

"Good," Tom's smile said. He turned about and strolled through the automatic sliding doors of the bank lobby. Remy watched him enter, making no move to follow, in no hurry to be disappointed. *If I had half a brain, I would turn down this new job in Guangzhou, tuck my tail between my legs, return to Florida and move in with my family.*

He was alone. He looked up at a sky white with formless clouds. A day without much light or shadow. He thought of her, of how close she had been to doing the right thing. How she had broken up with him over nothing, clearly nothing at all, just two weeks prior, obviously trying to shield him from this blow. Of how she had paused and warred internally with herself before she made the critical decision to transfer the funds. *That was no act.* He remained confident in his ability to perceive the intimately guarded, though his batting average was certainly under one-hundred percent. *That was no act,* he thought again. *There is goodness in her. She can be swayed over to what is right and good.* He loved her still, one day after she had robbed him, one day after he watched that creepy, expressionless face of hers turn away and leave him to deal with the demon she had summoned.

He thought of the new employer that had required an immediate ATM receipt showing payment from his bank account to the moving company in order to process a full refund. Of how Monica had secured the moving company's services. Of how she had championed the cause of rushing to provide proof of payment that same day, despite his hesitancy. Of the part she had played, and of this new employer that undoubtedly did not mean him well. *They are surely connected,* he thought, *as is Tom and even Mike somehow.*

He thought of his last trip to Macao. How it was only on that one trip with Monica, that he had lost more money than he had spent playing poker. It was the only time he hadn't left Macao with winnings. At the time, he had chalked it up to poor luck but as he recollected the event as he ascended the steps of the bank, he remembered her insistence on joining him at the table for poker, how she had sat directly behind him, had wanted to be shown his cards to learn the game, though she'd never expressed interest in learning before. It had felt wrong then, like an outside presence was working against him, which she had later claimed was ridiculous. "You being paranoid," she had responded.

He thought of a trip to India without her. He'd asked for a sexy photo to tide him over from being without her for two weeks and she had provided exactly that, her in red lace and little else. Instead of a selfie, though, he had received a photo of her reclining in a rather nice arm chair in a room he did not recognize, scantily clad and with a hungry look in her eye. When asked, she answered her friend -- a female, physical education teacher from their shared school -- had taken the photo. Remy had been so distracted at the thought of these two women in such a situation that he'd completely ignored the possibility of treachery. Later on during the Indian vacation, he had fabricated a tale of a lost passport and wallet and needing to prostitute himself for money for food and travel fare back to China, meant as a silly story, juvenile really, a cheap and easy laugh. He had been met with a long, somber silence that felt as if a cold wind had blown through their dialogue. "You must do what you need do," she had said in an icy voice Remy had barely recognized. He couldn't bear the tension and stated his ruse, a poor joke. She hadn't laughed then and the conversation ended shortly thereafter, the awkwardness unresolved.

"Well, she did not find that funny at all, Mike." Remy said, clicking the *end* icon on his phone.

"Really," Mike had replied unquestioningly, unsurprised. But the unease had quickly melted away in the midst of the vacation. As Remy stood outside of the bank in which a triad thug dubbed Tom had just entered to undoubtedly discourage bank employees from being helpful in locating suspects, the awkward silence following that trivial joke seemed a much more revealing incident. *Mike,* Remy remembered, *has been a part of this for quite some time. Whatever this is.*

He thought of Monica's odd behavior, of how she would stay out late into the evenings, not returning to their shared apartment until well after ten o'clock, even after the Tan issue had been resolved. Of her cryptic answering of what she had been doing out at such a late hour. How she had always dashed into the shower first thing upon coming home. How she would often stay out until midnight or so on the weekends, "With friends," she would say. Friends

Remy had never met. He thought of how he had grown tired of hearing suspicious answers. How he had begun to combat the growing unease and investigate.

Spying, the thug had put it. When Monica left the apartment around seven o'clock one evening, called away for some reason or another, Remy had paused a video game and wished her well as she gathered her purse to leave. He held her hand, pulling it close and kissing the back. "I love you," he spoke, meaning the words, before returning to gaming. She left, but as the sound of the closing door whooshed throughout the apartment, he was already on his feet, padding over to the door swiftly on silent footsteps yet again, such activity having become habitual. Not two seconds had passed and Monica's retreating form was exiting the fishbowl field of vision that the front door peephole provided. He listened to her heels click purposefully down the flight of stairs and then dashed to his room, doffing his pajamas and donning grey sweatpants topped with a darker grey hoody. He slipped on sneakers one at a time, hopping along on one foot and then the other.

His balance true, his body focused on the task ahead, he slipped out of the front door, closing it quietly behind him, focusing on the clicking of those heels, judging the distance to his target, the speed of its departure, the direction. He took note of the lighting as he moved through stairwells and hallways, of what direction his shadow projected and where, adjusting movements to be optimally concealed as he pressed onward toward the sound of the click, click, clicking of the heels. He kept her close enough to be tracked and as far as possible so as to not reveal himself in the process. He took care where to step, avoiding litter and debris, so as not to give away his presence, timing his own footfalls with her steps.

Remy remained motionless, immersed in shadow one flight above her as he watched her walk away below, feeling very much like a ninja. Along the flat surfaces of the parking lot, pursuit was different. Crouching while slipping from one shadow to the next. Silently dashing through well-lit areas. He crouched in shrubberies, behind cars, along a fence, the other side of which housed a familiar toy poodle trotting around doing nothing. She had stopped on the far end of the lot, well out of the visual parameters of the kitchen window back home that Remy would gaze out of from time to time. She opened her bag, took out her phone and placed a call. She spoke swiftly in Mandarin, listened for a reply, and hung up without a goodbye, all business. *Normal people say goodbye*, he had thought. *But then again, normal people don't crouch in shrubberies observing someone not say goodbye.*

She waited for a few minutes before the usual sports car arrived. The car rolled up and slowed to a stop. A man Remy's age, early-thirties, opened the passenger door from his position as driver. Just the two of them. He smiled brightly and Monica tucked herself inside the passenger seat without emotion. No music played in the car. The car door closed, the interior light flickered off, and the car drove off. Remy crouch-ran between a couple of parked cars and took in the license plate, memorizing the Chinese characters, the first symbol marking the province, the remainder an alpha-numeric sequence.

Monica had returned home around midnight, finding Remy in his pajamas playing video games, right where she had left him. She pushed away Remy's kissy advances. "I shower first," she had said, scolding his ardent efforts. He had had little desire for passion that evening but a ruse was a ruse and he would see it through to completion.

"Where were you?" he had asked, nibbling gently on her neck. "I missed you."

"With friend." The standard reply.

"Oh, did she pick you up or did you take a taxi?"

"Taxi."

Remy hadn't missed a beat. "Oh, you should let me know next time and I'll drop you off where you need to go."

"No. It far. So far. Your motorbike no take me there. So much wind in hair."

"Or we could take a taxi together. I would very much like to meet these friends of yours."

"No. Everyone speak Chinese. You no like."

"I wouldn't understand much, so yeah, I guess I wouldn't like it." Outfoxed, he turned his mind to other things, remembering the recent tailing, of observing without being observed. *I snuck up on a dog. A poodle. Those things bark at everything and it had no idea I was there.*

"Why you smiling?"

"Just glad you're home again, Moni. It's boring without you."

"Go play your games and I will be back and make you exciting." Seductive, spicy, hard to resist.

Remy gave the nape of her neck one last smooch and complied with her commands. He tailed her a few more times after that, always that same car, always that same driver, never music playing in the car. Always a lie about a taxi. He had assumed she was secretly dating, preparing to transition to a new man once the school year ended. That had been bad enough, a dark secret that he couldn't share and that he hated deeply. But as Remy stood outside of the bank, recently robbed and immersed in the terrible unknown, a new thought came to mind.

A pimp, he thought the words clearly, almost audibly in his head. *I was dating and living with and am in love with a prostitute. That explains the driver, the lies, the constant showering, the late hours. That explains the connection to a guy who can just waltz into a police precinct and take control of the entire operation. It explains an emotionless face, a separation of self. It explains the Macao poker loss, the only poker loss in five trips to Macao, the only trip I took with her. I guess she was working with someone there. Which would make this an international issue.* He filed this away to be pondered later. *Her discomfort when I mentioned prostitution in Goa, India. It explains why I'm pretty sure I overheard a Russian fellow whisper into her ear at a karaoke party something about his friend's wife leaving him and wanting to meet her.*

Remy had lost his cool then, unable to connect the dots, hoping she was being propositioned incorrectly, that he was defending her honor, but also somehow knowing such a thing was improbable. Not wanting the truth to be the truth. Clutching onto any small chance because otherwise there would be nothing left to hold onto.

The clouds swirled and boiled above, a reflection of his own inner turmoil. She had broken up with him yet again not long after that but had returned later with fresh bruises and a distant heart. She had hesitated and almost resisted the theft at the ATM. There had been pleasant nights in the kitchen washing dishes together, listening to music, kissing a cheek. There were so many nights they lied asleep draped in each other's arms, wrapped up in one another. *Maybe she's trapped in all of this,* he considered. *Maybe I can pry her free and into a better life.*

Besides, he thought, turning toward the bank, marching forward, ascending steps that led to the sliding glass doors of the lobby. *I can't let that guy win. There's a mystery to be solved and I will solve it. This new school in Guangzhou demanded a receipt and is certainly a part of this movement against me. I will go there. I will study my enemy. I will collect clues and evidence. I will crack this case wide open and bring the attention of the very world crashing down upon their heads. I will eradicate this evil. Such is my mission. Such is my task.*

Automatic doors slid open as he approached. Using a middle-aged couple entering to conceal himself, he entered the lobby. He broke away and took a seat next to a rather plump, elderly gentleman who was fixated on a television screen displaying looped advertisements promoting the bank. Concealed reasonably well in plain sight, he used his peripheral vision to take in the scene. Tom stood regally behind a counter that separated bankers from customers. As teller interactions with customers concluded, he moved in to speak to a few, each showing obvious discomfort in speaking with the man. Not once did Tom show identification. Ten minutes later, equipped with several banking printouts, he finished making his rounds and turned his attention to the crowded lobby, finally spotting Remy in the mix.

He threaded through the customers and explained that a false identity had been used to set up the bank account in which Remy's funds had been transferred. No, the cameras were not able to record the incident at this ATM or at the ATM where the perpetrator received the transfer. The video footage wasn't saved from day to day. Did the transfer occur domestically or internationally? He couldn't answer that. What was the receiver of the wire's name? It didn't matter. The name was an alias. How did he already know that the name given was an alias? Because that's how it's done. That's the normal way to steal money through a bank transfer.

A conversation went on in which absolutely no clues or solid answers were divulged. Remy's questions were balked at every turn, his only solace being conveniently positioned so as to allow a full view of the proceedings. The predominately female banking assistants went about their business adorned in professional skirts and blouses, taking care to avoid eye contact with Remy and Tom while never letting the two men out of their sight. Subtly persistent in their ogling. They knew well the danger Tom embodied. Yet, in the midst of this flock, there was one more angry than fearful, one with a steely gaze. He quickly memorized her face, and when Tom began to notice attention drawn elsewhere, Remy stormed out of the bank dramatically, replaying the woman's face and other defining physical characteristics in his mind's eye as he bluffed a tirade.

CHAPTER XXXI

USA

"Cleaning and putting away dishes from the dishwasher are obviously not crazy concepts, Chuck. What is crazy is wanting me to remove the dirty dishes you put in the dishwasher before I start the machine. The issue isn't that you don't trust me to switch on the machine properly, slightly insane though that may be. The issue is your alpha complex." Remy spoke the cutting words from as unobtrusive a position as possible, sitting down, arms splayed wide, serious about the cessation of the issue but not wanting to hurt Chuck's feelings. He kept his voice pleasant and light.

"You're upset that I washed your bowl and put it away. That's pretty crazy, Chuck. You don't accept rides from me to visit cafes or bars. You've driven me places but refuse to be a passenger. You reorganize things I've organized just to be the one on top, to be the last one who changed it. You open windows that I close. You close windows that I open. Not because of a desire for fresh air or because you feel chilly but just to be on top. You've repositioned the nightlight four times and it's not even yours. You couldn't just leave it where I plugged the thing in. You say you needed room in the freezer, so I made room. You had half of the freezer cleared, plenty of room, and yet, you shifted things around your way. The only way. It must always be your way, Chuck. How many times have you moved my condiments around inside the refrigerator? It's weird, Chuck."

And Chuck responded in anger, his fragile pride injured, cackling bitterly as he retorted. Regardless that he stood over a sitting man, that he entered into Remy's room, still, it was Chuck who felt prone and vulnerable and so he lashed out in a gossipy, everyone-knows-this-and-that manner, using the concept of majority-rule to reinforce a personal opinion. He was not looking for a solution. He didn't like the idea of a compromise. He was solely focused on reciprocating the pain of his recently wounded pride.

Like how small-breed dogs are threatened by practically every strange thing that crosses their paths, so too with little people. Chuck's angry words washed over Remy while a growing feeling of disappointment welled within. He had hoped for more from the man. He had been the best choice from those he had inhabited the shelters with, the one least likely to lose his job or spend rent money on frivolity, but Chuck had been let go from work two weeks prior, one short month after moving into the two-bedroom apartment.

While he had at first seemed quite easy-going, Remy was finding Chuck quite overbearing now that they shared a home. From demanding to have the thermostat set at Chuck's own personal temperature, the one "everyone sets their house to", to downloading his own apps on Remy's Xbox, Remy had had enough. He enforced a compromise on the thermostat temperature -- the midway point between their personal preferences -- and initiated a no-download policy on his electronics. Chuck was not taking the news well and had recently become upset that his bowl had been washed and put away in the cupboards. He didn't own much more than that bowl and some silverware and was trying to reciprocate the discomfort he felt at having restrictions enforced upon him via the medium of a single blue cereal bowl signifying the sovereignty of Chuck's possessions.

Okay, Chuck. It's weird, but okay, Remy thought. *I'll dance around your fragile sense of self as best I can albeit undoubtedly an upcoming insufficient amount. Your bowl is off limits. Doom in the future, I'm sure, but I'll try to make it work.*

"Alright, Chuck. I get it. Don't touch your bowl. Message received. I feel you're just not seeing my point here, though. And now you're angry."

"I'm not angry," Chuck said with an uncomfortable smile, looking for an opening in the armor to land a verbal blade. "You drink too much."

"Okay, Chuck. You're just sort of lashing out now. We're done here. Please close the door on your way out."

He obeyed, grumbling to himself as he returned to the living room. Remy intentionally tuned out the negative frequency, focusing instead on the open window, to the blue sky and cottony clouds above, wishing for the umpteenth time that he lived in a better environment. *He's still the best candidate for a roommate even with those psychological problems. Psychosis is commonplace here and I don't want to find out if I can afford these bills on my own. In time, the dust will settle and we will live more or less in peace. Distant but peaceful.*

CHAPTER XXXII

CHINA

"May I help you?' she asked pleasantly.

When Remy entered the bank the following morning, it was as if a weasel had entered a henhouse. While professional bank tellers tried their best to act unobtrusively to the incursion, he cursed himself for being recognized so swiftly.

Having arrived a tad before noon, lunch breaks were beginning and tellers' minds were set on shift changes and upcoming meals. A time in which banks were usually quite busy tending to customers coming in on their own lunch breaks. The perfect time to enter in unseen. He'd expected to just glide right in, completely unnoticed. Instead, he stood in line awkwardly feigning as if he was unaware of their attention. Within a minute, the entire banking house had been alerted without anyone in particular muttering a single word. The focus was both intense and subtle. None of the customers seemed to have any idea something abnormal was happening.

The woman he had come to speak with had tunneled into the pile of hens, obscuring herself in colleagues while tending to a task. *I don't have much time,* he thought. *Someone will either escort me out of here soon, or Tom will return, or some other thug, or a police officer.*

The more time I give them, the more united against me they will be.
He excused himself politely and inserted himself at the head of the
line adorned with a bright, warm smile.

"May I help you?"

"Yes, I do hope so. I was robbed here a couple of days ago and I'm
seeking justice."

"Sir?"

"I would like to speak with her, please." He pointed into a trio
of women in which he could only make out the faint outline of
the woman whose face he had semi-memorized the day before. The
other two women cleared away leaving a reluctant and very much
alone bank teller who balked only slightly before she began approaching the counter.

"I not sure she speak English, sir."

"We'll make it work. Thank you," he replied, breaking off and
approaching the hatch that separated bank tellers from public customers, jiggling the latch as if to open it. A bold move that brought
the teller's complete focus to bear on Remy.

"Sir, not coming in," she stated firmly.

"Oh, really? Silly me. Come out here than," he said with a smile
that he hoped looked reassuring. *Nothing about this is not insane,* he
thought. *But at least I have the right woman's attention now. And
she speaks some English.* "I need help," he added. The isolated teller
stared back at him, hints of annoyance and worry, anger and confusion dancing about her facial features. "Please," Remy added, the
word softening her features. She looked about and noticed the two
to three-meter radius of empty space that had formed around them,
a buffer zone, all eyes save Remy's cast to other places and other
people. He was both invisible and also the focal point of attention.
She accepted this oddity with a smirk that he found endearing. She
spun a key into a lock in the teller/customer partition and entered
the bank lobby. Dutiful, she immediately spun about and relocked

the thing. Remy motioned to a corner of the bank and they walked slowly in step.

"I come here seeking answers," he began.

"The police come. They told you answers, yes?"

"No. You mean that thug? No, he did not ease my worried mind. It's interesting that you use the word *police* because that's a funny story all in itself."

He stopped at the corner of the bank and turned to face the teller.

"You know, there's a chance that that man who came in with me yesterday might not have had my best interests at heart. Just a tiny chance really, but something to think about."

He winked and she smiled and for a moment the weight of the world was manageable. The levity was fleeting, however. She soon became aware of her colleagues' subtle attentions and began fidgeting nervously. Remy's mind reset to the gravity of the unsolved theft, of the battle he had been thrust into, all glibness perpetually fleeting, always returning to that crime, to the conflict, to Monica, to opponents.

"I'd love to dig a deep hole and throw that man in it but I digress. He is but a pawn. A big, thick pawn, but a pawn. I seek bigger game. And my money. Where is my money, Rose? You look like a Rose. Do you mind if I call you that?"

"I not understand all English."

"Undoubtedly. Truth be told, while the words make sense, they fall oddly upon my own ears, Rose. I've read detective books and enjoy a good mystery, but I never thought I'd be where I am right now. I still don't fully fathom the details." He realized he had been speaking mostly to himself and returned focus on the teller, finding her dazed. "Oh, don't worry about that. Don't worry about any of this. After I leave, you can tell the others that we talked about whatever it is you come up with. I recommend the truth, that you didn't understand much of what I said, but that's up to you." Remy locked eyes with her. "Who has my money, Rose? Where can I find it?"

"I don't know," she answered, looking so uncomfortable with the question that he instantly recognized the lie.

"If you don't know than I will never know. You're all I've got in this crazy place." And it hit him how true this was. He was acting on a hunch and it was the only lead he had except to tail Monica again, which would likely prove more difficult and less fruitful. *Far safer for this banker to please the overlords and not tell me a single useful thing. Why on Earth did I think this would go anywhere? I have a new job to move to in three days. Should be some leads there, I suppose. I'm sure they're connected to the crime, just not sure how to prove it. None of my stuff is packed yet. I don't know how to send my belongings over. Finishing touches at the old job still remain. I'm not sure how I will even get to the airport and here I am, acting like Sherlock Hol---*

"It go to Guangdong."

"What did you just say?"

"Guangdong."

"Like Guangzhou, Guangdong? Like the place where my new job is located? Where I'm moving to in a few days?" He bore a wide grin, his mind awhirl with possibility and open avenues.

Rose frowned. "You will go to work there? You will live there?"

"I guess so, Rose. I guess so. Guangdong prefecture, you said, right?"

"Yes." She saw the smile on his face, his eyes bright with thought. "Do you have home? Go home. You should go home."

"Home is this mystery solved. That's the only home I have now. How about a name? What was the name of the person who received the transfer?"

He could feel the attention of the bankers upon them. So could Rose. "I need go now." She turned and began walking back to the teller section of the bank. He walked briskly alongside her, asking again for a name or an address or a copy of a video recording from the ATM cameras. A time, a date, an IP address, a phone number, anything. She offered nothing more than what she had already given: Guangdong and unheeded advice.

"Then that is where I must go," he stated, realizing no further progress from the bank would be forthcoming. "Thank you. You're quite brave for doing this." He jotted down his email address on the back of a business card and slipped it to her.

"I'm sorry," was her only reply. She unlocked the divider separating banker from customer and passed through without looking back. Remy strolled toward the exit, pondering his next move. At the entryway, a middle-aged security guard with a face determined on finding trouble marched through automatic doors. He spied Remy and altered his course, latching onto his target. Remy looked up, visibly showing surprise bordering on shock. He pointed dramatically back the way he had come, miming that it would be best if the guard hurried to the back of the bank where all of the action that wasn't was. The guard rushed away and Remy continued along.

Was that guy connected to triads or the police? Or is there even much of a difference here? he asked himself as he reversed out of his parking spot. The electronic engine started up silently and soon he was merging into traffic that yielded for no one and obeyed no law. He returned home, packed what little he owned, and prepared to venture into the unknown as best he could, by expecting nothing.

Observe and react. Gather data proving the guilt of members involved in this banking theft, of this syndicate, rescue the girl if possible, and oh yeah, don't forget to teach classes. Monday through Friday, teach at the very school that is most certainly connected to all of this. And I'm sure it's no coincidence that Mike and Monica both happen to work at the school that I'm leaving here in Nanchang. What is it with these Chinese schools? What kind of students have I been teaching?

Heavy were his thoughts and heavy were the two suitcases, duffel bag, and large kennel containing the one-hundred-pound German shepherd that he hauled out of his home and into a van. He had discarded most everything else in his flat: blankets, cooking devices, the e-bike, minor furniture. *I must travel light now, not that this is light. I must be prepared to leave even this behind. A time may very well come when I only have the things in my pockets and this loving beast.* William's tongue lolled through a gaping maw, doing that dog-smile thing, loving the journey, to be on the road, to travel, oblivious of the concerns of his master.

William's pleasure eventually crept into Remy's concerns. Tension ebbed. Outside of the backseat window, the city of Nanchang flashed by, random images of people's lives captured in an instant and released as man and dog approached the airport.

CHAPTER XXXIII

USA

The white bishop glided across the board landing smartly on G6, checking the black king. White had started off defensively by creating a firm border from which a punishing attack was being delivered. Black had been retreating for the past fifteen moves. White pressed the advantage, leaving a knight exposed, ignoring the initial left attack and pressing in on the right. His opponent was pinned down, the only move available a rook sacrifice. Instead he held out his hand.

"Good game."

Remy shook hands with the man. "Good game," he reciprocated. "Feels good to win one. I'm going to grab a beer. You want anything from the bar?"

Cordial in defeat, his opponent's smile was warm and true, "No, thanks."

Remy sauntered off, pleased to be out of the apartment. The original plan was to meet with a few others to discuss the ins and outs of political correctness: should we be more mindful of the negative impact hurtful words have on other cultures, and if so, to what degree does this encroach on civil liberties such as freedom of speech?

An engaging conversation, maybe a little debate to convince the fence-sitters. Sounded pretty good. Spending twenty dollars on dinner did not. It was with reservation that Remy entered into the Vietnamese restaurant. He strolled in and turned his attention to the center of the main room while he peripherally took in the large banquet table along the far wall.

A dozen younger to middle-aged men and women sat with stiff postures and formal demeanors. One was speaking while the remainder listened attentively. A slow, uninterrupted response followed. *Dry as plain toast but likely an intelligent gathering,* he thought. Weighing the dull gathering against the wickedness of the employees he worked alongside -- cooks that threatened servers for ringing up food orders, an employer that effectively told him to just accept all the negative and not complain or he would be fired from the pub, customers, half of which didn't tip properly and had far greater expectations of a server's responsibilities than Remy found healthy -- he determined he just wasn't in the mood for a large gathering.

Life in America saddened him. Perpetual disappointment plagued him. He had given up on being able to move his people toward a better path. He was getting too old to entertain notions that he would one day rise up in ranks and lead. An impoverished existence seemed inescapable. Rather than spend twenty dollars on dinner and a stiff conversation, he turned about and walked out, likely unnoticed by the group. Having ventured north into Orlando and in no hurry to return to a residence shared with his unemployed roommate, he decided to drop by a local café hosting a chess meetup.

It was a unique place with overpriced beer and moderately priced coffee. The décor appeased the many millennials that frequented the establishment: an eclectic mix of modern art, potted plants, artistic endeavors into furniture-making, and black and white autographed photographs of popular people framing the walls. On one of which Britney Spears -- an Orlando legend -- lied rather seductively across a sofa in a provocative outfit, beaming a shiny, white smile. "One of my favorite spots in O-town. Love ya!" was scribbled across the bottom corner of the shot.

"I wonder what these things are," he said aloud absently, bored with the long line. Above him, fifteen or so profiles of the head of some creature dangled on thick strands of twine, creating something akin to a baby mobile.

"Fish," the twenty-something girl ahead of him responded. She was short and slim, with pleasant facial features and wavy hair. She had dolled herself up, her hair curled and shiny, facial makeup subtly accenting her features. She gave a glance back to Remy and then returned to staring noncommittally ahead.

"Can't be fish. Those things have ears."

"I think those are fins."

"Like dorsal fins? Along the back? Can't be that. It's too close to the head. That has to be ears."

"Pretty sure they're fish."

"Maybe a fish with ears? Some sort of mammal-fish. You know it looks more like a raccoon wearing goggles, though that would be a bit redundant."

"Because they already have the burglar mask on."

"Yes! That's it exactly. Very good."

She turned about fully and Remy took her in. Then she abruptly trotted off, right out of the line and back into the café crowd.

"Am I that menacing of a character? I seem to have scared that one off. Such an easy thing to do in this place." He didn't mean anything as small as the coffee shop. He was thinking more of America, or possibly Earth, the inhabitant thereof far too fragile for his tastes. "I tell ya, I'm not so sure I belong here."

The newly appointed woman ahead of Remy gave him a sideways glance, opened her mouth to speak, thought better of it and returned to staring vacantly ahead. He waited silently until eventually becoming the head of the line.

"What can I do for you?"

"You can tell me what these animal heads are."

"Fish."

"Are you sure? They appear to have ears, you see. Do you know the artist? Are you certain?"

"The artist's name is Robert Umliddle. He's done a number of things around here. Including these fish."

"Alright, barista. You win. If the artist says they're fish, than fish they are. Now, I would like one of your finest, cheapest beers. Let's say, hypothetically speaking of course, that I am impoverished. What's the best bang for my buck?"

He left the line with a cool pint of Polish beer bearing an image of a young lady dancing the Polka. The beer was good, light on the hops and barley but still quite flavorful and refreshing. He sat back down in the same seat he had left. Confident in his prior victory, he promptly lost the next two games to scorching offensive maneuvering. The conversation during play danced from online dating, to the internet, to artificial intelligence, to evolution, and possible distant and not-so distant futures. Glad to connect to the world outside of Chuck and work, he bid the players farewell and returned home, a place undeniably better than a homeless shelter. *I am grateful for these things,* he thought. *Truly grateful. Of course, this would be the time in which it all begins to crumble around me. Enjoy it while you can,* he reminded himself.

CHAPTER XXXIV

CHINA

Looking down upon the dense urban sprawl below him as the plane made its final descent, Remy was heartened. Guangzhou's population hovered around thirteen million, roughly fifty percent higher than New York City. Some cities boasted similarly high populations but were so spread out that, though the numbers were there, the city itself didn't feel especially urban. Some cities reported populations of lower than five million but gave off that big city vibe due to housing that number in tight, condensed spaces. *It's really all about population density,* Remy concluded as the jet spiraled gently downward to land.

Taking in the last of the city by air, he noted a multitude of high-rises packed tightly together in the distant, tilted horizon. The downtown roadways were too far away to see with clarity, but Remy assumed the standard Chinese design would apply to Guangzhou as well: concentric circle highways that emanated from central downtown, connected in turn by perpendicular roadways connecting the outer circles. *Like a spider's web,* he thought, shrugging the idea off as soon as it flitted by, much as if he had actually walked through one, not liking what that made of him in such an analogy.

There will be trouble in the days to come, he thought, *but in such an expanse of people there will be some lawmen, some do-gooders. It is one thing to come from Nanchang, a smallish city by Chinese standards, and experienced what I experienced: triads dominant over law enforcement. But Guangzhou is much, much larger. In all of this urban sprawl, there must be some good. Someplace to turn to if it gets nasty. Surely, amidst the many consulates and international businesses there will exist a haven or two. Hong Kong and Macau roughly a hundred miles that way. There must be less maneuvering room for triads to operate so brazenly. It's one thing for a lone thief to establish a false identity, receive a transfer, cash it out, and then fade into the shadows. That could happen here easily. May even be happening right now, though by the time I'm finished with this place such a thing will not so easily occur again.* He smiled coldly. *But there's just no way that a police station gets commandeered by triad here. I'm closer to the case, in an ideal position to gather intel and follow the trail, and my enemy must have a weaker grasp of this territory than Nanchang. Things are looking up.*

But in his core, he knew the plane was landing in a city that housed a school that had simultaneously employed him and also been directly involved in his theft. And while Hong Kong and Macau offered international avenues of escape, he was aware of the long history of triad activity within these two once-European colonies. The danger was very, very real and he was rapidly descending into it. The coldness of this reality had been pressing upon him, heavier and heavier, from van to check-in counter to boarding gate. As the plane's wheels made contact with the runway, it felt as if icy fingers clutched and kneaded his guts. He held on to all the positivity he could muster and gradually the terror of what may lie ahead subsided. *Fear is the greatest of enemies,* he reminded himself, unsure if he had learned this from a fictional mongoose named Rikki-Tikki-Tavi or from one of Winston Churchill's rousing speeches.

He disembarked, stepping off of the folding steps of the plane and onto ground that felt hostile. Normally, he was quite pleased to find firm earth beneath his feet after a flight, but not that day. The place felt wrong, irreverent. Like celebrating in a cemetery, there was something aching in his spirit that had no name. He stopped midway to the airstrip bus that was collecting passengers for the jaunt to the main hub of the airport terminal, turned about and doubled back toward the plane, acting on an inner voice that screamed, *Evacuate. Let it go, let it all go and walk away. Rebuild somewhere safe. Go home. Return to America. Go anywhere else. Don't do this.* It was this instinct that pulled him around and back up the plane's stairway, marching up against the flow of exiting passengers, knowing he couldn't possibly be allowed back on the same plane but approaching just the same. Halfway up the steps, his mind regained control of his body and he doubled back again to join the flow of people cramming themselves onto the crowded airport bus.

He waited at the carousel, watching the same luggage revolve around for the fourth time. A dark blue duffel bag crept by again and was scooped up and off the conveyor belt by an airline employee. Remy approached.

"Excuse me. Do you speak English?"

"No. I no speak."

"Okay, great," he continued, unperturbed. "I'm waiting for my dog. My dog." Repetition, unlike speaking louder, had proved a helpful device to convey meaning in foreign lands. That failing, he switched to speaking Mandarin to the best of his ability, which is to say poorly.

"No dog here," she replied, continuing her task, scooping up a grey suitcase.

"Yes, that's the problem." He spied a bag she was intent on and grabbed it off of the carousel for her. He shuffled it back towards her and handed it over.

"*Xie xie.*"

"You're welcome. So, where are the dogs?"

"Where are the dogs?" she echoed with an expression clearly stating this was a spectacularly foolish question to ask.

"Yep. William. Looks like a wolf. Heart of gold. About your size. My dog. Where's my dog?"

She didn't quite shrug, though the body language amounted to the same thing. Spying another target, she spoke while straining to handle a pink handbag that was far heavier than it appeared. "Not here."

"Well, only ten thousand other places he could be than. *Xie xie* for nothing," he replied, not at all unpleasantly.

He abandoned the carousel and eventually found assistance at an information kiosk that informed him that all animals pass through a quarantine zone before they disembark. Someone else pointed him to the actual destination where this occurred, a building on the edge of the airport property, alongside warehouses housing freight shipped via air. Remy asked if he could walk there from the airport. "Far," the man answered. "You need taxi."

"I was hoping to avoid the highwaymen, all pun intended," chuckling at his own joke, needing the laugh. "Taxi drivers charge whatever they want in this nation. Always too much money."

"Yes," the man agreed, "but you need taxi."

"Do you have any recommendations? Who can I trust to give me a good price? A fair price."

"Everyone," the help desk clerk answered with a wry smile.

Outside of the arrival gates, Remy was immediately accosted, surrounded by men who looked hungrily to the burdened foreigner uncertain of his surroundings. Handshakes turned into tight grips, as drivers began pulling him toward curbside cabs. Each member of the pack wore a smile of well-concealed disdain. They began quarreling with each other over who had seen Remy first, who had dibs on the man, wholly unconcerned with Remy having any say in the matter. Three were arguing loudly as a fourth came sneaking in from the side and began ushering Remy away to his taxi, "Good price," he whispered conspiratorially, beckoning Remy to follow him. "Come, come," he hissed.

"I hate all of you," Remy stated flatly, setting down his duffel bag and stretching his shoulders. "I hate this guy because he's trying to sneak his way in when he wasn't even part of this wolf pack. Not that mobbing someone is the right thing to do, but this guy didn't even wait his turn. And these others are just bullies. Not accepting no as an answer. Quoting me prices far higher than a meter would read. Telling me it's a good price when it's three times higher than what any of you would be charging a Chinese citizen."

The argument had stopped. All the taxi drivers that had converged were taking in the show, though they understood little of the wording. This sort of thing had never happened before.

"Bullies," Remy spoke evenly, locking eyes with the men one by one. "And a little sneak-thief over there, trying to lead me away while the big dogs fight. You aren't role models, you know. I don't like any of you."

One of the men picked up on this last part, "You not like me?"

Remy hadn't expected his words to be understood. "Well, I guess I don't know you, personally. Maybe you're a terrific father to your child. I don't know. I don't want to use any of your cabs, though. And I don't trust a single one of you. Sorry."

"Sorry," the man repeated, knowing this one word, though uncertain how it fit into the string of unknown English.

"You know what," Remy stated, cheering up, "that's a perfect way to end this encounter. Good day, gentlemen." With that, he picked up his belongings and marched away, not knowing where to go, just knowing that he should move away. He ended up on the outskirts of a small bus depot. Behind a pillar, he set down his burden and watched the taxi driver mob descend upon another helpless traveler. He searched his mind for another way to get to the quarantine department and finding none, set out to do the irksome. For ten minutes, he watched the pack's comings and goings. Observing how the same three men that intensely argued with each other were actually well-acquainted and on reasonably good terms with one another. That the sneak-thief driver never returned. That they all smoked way too many cigarettes. Still not a group he cared for much at all.

The older the man, the better. I would feel better putting too much money into the hands of an older man and an older man is more likely to be wiser, to be above the trappings of this material world. More likely to be truer and cheat me less. He found a driver in his mid-fifties, on the outskirts of the taxi herd, a man connected to the group by only one other man, a loose acquaintance Remy surmised based on their limited interactions. *This one may be new to the taxi game and thus less negatively influenced to lie and cheat. The farther removed from this mess, the better.* Having decided on his target, he returned to the herd. They quickly surrounded him, shaking his hand again so as to latch on and pull him toward a particular cab. One man refused to release the handshake, the driver physically pulling Remy away and toward a taxi. Remy tightened, adopted a martial stance, and released himself from the grip in exactly the same manner as he had done just one week prior from the thug faux officer.

"Enough!"

The word reverberated throughout the scene. Twenty-some people turned to the source of the sound, including a security guard who began approaching, causing the herd of drivers to dissipate like smoke in the wind. *But it won't last. I must act now.* Remy jogged up to the older driver. "Excuse me. Take me to this place," unfolding a map given to him inside the airport and pointing to the circled building where he was told William would be. "Take me here," he repeated curtly. The driver nodded timidly. *Good,* Remy thought, *better that than him robbing me.*

"Don't worry, old-timer. I'll pay you fairly." The man smiled placatingly at the remark. Seeing a legitimately pleasant demeanor in Remy, he relaxed. "That's right. It's all good. Good enough, anyway." Remy set his bags in the trunk and plopped down in the passenger seat as if that were the normal thing to do in taxis. They shared a second look at the map, exited the parking lot, and arrived at the animal quarantine shelter shortly thereafter where Remy waited for hours for William to be processed, spending most of that time outside of the vehicle, being uncomfortable waiting so long and hoping to expedite the issue by pacing about in front of the building where he was being held. After showing a receptionist William's traveling paperwork, he had been told to wait outside until the examination was complete. He had grown restless after half an hour and accepted the driver's offer of a cigarette gratefully, choking down the smoke and exhaling awkwardly. He felt comfortable enough with the man to lay down in the grass outside of the complex under a tree, fairly sure his possessions were safe in the trunk of a taxi whose license plate number he had memorized just in case. He stretched his tired limbs among tall blades of uncut grass, knowing the back of his shirt and pants were now soiled and not caring much.

He was looking straight up, through the branches of a tree that quivered in the wind, rustling leaf against leaf, making music of the breeze, when he heard someone approach. He was exhausted and content to sleep under the tree though the hour was just somewhere around five p.m. He was too tired to discern if it was the taxi driver or the animal quarantine specialist.

"Hi," said the young man, a college student Remy assumed due to his youthful disposition and command of English. "What are you doing?"

"I'm solving my own crime, a banking theft that involves a host of characters. And trying to get my possessions to a new address that I have yet to see, paid for by an employer likely connected to the whole thing. I have an address that my cab driver doesn't understand and that I've only seen a few times on Google maps. Somehow, I need to go there, but first, my dog. I need my dog."

A pause.

"How about you? Who are you and what're you doing here?"

He announced his name and they shook hands. He said he'd been called in to help translate, though he did little in that regard as they didn't speak of William's health or documents. Remy had a good feeling about the young man, though. They chatted amiably about trivial things for a while and then the young man said something strange, "You need a friend here. I will be your friend."

He was correct, but to hear it from a stranger, to know that a complete stranger knew Remy's plight well enough to make that outrageously factual statement was a little more than he could comfortably process.

"No offense, but the fact that you know of me and I don't know you puts you more in the opponent category than the best friends forever one."

"Alright," he said, "Good luck." And he turned about and began walking away.

That Remy liked even less. "Wait, wait. I've been rude." He stood and walked over to the young man.

They rejoined and chatted about comic book characters and the weather and cultural differences and whatnot. As the conversation faded, he presented his phone number. Remy hesitated to record it.

"Do you know anyone here?" he queried with a smirk that said: *you don't know anyone here.*

"You know the answer to that," Remy replied. "And that's the problem. Put yourself in my shoes. If you were wearing my shoes, if you lived my life, what would you think right now. How would you feel about this?"

"Wearing your shoes. That's good. That's funny to say, but I understand." He paused to think it over. "It scary, I guess. To be in strange place."

"Now you're getting it."

He departed and soon afterward Remy was summoned to the front of the quarantine office where he was reunited with William. They were happy to see each other and wrestled merrily with one another in the tall grass outside of the building. Remy pinned down the fifty-kilogram shepherd but he quickly rebounded, squiggling free and pouncing upon Remy who tried to pivot out of the way but being too slow was bowled over by the beast. They moved in circles as combatants do in martial arts movies, in the end crashing together in a sort of loving embrace. Tired of this game, Remy kissed the top of William's head and off he went, sprinting over to give the newly terrified driver a good sniffing.

Having passed the sniff test, William took a seat in the back of the taxi, where he at first turned this way and that, taking in the scenery as the vehicle sped through the streets, but soon curled up and fell asleep.

The driver insisted on calling the contact number the school had provided in order to know where to go, apparently unable to decipher Remy's handwriting in Chinese as to his new address. Prior to departure, Remy had studied a smidgeon of Guangzhou geography. Not much, but enough to know the rough direction they should head from the airport in order to arrive at the new school and the neighboring apartment. South. More or less straight south. After speaking with the representative from the school, the driver took off from the airport along a wildly meandering route. From Remy's research, the trip should have taken a little more than half an hour. Seventy-five minutes and several nonsensical circles later, a disappointed Remy said, "Really? That's what you choose to do?" The driver smiled as if he didn't understand at all. "You waited a couple of hours and shared a smoke with me. And now here you are driving in an intentionally misleading and confusing path, probably at the behest of my new employer who is most assuredly connected to my theft." Mirthless chuckling. "Good luck figuring all that out, driver. In any language."

He arrived twenty minutes later, an hour and a half after leaving the animal quarantine shelter though the traffic had not been congested and the roads had been clear. Little of what Remy saw made sense to him. There was a vast courtyard separating the parking lot of the apartment complex and the apartment building itself, a tower that cut upwards some sixty meters or more. The courtyard looked like the kind of place where children would play and middle-aged women would practice Tai-Chi dancing in the early evenings. A courtyard in which the inhabitants gathered to socialize in the evenings. A buffer between the busy city streets and residential living.

When he arrived, he found the courtyard filled with forty or so people clearly facing off against one another in the midst of a milling group. Nightfall had come and it was dark but he estimated around a hundred in total were involved in the standoff, nothing playful in their stances or demeanors. Though unseen, he felt a presence of spectators among the open windows of the surrounding area. The cause of the conflict remained a mystery as he wasn't fluent in the language that flew across both sides.

There was certainly a disagreement centered on two men in their thirties, an issue so tense that it almost came to blows. Two large groups of youngish men toeing an invisible and quite real line, disagreeing intently on something. If the clash had something to do with Remy's arrival, than he had a substantial backing. Armed with only basic Mandarin language skills and now residing in China's south, home of Cantonese speakers -- a language he understood even less than Mandarin -- the words fell on deaf ears. More to the point, he was exhausted. He gave the near riotous group a wide berth as he entered the complex hauling two suitcases, a duffel bag, a kennel, and William.

The coordinator from the new school was waiting at the apartment door. Likely the speaker on the other end of the phone conversation with the cab driver, probably the same one who insisted that the cabbie not take the main highway and instead drive about in the most confusing and time-consuming manner possible. Perhaps even directly connected to the banking theft. Remy smiled as if he could do this all night, as if it were just another day in the office, thanked her for her time, accepted keys, dragged his belongings inside, and promptly fell asleep fully clothed on the living room floor.

CHAPTER XXXV

USA

I have a blender for smoothies and margaritas. I have an LCD widescreen television and an array of television programming at my command, just a click away. A swimming pool a stone's throw away. I'm reasonably healthy. My car runs smoothly. My teaching license was just reinstated. I should be much happier than this.

To survive a life-threatening situation is a life-changing event that doesn't translate into words effectively. Such an experience must be felt to be understood. The anguish of the situation. The joy of not succumbing. The triumph of cheating death. He had been faced with such adversity for so long that life without it had become foreign, gray, and dull. He imagined the years rolling by, serving tables, maybe teaching again, paying bills, buying cheap groceries, a panic here and there when faced with an unforeseen medical or dental need, but eventually paying that, too. A car part in need of replacement. Perhaps a minor fender bender. The bank account low and getting lower at times, rising at others but never remarkably. Apartment living. Driving an old car. Turning fifty. Sixty. Too poor to retire. Seventy. Dying in the same position.

It was all so mundane, the months turning to years and decades marching by. The days were already bleeding into one another. He didn't dread Mondays. There was no TGIF mentality, no expectant joy of upcoming days away from work. He couldn't have cared less about hump day. The arrival of his own birthday had failed to spark any interest. There would be no celebrants. And while he was not suffering, the nothingness grew heavier.

He sat and pondered days past, important moments encapsulated in memory. *Memory seems to be the only place to find importance. The best bits of life have already occurred. I'm just riding on the wake of what was, an echo that grows evermore faint.*

CHAPTER XXXVI

INDIA

He had survived a fifty-mile an hour motorcycle accident in the beach town of Goa, India, receiving heavy wounds to both palms. The skin had abraded away leaving bare flesh which had also begun ebbing away until Remy made the decision to detach from the skidding motorcycle, tuck and roll, popping up on the other end of the highway and into the intersecting path of an oncoming motorist, pivoting neatly and narrowly avoiding a secondary collision by a matter of inches. A roadside farmer had stood frozen, transfixed, farming tool loose in hand. "God walks with you," he spoke absently in perfect English, dazed.

"Thank you," Remy had replied, unsure what to say in such a situation. He limped over to the motorcycle that had slid a hundred feet from a pothole the size of a goat where the accident originated, adrenaline rushing, forcing breath in and out properly, deeply, keeping steady and calm. He steeled himself and hauled the motorcycle back upright. It was heavily scratched, and one of the handlebar mirrors had gone missing, but the frame and wheels seemed fine and the seat held his weight. The engine turned over. Remy rotated the throttle, gritting his teeth as skinless, eroded flesh formed a grasp around the handles.

Mike pulled up alongside him on the shoulder of the highway. "Are you alright?" he asked. "I mean, you obviously aren't but can you drive this thing to a hospital?"

"I don't have money for a hospital, Mike. I'm a teacher. Besides, what would they do at a hospital? These are all surface wounds. Nothing needs stitches. I just need time and soap. And a bottle of whiskey for the pain." He looked down, taking in the wounds. "Maybe two or three bottles."

"Show me your hands, Rem." He grudgingly complied, wincing as he removed them from the handles. He had already begun adhering to the surface with some sort of mixture of blood and a sticky, watery liquid emanating from the chewed-up palms.

"That's real bad, Remy. Can you make a fist?"

Remy began the motion. Blinding, stinging pain flooded his optical processor, and he stopped. "Yep. More or less. I think the bones are fine. I'm just missing a lot of skin and some flesh now."

"Oh, is that all?" Mike replied smiling. "You should put some bandages on your hands."

"Sure. Let's stop at a drugstore."

"A drugstore? Sure. A drugstore. I'll ride slowly."

The farmer remained inanimate along the roadside. He waved over to the departing foreigners. "God walks with you," he called again as a farewell of sorts.

The pain was too intense to allow him to ride a motorcycle safely, even at slow speeds. He stopped a couple of miles down the road, tearing off strips from his recently tattered shirt to wrap around his palms, giving him the appearance of a kickboxer, albeit one who throttled a motorcycle gingerly, using only fingertips. They found a drugstore and he purchased all of the bandages and gauze in stock along with a large bottle of hydrogen peroxide and a bottle of rubbing alcohol. The clerk had been insistent that he go to the hospital and he had only stopped her from placing a call to an ambulance by alluding that he would ride there himself, which he did not.

He spent the entirety of the vacation, almost three full weeks, in pain. Once the adrenaline wore off that first day, the pain had become very real and consistent, feeling as if he held onto hot coals twenty-four hours a day, making sleep impossible for the first few days until sheer exhaustion rendered him unconscious for one thirty-hour stretch of near coma-like sleep, awaking to bandages in need of changing. Unwrapping them, he found a grey, thick film covering his palms that did not smell especially healthy and was taking over the place where skin should be on his palms. Knowing what he should do next but unprepared for the pain it would cause, he found painkiller from a wandering merchant along the beach, a small bag of white powder he was told to mix with water and drink down quickly which turned out to be MDMA or something quite similar. He returned to the hotel room with a newly acquired mesh, dish-cleaning scrubber, became heavily intoxicated, and scrubbed off the film that shouldn't be covering his palms. He remained conscious long enough to finish both hands, pouring first peroxide then alcohol over the wounds before promptly falling unconscious on the hotel bathroom floor.

When he awoke, the wounds looked and felt better, and afterward, would heal so completely that one would never know such a trauma had ever occurred. The lines that palm reader's believe hint at possible futures would in time all return to their previous state, not even a scar to show for the experience. He spent the remainder of the vacation in constantly dulled pain, the same vacation in which he had joked of needing to prostitute himself for money and had received an unexpectedly somber response from Monica Hu. By the time he returned to Nanchang, China his palms showed just hints of abrasion, and a month afterward, not even that. But not all wounds were to heal in the same manner.

CHAPTER XXXVII

CHINA

He awoke fully clothed to William's stoic gaze and wet-nose muzzling, the culmination of which communicating a need to venture outdoors for biological necessities. He followed the hound out of the apartment and into the elevator, down seventeen stories to the lobby and courtyard below. No trace of the warring clans that had populated the area last evening. Just a group of single mothers overseeing playing children and grandparents overseeing the overseers. Pleasant smiles all around. William, focused on finding a bit of grass and dirt, tromped through the edge of the scene with purpose, eyeing the ball being kicked around by toddlers with longing desire along the way.

Remy was taken aback at the normalcy. For a moment he began to doubt what he had witnessed the night before. *Could it have been a trick of light and sound? Perhaps I exaggerated the number of attendees of whatever that was.* He found the memory freshly stored and reviewed it. *Nope. It all checks out, though one would never guess it now, looking at this.* He walked around the outskirts of the courtyard, totaling the size of one city block, surveying the perimeter. No external fire escape, two service entrances/exits presumably locked, a playground complete with adult exercise equipment in front of a walk-through garden featuring a miniature waterfall, the runoff irrigating elegantly throughout the garden, an overpass nearby, a strip of two-story buildings: mom-and-pop restaurants on the first floor, housing for mom and pop on the second.

The smell of veggies and meats frying in a distant wok caught William's attention and having finished his toileting needs, he promptly began marching off toward the aromas, Remy in tow, focused on breakfast. Savory pork, gingered hard-boiled eggs, dumplings, and pickled greens wafted through a soft breeze triggered an unconscious belly rumble. After a muddled conversation in Mandarin, he returned to the new home with hands full of freshly-cooked meals, enough to satiate the two of them for the day if need be. William left the rice more or less uneaten in his bowl, preferring the dumplings and eggs and strips of pork. Stomach full and more or less content, he slipped out of the apartment while the hound napped.

Remy generally enjoyed travel, the potentiality that came in relocating. A new person in a new place. Seeing new things. Meeting new people. Better understanding a little portion of the world through the society that inhabited it.

He didn't know much of the metropolis he found himself in while Guangzhou had been expecting him. He had recently uncovered evidence that the theft definitively occurred in the same province of his new employment so he strolled down her streets with mixed emotions: apprehension seasoned with curiosity. Caution was with him as he surveyed the surrounding neighborhood, locating access points and possible escape routes, but the sunniness of the day, the contentment breakfast had brought, the cheery disposition of the people he passed swiftly tranquilized him. Deterred from the logistics of his very unique and pressing situation, he took the day off from his plight and just enjoyed sightseeing. He didn't double-back and find a clear route to the airport, the final goal of any sensible escape route and one that had been intentionally confused. With the previous day's madness pressing ever inward and the realization of where he was and what he was doing, very much alone and feeling it, he simply could not soldier on another day. Not that sunny day.

He enjoyed the day off, putting the serious business of international detecting aside and just feeling the warmth of sunshine on his skin, the gentle coolness of the breeze. Trees with roots growing from high branches, an oddity he had never seen before, lined the borders between bustling sidewalks and congested streets. Trains and subways took him this way and that. Sidewalks led him to department stores where he browsed wares he had no intention of purchasing, passed a street performer accompanied by a dancing monkey on a leash, passed a beggar so badly burned in a past blaze that his face had been transformed into a flat, smooth surface bearing only nostril and eye holes and a mouth full of broken teeth. Passed high-rises and shops and glass displays and bus stops and eventually, passed his own troubles and concerns and plans and losses.

I am here, he thought with wonder. *Not sure exactly what comes next. But here I am.* The thought was empowering. *Perhaps my tenacity will be rewarded. Perhaps, higher-ups will look upon my boldness with respect and return my money to me.* The return of his stolen savings had come to symbolize the dominance of the greater good, a belief that what was right would prevail. The money must be traced. It must be returned. He would die in the process if need be to make that happen. Remy was well aware of the impertinence of flesh and bone, that the mortal shell does not last forever and could think of no better use for a life than ensuring truth and justice won out in the end.

He whistled a jazzy tune as subway doors opened and folded closed behind him, depositing him back to Tianhe station. Ten minutes later, he opened the door of his new apartment to a rapturous hound overjoyed by his simple return and enjoyed an evening completely detached from the tremendous burden that had become his life.

CHAPTER XXXVIII

THAILAND

To decide that he would die in the process of finding his money if need be was neither a simple nor a light decision. He had felt the grip of death just a few years before arriving in Guangzhou when he attempted to swim across a stretch of sea to a seemingly nearby island from a deep-sea fishing ship and, in the process, had become caught in the pull of a riptide that locked him in a parallel current alongside the distant shoreline. He scrambled and dashed about the surface of the ocean, pressing himself to swim harder and break through whatever tidal forces were propelling him back into the sea away from the shoreline. Like magnets repelling, so was Remy and that beach. Within ten minutes, the island's position had slid along the horizon and was no closer. A backwards glance showed the fishing ship even farther away than the shoreline.

Panic had overcome him then. Terror disrupted his breathing as he realized that drowning had become a very real possibility. Exhaling too much, inhaling too little, choking on another bobbing wave, he slipped beneath the ocean's surface as another relentless swell rose and plunged and took him under. Overcoming the panic, finding a calm somehow, he surfaced and began swimming once more toward the shoreline. And again, he was repelled. Then terror returned, more insistent this time, only barely contained through sheer force of will. He floated as best he could while trying to quell the panic, searching his brain for an answer to the deadly problem, something other than swimming fruitlessly and sinking into the sea overcome with exhaustion. Calling upon a reserve of strength rooted in hope, Remy took a deep breath and dove, swimming deeply under the water's surface.

He half-remembered the details of a science lesson learned long, long ago about the ocean floor not being as deep near shorelines as he dove deeper into the currents that prevented progress to the shore. The plan was to reach the bottom of the ocean and propel himself off of various obstacles – stones, coral, the ocean floor itself - toward the distant beach. Remy was sure he could fight the current if he could just kick off of something or pull himself along the bottom. *The current should weaken the deeper I go,* he had thought, repeating the thought to himself again and again in an effort to remain calm as he continued descending into the dark coolness of the sea's depths. Breaststrokes took him deeper still, through increasing water pressure that made cutting through the water all the more laborious a task. Downward until his lungs felt like they would burst and his vision dimmed in water that had grown so dark that the surface was just a dull glow in a direction that felt like all the others. The water had grown cold, not cool, but cold, a far cry from the warm tropical environment of the surface. True panic took him when he realized that he had misjudged the distance to the ocean floor. He halted his progress and floated motionless many meters below the swells of the sea's surface above. He looked with dimming vision to where he thought he remembered up being and spotted what appeared to be a part of the watery world more illuminated than the rest. He exhaled a precious bit of air to examine the trajectory of the bubbles that journeyed upward and gave chase as best he could. *That's the way to go,* he thought, half-swimming, half-floating back to the ocean's surface.

He didn't come up for air as drowning people do in the cinema, thrashing about and gasping. He was too tired for that. His chin and jaw broke the surface immediately triggering a long gasp for air around the rise and fall of another relentless swell. His vision had dimmed substantially despite the sunniness of the afternoon. Half of the next breath involved a fair amount of seawater and he desperately wanted to take another but gravity and riptide and exhaustion and sea swell pulled him back down. He wriggled upward once more, arms and legs basically unresponsive, barely breaching the surface, and took in as much water as air with the next inhalation. Sputtering and coughing, he sank once more. *This is drowning. This is death. Only help will save my life.* He moved upward once more, snaking his way up by wriggling his body, weakly carving a path through the water. He broke the surface again and said, "Help," realizing as he began to sink again that since the nearest people were perhaps a hundred meters away, his request went unheard. The word tasted bitter in his mouth and he was a little pleased that no one seemed to hear. Embarrassed, he debated internally if death was better than yelling out for help. With the last bit of reserve, he broke the surface one last time. There was only time to shout a word as loudly as he could muster, which, having used every last bit of strength, was not very loud at all.

"Help!"

Then, he sank for there was nothing else he could do.

Downward, he drifted, watching the light of the surface world dim, the light of life fading away. If there was a difference in the two, he was too tired to pay it any mind. Too tired to keep his throat and lungs sealed shut. *Sleep will fix everything,* he thought dreamily. *Everyone feels better after a nap. Besides, maybe I can use the oxygen*

in the water somehow. There was a distant, fleeting thought about in-
fants and wombs and breathing liquid as he opened his mouth.

Everything had become dark and still and distant, and truth be
told, he wasn't even there when his body was violently snatched up.
When his torso was pulled into oxygenated air, he did not inhale and
while his eyes were open, they saw nothing. Mike took the heel of
his hand and brought it down hard against Remy's cheek. No response. He shifted his weight and delivered a second blow: a strong
smack across the other cheek. Remy reeled from the sting, inhaling deeply while simultaneously projecting water from his mouth,
a painful process akin to the feel of vomiting salt from one's lungs.
Mike shook him with a free hand, the other looped firmly about
Remy's waistline, kicking hard to keep them both above water level.
Remy's initial reaction was to break free and dash off toward the
shore but, being so weakened, this attempt was easily cancelled in
Mike's grasp.

"Stop it. Just relax. Relax," Mike commanded, churning through
the water at a nice clip.

He couldn't speak, couldn't think clearly, but he obeyed, collapsing into the embrace and soon finding footing in shallow water.
Remy detached from Mike, moved to stand on his own two feet in
the waist-high waters of the beach and immediately dropped, plung-
ing into the water. Nothing worked. Mike scooped him up, looped
an arm over his shoulder, and marched him onto dry sand where
Remy collapsed on his stomach, gasping and coughing and gasping
again.

Eventually, his arms and legs grew responsive enough to raise his
torso out of the sand and onto his knees and elbows, a maneuver
his body only agreed to because there was more air to be had. Much
later, he was able to sit upright and gradually grew more aware of his
surroundings. People of varying nationalities, though mostly Thai
and Russian, surrounded him on the beach, trying their best to not

stare openly at the nearly dead man as they playfully splashed about and chatted.

Spying Mike nearby, Remy solemnly said, "I owe you my life."

"Don't worry about that."

"I am worried about that. I don't know how to repay something like that. But I will somehow. Do I give you everything I own? Would that be alright?"

"What're you talking about? Just breathe and get some rest."

"But there's this debt now. What do you give a man who saved your life? How does someone repay a debt like that?"

"You don't, Rem. You just live."

"I don't like that answer. I think you should take all of the money I've saved, at least."

"You want me to take all of your money?"

"Then maybe we'd be even. But that wouldn't really solve it, would it? A life is worth more than the money one's saved. I hope." Remy tried to laugh at his insignificant financial standing but found that physically impossible. A cough passed through a feint smirk instead.

"Get some rest, Remy. It's a long swim back to the ship."

"I think," Remy mumbled, winded and sleepy, "that I will take one of those smaller boats back to the ship." Which he did some time later. The rest of the journey went by sleepily, the ship docking portside as the sun began to set across the warm waters of the Pacific.

"What can I give you? How can I repay this? You saved my life. What do you want, Mike?"

"I want you to shut up about it. How about that?"

"Doesn't seem like an even trade to me. But okay."

Negotiating themselves across a gangplank that bobbed with the motions of the ship toward the stability of a dock on the opposite side, Remy brightened with a thought, "I could at least pay for the next round of pints."

Mike turned back, having reached the dock and firm-footing first. "You could pay for the next three."

CHAPTER XXXIX

CHINA

Remy stood and stared through the window of his kitchen across the skyline of Guangzhou, remembering that day. Remembering Mike and his cryptic, accurate warning of the bank theft. *The same man who saved my life was aware of my upcoming theft, warned me, and did nothing to prevent it?* He tried to find some connection, to understand a deeper truth, but could make no sense of it. *If Mike had wanted my money, I would have handed it over to him that evening willingly. And yet, he was in the know of what was to happen. He knew the plan ahead of time but wasn't part of the thieving? Why?* His left leg buckled and he looked down as William's large head retracted from headbutting his thigh. The hound looked up, pleased with himself, mouth open, tongue lolling. They shared a smile of sorts and then William sauntered off to lay down, leaving Remy alone to brood.

CHAPTER XL

CHINA

He thought of Monica every day and each night. The loneliness had become very real as the first few days turned into the first weeks apart. He mingled and flirted with women in pubs and bars and nightclubs, as well as staff employed at the massive school in Guangzhou in which he taught. Had even chatted up the same assistant who had instructed the taxi driver to take the circular, confusing path from the airport, as much to glean some insight from her as a remedy to loneliness. Americans, India-Indians, Brazilians, Israelis, British. He utilized an online dating app, sifting through scores of smiling women with left and right swipes. Nothing remotely interesting materialized.

Certainly, it didn't help that he viewed these women as a potential hazard, and more to the point, himself as a definite one. A lose-lose situation. If a woman displayed meritorious qualities, hinting to be someone Remy could care for and respect, then he took it upon himself to keep his distance, to keep the trouble that whirled about him far away from a would-be mate. Thus, only women who definitely had something to hide, unscrupulous sorts, did he bring close. Such women were justifiably subject to the troublesome elements of his life and indeed were likely of the same ilk that had brought about his theft in Nanchang, or so he hoped. Through these outings, she remained. No one understood the madness of his plight like her. Beyond that, which was monumental in itself, he missed her. All of her. Even though.

When he dialed her phone number and heard her speak on the other end of the line, his heart softened and soared. The impossible task of solving his own crime -- sniffing out gossip in shadowy places, lining up meetings with people who knew people that may be criminals, dangers and troubles beginning to congeal about him -- all seemed much smaller and farther away when her voice danced through his ears. "I love you. I miss you. I need to see you again," Remy spoke, the words pouring out. Mysterious and deceitful and downright frightening though she was, he loved her and was gladdened when she soon agreed to come visit the following weekend.

She looked beautiful, of course, pulling a small pink suitcase up the subway stairs. So beautiful in fact that Remy stood there transfixed, beaming happiness. She pulled the bag capably, exhibiting fine posture and balance. By the time he was aware that he had been staring and not helping, she had already reached the fifth to last step. "You're doing great," he called out. "Just a little further." She looked up and grinned.

"Thank you helping me."

"No, no. Thank you for stealing most of my savings. I mean coming to visit me."

Her grin disappeared and he immediately mourned its loss. His search of lost funds was going nowhere. No bank in Guangzhou had offered any information or even pretended to check up on it. No one in the police stations Remy had visited spoke English, understood his Mandarin, or cared to attempt communication using a translation app. The teaching department of the new school, while undoubtedly playing a part in the theft, was both unyielding of clues and mildly threatening. Several of the foreign staff in his office didn't seem to actually teach at the school. These men kept Remy at a safe distance, becoming curt and abruptly leaving the office once his questions began to probe into nonacademic territory.

Most of the out-of-place teachers were thick, brutish types, save for one man younger than Remy, shorter and thinner, a constant drinker of hot tea and a computer guru whose desk was positioned cattycorner to his own. Patrick. All signs pointed to this man being behind the development of the false website that was immediately retracted from the internet after the banking theft, a website that according to the thug that had replaced the investigating officer had left no evidence behind as to where it had once originated. Close and yet completely without any proof.

Patrick was perfectly comfortable explaining how a wire theft could have happened, and in time, explained exactly how Remy had been robbed, the blatancy of it all infuriating. Each passing day the belief that his theft would ever be redeemed grew ever more distant. He was in the right place, in the same province and likely the same city where his savings had been transferred, at the same school that had needed proof of shipping payment and thus had triggered the theft, working among those responsible and with absolutely no evidence to link anyone to the crime.

He was out of his element and being toyed with and he knew it. Only grim determination kept him going, one day after the next, searching for proof and finding none. He was alone and surrounded by sharks in deep water. Still, he swam on, searching. He was exhausted of being on guard everywhere at all times and then she arrived, trudging up those steps, just stunning, and it all melted away. *The heart wants what it wants,* Remy thought. *Pretty sure my heart hates me, but it's so good to see her again.*

"Sorry about that. I want you to be comfortable, regardless of what has occurred between us. I do love you, you know. Idiot that I am."

"Yes," she said smiling once again, intentionally leaving out if she was agreeing that he loved her or that he was an idiot. She allowed him to haul the mini-suitcase the next four blocks to Remy's apartment. Like every night except the first, the courtyard was filled with middle-aged and older women practicing tai-chi, children running around being children, and grandfatherly types looking on, supervising. A very family affair. *Really puts the community into communism,* he had often thought, observing from a distance while walking William. The security guards manning the lobby raised eyebrows when Monica and Remy ventured through. As the elevator door slid shut, he turned and kissed her passionately, with great sincerity and forgiveness. The taste of her, the smell, like home.

"Okay, okay," she shushed, wriggling free from his roaming hands, "I need take shower. I stinky."

"You are not that. Well, maybe a little. But it's you and I like it."

"No."

"True story, my dear," he replied, opening the front door. Once again, he was met with deflecting hands and a pivoting body that was already on the way to the restroom he had yet to introduce her to. He sighed as the door fastened shut. *Plenty of time for love later.* And of that, there was much.

He woke during the night as her hair flashed across his face during some sort of sleeping convulsion. Finding the nape of her neck exposed, he took it upon himself to cover it in kisses. She nestled in closer, shifting her hips more tightly against his own.

He awoke hours later, her arm draped across his chest, his own lodged deep beneath her torso, tingling painfully due to restricted blood flow. He slowly inched his arm out, trying his best to not wake her as fresh blood flooded the dry appendage. This too somehow elicited more hip-shifting.

Hours after that, the sun having just barely crept out of the darkness of night, he came to as she slept on her side nearby, breathing heavily, just short of snoring. Enough light filtered through the edges of closed curtains to illuminate her form in a dull glow. He swept her hand into his and pressed the back of her hand against his own cheek. He inhaled deeply, perfectly content as sunlight brightened the room. A slightly snoring William in the corner, the sound of a neighbor's door shutting, footsteps down the hallway. *Life without her isn't much,* he thought drowsily, kissing the back of her hand again and drifting back into peaceful slumber.

CHAPTER XLI

USA

Remy glanced down at the object in his hand. A skewer would be the best way to describe it. A wide, circular metallic base supported a thin, silvery spike that jutted upright at a ninety-degree angle. It was designed so that bar staff could keep a log of beverage receipts but it was also a convenient tool for prying open the battery lid on the electronic machines that served as menus and ordering devices atop each table.

It had been a busy night. A digital clock on the wall showed the time in red numbers – 1:17. The last time Remy looked at that same clock had been at five-thirty. Since then, nothing but tables and orders and vulgar, threatening cooks and customer after customer after customer. He needed rest, but there was still work to do: a few more tables to serve, a few more dollars to collect in tips. He had smoothly lifted the skewer without so much as breaking stride in passing the bar on his way to eject batteries from tabletop devices in the front of the restaurant, always multi-tasking, doing three things while working on a fourth. The challenge this presented pushed all memory from his mind so while work was grueling, taxing on mind and body, he was pleased to not be reminded of China and her. With the pressure of a hundred people's orders and reorders and seating needs and bills and payments fading from the fore, hints of memories began pressing in. All that once was, all that was lost, came crashing down.

He had inadvertently slowed to a crawling pace. Instead of stabbing the skewer into the side of a device and ejecting a battery in need of charging, he slowed further and stopped in a portion of the dining room no longer in service. He tested the tip of the skewer with the tip of his index finger, finding it far less sharp than imagined but pointy enough. *Thin enough to fit easily between my ribs. What would happen if I just plunged this thing into my heart right now?* An image flashed of a self-staking, of blood pooling, not showing easily at first on the black button-up shirt he wore but eventually dripping down the waistline and onto the stained carpeted floor in branching rivulets. Collapsing, lacking in that most precious of commodities.

He looked around and finding no one about rested the point to the left of his sternum, placing the instrument directly between rib bones over his slowly beating heart. *It would be so easy now. It would just slip right in. No more memories. No more Monica. No more poverty. No more life.* His right hand opened, the base of the skewer resting on the open palm. Rigid. Tense. Ready.

"Are you done with that or what, Rem?"

Startled, the skewer fell and bounced away as he spun around.

"Good one, Rem. Real smart. Other people need to use that, you know."

"Do they? Okay," he replied, fumbling to find the steel spike. He scrambled to recover it from under a table and looked up at a dubious coworker.

"Are you alright?" she looked on with concern, one of the few good ones that worked in the pub.

"No. But I'm better than you. Not that that's difficult," Remy answered with a grin, handing over the skewer. He held onto it a little too tightly though in the exchange, the spike coming free from his grasp only after a second firm pull.

"Go f^&! yourself, Rem." She said jokingly and walked away. He looked down at his empty hand, reimagining the skewer, wondering how far that would have gone. Out of the corner of his eye, he spotted a hand in the air, a customer in need of something, and with that, he was off.

CHAPTER XLII

CHINA

The kitchen was warm and though the windows were wide open, the smell of cinnamon, sugar, and cooked bread danced throughout the apartment. Remy whipped a bowl of milk and egg and spices, preparing for another baptismal slice of soon-to-be French toast. William stood next to his food bowl in the kitchen, watching, waiting. In the living room, Monica primped, curling her eyelashes while a documentary continued on, ignored by all. Every bit the happy family.

"I'm not getting anywhere here."

"I thought you going to police. Going to fix crime."

"Yeah, if you want me to spit in your French toast just keep talking. Half of this I do to save you, you know." He brought the bowl to the living room, still whipping the contents. "Do you even want to be saved? Would you even know what that would look like, I wonder?"

"I no understand," she said as she rubbed facial cream into her cheeks.

"Right. You don't understand. You don't understand that your life is a sham. That you just robbed the best thing that will ever cross you path. That your *friends* are the lowest of low-lives. You don't understand any of that, right?"

"What you mean?" she asked without wonder.

"I mean, you're a damsel in distress and I mean to rescue you. But first I must apprehend some criminals. Make the world a safer place for decent people. Not people like you," Remy chuckled at his own joke, as he slid in and stole a kiss on her cheek in apology. "Decent people."

"You criminal."

"Blurred lines, my dear. Blurred lines. Something any undercover detective would tell you."

"You no detective."

"Eat your breakfast."

He flipped golden brown French toast onto a clean plate and gave it a good coating of maple syrup. Adding a fork, he set the plate down next to her, currently engaged in applying lotion from head to toe.

"Thank you."

"No, thank you," he replied, returning to the kitchen to create a similar meal for himself and William. "Without you, I would have a normal life. No one to save. No case to solve. Just peace and quiet. You saved me from boredom, you know. I always thought I was meant for better things, and you my dear, represent those better things. I will either save you, or divulge the participants of a criminal syndicate to the public, or both. Or neither, I suppose. I mean, I'm still aiming to get my money back, but that does seem distant at best these days. On the plus side, if I die along the way then my death will shine a light on something that has been operating in darkness for far too long. And if I survive, then I'll continue to spend all that I am on ending this thing that has caused so much harm. Either way points toward disrupting evil, to prevent another from feeling the hurt that you and your brood have instilled." Her fork hovered in mid-bite.

"Oh, don't look at me like that, like you're innocent of all charges. Please. Come on now. We're better than that."

She continued along with the forkful of sweet bread, chewing slowly.

"And you," she said swallowing, "You no guilty? You good man?"

"Yes. Yes, I am. Do enjoy that breakfast I'm serving you. And even if you were to prepare breakfast for us, preposterous though such an idea might be, I would never, never rob you." He stopped cooking and walked over to the dining room. "Do you understand that? I would never do what you did to me. Not if my life was threatened. Not if I was tortured. Not if someone else filled my head with lies about you. I wouldn't do it even though I know about the black sports car with this license plate," Remy recited the alpha-numeric sequence he had memorized long ago. "Not even then."

She stopped eating altogether and slid the plate away. "You no know what you doing."

"No, little one. It is you who has no clue what has begun. I am prepared to die for this. You are tiny and unprepared."

"I want go home now," she said as she began tossing makeup accessories clumsily into a bag.

"So do I, but I have a job to do first. To prevent this from happening to the next guy."

"You no understand," she said, and in her eyes he saw that she did in fact know something very pertinent that he did not.

"I'm all ears."

Nothing.

"This would be a great time. We could be a team, love. You and me forever, until the end of our days. Just work with me. What don't I know?"

She returned to the French toast. "Many things," she spoke while chewing around a mouthful. "Nothing."

"I don't know nothing? And I don't know many things?"

She gave him an approving look.

"I hate your face," Remy lied playfully, returning to the now burning side of one slice of battered bread. Hating to be a mouse in a game of cats, he lashed out. "Have I ever told you about World War II? How pitifully your people resisted the Japanese? Wow, that was fruitless, right? Like throwing stones at Vultron."

She didn't know what Vultron was but she knew enough to hate the comparison. "We weak then, poor and fighting inside. Together now. Why you say this?" she spat, the anger blatant in her voice. She stood and moved to the bedroom to gather her possessions, set on leaving.

So patriotic, he thought. *Just like that thug that took over at the police station. That was the only time I thought he may snap and strike me. Not so bizarre, actually. The Yakuza back in Japan were radically patriotic. Makes a sort of sense, actually. They condone their own evil as being for the betterment of the nation. A shadowy means to a noble end. Hurting others, sure, but aiding their own homeland by bringing in funds internationally from drug sales, prostitution rings, robbing foreigners, etc. Any weakening of foreign powers raises their domestic status.*

But then why are there Canadian and American and British teachers at this new job? The handful of Western teachers in this new office that don't appear to be teachers at all, could be some sort of rebels. Cyber-criminal rebels. Anonymous, the hacking group? Or some derivative thereof. It would benefit China to allow them to operate freely within her borders, cracking into the Sony Playstation network, into foreign governments' files, into banking institutions, bouncing their IP addresses every which way while enjoying a cup of hot tea right here in China. He thought of Patrick, so smug and quite the savant. Of the tech-heavy nature of his own theft. *Needing to shut down a mobile phone before Mike would even hint at an upcoming problem, advice I failed to heed. Maybe the security cameras actually were shut down the day of my theft. Can a hacker do that remotely now? I bet so. Anonymous explains the inclusion of Mike and other Westerners in all of this. Whatever this is.*

Lost in this new train of thought, staring blankly at the wall across the room, Remy came to as Monica crossed his path, rolling her pink suitcase towards the front door.

"Hey! Wait. Don't do this. Don't leave. I wish you would tell me more. I know that you know more. I know. I followed you for a few months so I---"

"You did what?!" Though the volume of her voice did not change -- she never yelled or screamed, didn't even speak loudly -- but there was something in it that exclaimed.

"Yep. I know you've been lying to me for a long time. I know you robbed me. I don't know why you're here right now, though. That makes no sense to me. Why return to a man that you robbed? Why risk it? It makes no sense. Unless, you love me." He lowered a slice of bread into the batter and returned to the living room. "Is that it?"

She turned to him from the front door, no longer intent on exiting. "What you see?"

"Ah, pussycat. Now we both have something the other wants. Sadly, the truth will come much more readily from me. You seem to be allergic to the stuff."

"What you see?"

"And hear. But how did you put it? Many things. And nothing. It's hard to remember right now. Sit. Eat your food."

She sat but did not return to her meal. Eventually, she spoke once more in a far-away voice.

"You no know what you doing."

After breakfast, he slipped his arm around her shoulder, pressing her just a little closer. He kissed the side of her head lovingly. She smiled and they agreed on a film to watch, relaxing comfortably with one another as lovers do.

"You know if we were married, there would be one less problem in my life."

"Less problem," she chuckled at this idea. "In China, if you go to wedding, you should pay some money. To man and woman, wife and," she paused, searching for the word, "husband. As gift." She chuckled again. "Maybe you marry me and you get your money back."

"The same exact amount, too, I bet."

"Yes, that's it. Very funny."

"Yeah," Remy agreed dryly, "You're hilarious."

CHAPTER XLIII

USA

Working up the final bit of needed nerve, he guzzled down the remainder of the glass of whiskey in one long pull and clicked the *call* icon. Her contact information filled the laptop screen. Skype's spacey ringtone sounded throughout the apartment in the wee hours of the night. His screen flashed and rang several times before clicking over, displaying an established connection of twelve seconds though only one second had actually passed. There was quiet mumbling on the other end.

"Is this actually happening? Can you hear me?"

A few seconds of lagged, incoherent words and then the connection was severed. The total talk time displayed sixteen seconds on his screen.

"So that's it then," he said to no one. He had tried reaching out to her in a multitude of ways over the years: Skype, Email, Facebook, QQ. No response. No reply. No call. Nothing.

Each failure to connect with her took a little more out of him. He shuffled tiredly to the kitchen, filled a glass with ice and bourbon and melancholy, and slid open the glass door that led to the balcony. A muggy night washed over him. He sat down hard on a cheap plastic chair, body aching and sore from the labor of serving tables. He alternated between hiding his face behind his hands -- a face more worn than ever, skin loosening, permanently creased in those places that mark one's age -- and sipping bourbon. Some time later, most of the contents of the glass consumed, he caught himself staring at the back of his hands, at the wrinkles and scars, the veins, the speckling of white hairs, all evidence of time's unyielding march forward. *I grow old,* he lamented. *Old and alone.*

CHAPTER XLIV

CHINA

"I'm sorry, I must not have heard you correctly. Are we actually talking about this now?"

She answered with a joyless smile. She did not speak but the smirk spoke clearly: *Yes, you heard me correctly.*

"So, let me get this straight. You don't want me to notify Interpol of my bank robbery? Why, that just doesn't make any sense at all," he said sarcastically. "You're the love of my life. Surely, you wish those responsible for my robbery, and your own if I may remind you, brought to justice."

"No my name."

"Meng Ni Hu. That name? Don't state your name? Don't state that Monica Hu -- Meng Ni Hu -- who worked at Jiangxi Middle School in Nanchang, China in the 2011-2012 academic year, was an avid partner in the coercion of most of my savings being stolen via a bank transfer. That she furthermore called in a thug with credentials the likes of which I could not have fathomed to rescue her from an interrogation led by a legitimate police officer engaged in his sworn duty: upholding justice. And then there's the semi-riot upon my arrival after a taxi driver intentionally took an abstract path from the airport back to this place: home, I suppose I should call it, though that doesn't feel right at all. Come to think of it, I still don't know where the airport is." Remy stopped, staring off while mental images of the ride over from the airport flashed by internally. *So many twists and turns and back streets.* She stood and approached him, swaying subtly in all the right places. She nestled into his embrace, as a cat does, jolting him back into the present.

"No my name. Okay?"

She was close and gentle, but something in that voice was icy, hinting at much more than the words defined. *This is not an option. You will not use my name. If you think being robbed was bad, it can get worse.*

"I don't think I've ever been threatened before. Forgive me, I'm unsure how to respond." He paused, pretending to think deeply. He brightened, "Oh, yes. Go f$*^ yourself. That's it. That feels right."

She stiffened and sauntered back toward the sofa. Halfway, she turned about, and with a voice equal parts icy daggers and real sympathy, "No, Remy. No do this."

The combination of compassion and mercilessness unnerved him. The glass he was cleaning slipped from his grasp and clanged about the sink noisily. Recovering the soapy glass, he responded most uncharacteristically.

"Okay. I won't use your name."

She immediately brightened. Instead of returning to the couch to lounge she crept closer until he took her up into his arms and into the bedroom where they frolicked. Later, he kissed her forehead while she slept before slipping off to the bathroom for a quick shower. He left the door slight ajar, looking forward to returning to nap with the one he loved, and sort of hated, and definitely battled with, but above all else, adored.

He was rinsing the shampoo from his scalp when a voice not entirely his own came to him. *Go, now. Check on her.* The foreign internal intrusion was alarming but he complied nonetheless. He stooped over the rushing faucet, hands poised to twist the valve shut. *No,* voiced the foreign presence, *Leave the water running. Don't even dry off. Be stealthy and be swift.*

He paused, hands hovering above the tap, complying to something other than himself. He left the water running nonsensically and slid the glass partition aside as quietly as possible. He did not pause to dry himself and crept to the door, nudging it open carefully so as to not trigger the creaking hinge, and tiptoed nude and soaking wet into the hallway. *Such foolishness,* he thought, and almost laughed. *If she comes out of the bedroom now and sees me like this, what shall I say?* He poked open the bedroom door and found it empty. A nest of sheets and blankets, twisted and rumpled, lay on an empty bed. *Odd. I suppose she's pouring herself a glass of water.* He tiptoed forward, even more stealthily than before, taking note of where his shadow fell, senses focused toward the front of the apartment. *Activity ahead,* his senses told him, the inner voice his own.

He pivoted and slid along the wall so his shadow would meld into preexisting ones. *Business time again,* he thought, reminded of the tracking he had done just to watch her enter a black sports car repeatedly over the course of months. He had become something more than a teacher over the past year. All of that came to the fore as he crouched, nude and wet, and peered over the edge of the hallway wall into the living room.

Click, clack, clackety, click, click, clack. Monica was almost nude herself, wearing panties and nothing more, perched over his laptop, completely absorbed in her work.

The screen was divided, split in half vertically. The left, a normal webpage, the Google home screen. The right, a complex series of formulas and grids the likes of which he had never seen before. Flashbacks to a distant time when he'd programmed primitive computer games as a sort of hobby crossed his mind. Titles preceding parenthetical numeric and alphabetic computations. Computer commands. Not normal web-viewing. Whatever she was doing, she was intent, poised and focused on her work. She wove her fingers around the keyboard expertly, ignoring the mouse altogether. Remy had no clue that she possessed such a skill. He crouched against the edge of the hallway, transfixed, taking it all in, simultaneously proud of her and angered by her deceit.

She may have already done something like this several times, he thought. *A wiser man than me would flee this place. Just take the laptop tomorrow to someone who can make sense of what she's introducing into the software or deleting or checking or whatever it is she's doing. Surely this must be evidence.* But the more he thought about it, the more he realized he didn't know exactly what it was that she was doing. Perhaps that was the very evidence he was looking for, or maybe it was nothing. But once he left, he knew there would be no turning back. Doubting that anyone in law enforcement -- Interpol or otherwise -- would be persuaded to examine his laptop thoroughly for traces of criminal activity armed with only a story to tell, he determined that he needed more evidence and returned to the bathroom. He snatched a dry towel from the wall rack and doubled back to his observation point along the edge of the hallway, finding her to be slowing down as he returned. She was ex-ing out of multiple pages, straightening up in her chair as he faded back, shimmying backward while mopping up wet tracks. He felt pretty sure she entered into the hallway as he silently pressed the bathroom door back into a mostly closed position. He reentered the shower, so as to rewet himself, calling out, "You okay, love? Should I save some hot water for you?"

There was no reply. He stooped and turned off the taps, toweled dry and took his time brushing his teeth and hair, replaying what he had witnessed through his mind's eye. He entered the bedroom and found a seemingly asleep Monica, lovely and curled up in the same sheets that had so recently been just a twisted mess on a mattress. *I may very well die here,* he thought, covering the grim concern with a lover's grin, *in the process of bringing back proof to prevent this from poisoning another.*

He had no idea what that cost would be as he slid under the sheets and wrapped himself around his love and adversary.

CHAPTER XLV

CHINA

As the week progressed, they shared meals and watched films and chatted amiably. They went out a few times to pubs, nightclubs, the cinema, sometimes window shopping along the way.

He knew that she didn't divulge all that she was and so they toyed with one another: testing, feinting, probing. Trying to gather information from the other while protecting one's own secrets. There'd been a thrill in it in the beginning that had waned as he came to long for something more open and honest to develop between them. She refused to yield, holding onto that secret self of hers, refusing to discuss the black sports car or the thug that had somehow quashed the police investigation. While Remy wished she would just come clean, he held onto his memory of her cracking into his laptop as if it were an ace in a sleeve.

He had made up his mind: he would divulge her name and identity to Interpol though he had stated he would not. He felt betrayed by the hacking incident during the shower and was running out of ways to push back against the theft. A carefully constructed message to Interpol was one thing he could provide to move the investigation forward. Surely, the Chinese police department would be of no help.

In the last moments of the last day of her visit to Guangzhou, he broached the subject. She held her fully packed pink suitcase at the door, ready to go, a train to catch in thirty minutes, airport bound. He planned to have the email sent to Interpol by the time her plane departed.

"I will use your name." he stated flatly.

She turned to him, cross.

"I've thought about it," he continued. "I've been thinking about it for days now. Part of me would love to leave this alone. To pretend that none of it happened. No robbery. No thug posed as an officer of the law. No hundred-man standoff after an obviously intentional roundabout path from the airport to this address. No school that employs individuals such as yourself. A prostitute, I'm guessing, though it pains me to voice it. Technically an assistant to school administrators, but a prostitute first and foremost to the higher-level staff of the school: principals, vice-principals, and the like. It would explain the black sportscar, the driver a pimp, I suspect, delivering you to parts unknown for services I don't want to think about. It would explain why you said there was work to be done into late hours even after Tan left. I looked out from my kitchen window time after time after Tan left and saw no lights on in the school. Zhang's warning to me in the spring. All of this data gathered has guided me to this one awful fact. You're a prostitute. I take no joy in it, but that's who you are, right?"

Nothing. No admission of guilt. No denial. No anger. No sadness. No read whatsoever.

"It explains the weird way you responded to me joking from India about needing to prostitute myself in order to secure enough money to pay for the trip home."

Nothing.

"It explains a lot of things."

The mannequin face had returned, reminding Remy of that fateful day at the police station. She turned around and left, pulling her suitcase into the hallway. He followed her into the elevator, down the sidewalks that led to the subway station. Not a word was spoken. At last as train doors slid open and she wedged her way inside, he said simply, "Come see me again soon." He waved and bowed. Neither gesture was returned.

"Yes," she replied, her tone and expression the epitome of flat.

Life was about to become much, much worse, though he was wondrously oblivious to that fact as the subway doors closed and the train whisked her away to the airport. *I've collected no concrete evidence at all. Zilch. Playing poker here has been profitable and I do get the sense that some of these players know who I am, well, think they know who I am, know a story of me I should say, but those guys are guarded. Very guarded. Some of them literally have guards at the table. None are forthcoming with facts relating to the theft. No, this is not going well at all.*

He brooded on these facts, feeling apart from her with every heavy step, as he simultaneously wrestled with the wording of a soon-to-be-sent email to an Interpol officer. Arriving back in the apartment, the words rolled off of his fingertips. "*Quid pro quo, mon cheri,*" he muttered aloud, clicking the appropriate box on his computer screen and sending a detailed email to the international agency. An instant later, a confirmation message appeared informing him that his message had indeed been sent. His mind immediately flashed back to a vertically split screen -- formulas, parentheses, quotation marks, grids -- and he wondered for the first of many times to come if his computer was issuing honest statements. *Did that message actually go where it informed me it went?* He questioned himself, the first in a long a line of maddening doubt.

He turned his attention to his television afterward seeking entertainment and escape but could not shake a nagging concern of the possibility that what had been displayed on his computer screen and what had actually happened were not the same. *Paranoid*, he thought. *I'm being paranoid.* An animated penguin sang tunelessly atop an iceberg while Remy stared into and through the corner of the living room. Time ticked away as he remembered the past and pondered the future. *I don't get to be paranoid anymore. Any wild idea has some sort of purchase these days. Any crazy concept isn't so crazy if it applies to me.*

He left the unwatched movie playing and opened his laptop determined to access the vertical-split screen that she had been secretly augmenting while she thought him to be bathing. Unsuccessful hours ticked by. A digital clock attached to the stove read 2:13. Outside, the night was silent and moist, quite different from the air-conditioned apartment in which the animated penguin was repeating his offkey song as the movie looped a fourth time. A security officer continued dozing behind the lobby counter as Remy slipped into the vacant streets of Guangzhou searching for alcohol to still his troubled mind.

He found a convenient store a few blocks east, its neon sign blazing, the hum slightly audible in the depth of the night. Two young employees gave Remy a cursory glance as he entered before setting their attention back to stocking shelves. He exited with three liters of ale and one liter of rice wine. Needing the exercise, he curled the bags in different ways as he walked a few blocks back to his flat. He passed the still sleeping guard and entered the elevator, poking the number seventeen and wondering just how to surpass a set of restrictions he thought he'd located in his computer's operating system.

CHAPTER XLVI

USA

"I don't appreciate your condescending tone. You look down your nose at me and talk out of the thing at the same time. Speak out of your mouth, man. That would be a start. Everything you say is so negative. You turn every conversation into gossiping about people that aren't around. People I'll never meet. Do you ever have anything positive to say?"

"I don't understand where all of this anger is coming from. I assume it's because you've been drinking."

"There you go, Chuck. That's it exactly. All the way down your nose."

"I don't understand."

"No, Chuck, you don't. And you likely never will. Because understanding someone means that you have to step off of your high horse and share common ground. But you'll never do that. That's your problem. Well, one of them."

Anger was welling in the man. Remy sensed Chuck was on the verge of throwing a blow.

"Look. We're not meant to share a home. Especially one this small. We're doing the best we can with what we have and that ain't much." Chuck looked puzzled. Remy pressed on. "We're still the best chance either of us have to get out of this quagmire. This is better than the shelters. Prison is better than those shelters, for that matter."

"I still don't see why you're so angry."

"I'm not angry. I'm just telling you the unguarded truth for the first time. No anger here. Just a cold dose of reality. I don't want to share my life with someone like you, but I must. And so must you, I imagine. At least for the time being. So, let's just do our best to avoid one another as best we can. I work nights. You work days. We have that going for us."

Chuck turned and began walking the five steps needed from kitchen to bedroom. Remy saw the decision in his eyes and was pleased. He had had enough of Chuck often destroying positivity and asserting himself in the newfound void. He was tired of doing verbal battle with the man in his own home. Tired of defending hard won pleasant feelings. Tired of trying to compromise with a man who refused to meet him halfway. *Stop it,* the conversation had amounted to. *I'm tired of defending my happiness. Tired of you actively engaged in ruining what little good remains of this tattered life to feed your need for dominance. No more. Back off.*

Remy could hear his roommate mumbling angrily into a mobile device, already gossiping to some sad soul. More of the same. He closed the door to his own room, shutting out the annoying, droning voice. A sizeable portion of the weight of three months lifted as he drifted comfortably to sleep, a faint smile curling his lips.

CHAPTER XLVII

CHINA

It was one of those Super Mario Brothers days, the sky impossibly blue, the clouds flat on the bottom, puffy up top, numerous but never quite touching. Far below, Remy flashed a laminated identification card to a security guard who paid him no mind as he entered the gate separating school and city. The wall surrounding the campus stood three meters high, hedging in roughly one square city block's worth of academia. Two massive medieval-era, iron gates marked the only entry and exit points, south and east.

Passing through the southern gate, he merged into the thick pedestrian traffic that embodied Chinese high schools. Seven thousand teenagers strolled, strutted, marched, and lingered as a flow of pedestrians pushed its way into the heart of the campus. Some of the braver students practiced English in shaky dialogues with Remy as he moved through the crowd. He praised their language abilities, encouraging their efforts before separating from the bulk of the congestion and heading to the third floor of a building on the west end of the vast campus. Opening the ground level door to the stairwell, a small gathering of students shot up and hurried up the stairs alarmed at a teacher's presence. *Likely up to no good,* he thought as an electronic chime rang throughout the facility. Above him, a door opened and shut and the sound of teenage merriment was extinguished.

He hadn't slept well after Monica left. Not that first night, nor the nights after. Not often enough. Not enough hours in the rest. No REM. No dreams. After school let out at three, he walked a half-mile back to his apartment, graded papers and prepared for the next school day until dusk came. Then he turned to his second and third jobs, the unpaid ones, the costly ones: meeting up with shadowy characters to play poker in an attempt to gather word-of-mouth clues as to the bank theft and/or diving into the complicated world of computer operations to understand just what exactly Monica had been doing to his computer. Such was his routine.

Studying the ins and outs of his operating system was yielding more gain. He had thought that those who were not forthcoming in sharing what they knew of the crime would relax in time as they acclimated to Remy and perhaps let a bit slip, especially if he showed obvious signs of intoxication, but no matter how drunk he became at those poker tables no tongues wagged. He had no concrete evidence those who shared a card table with him even could provide a clue. Just a feeling he got in his gut from one or two of them. Conversely, he was awash in a deluge of information from his computer. It was sorting out the important from the ordinary that was proving challenging. The more he understood the pathways and parent/child permissions and remote accessing, the more questions emerged. *The deeper I journey down this rabbit hole, the deeper the rabbit hole becomes.*

Still, he had found some interesting tidbits buried in his laptop, things that shouldn't be and yet were miles deep in the coding and files that made up his operating system. One night, immediately after lifting restrictions on a series of files, all of the documents vanished, deleted completely from his laptop. Nothing to be found in the recycle bin. No return of the files after restarting. It was as if they had never existed. He was competing with some insidious force that had access to his computer, likely remotely, though there was no sign of that in the software. As he worked on solving his banking theft by delving into the coding of his laptop and mobile phone, nights with little or no sleep became the norm.

He spent many hours one night stripping security features from a file chain that sounded pleasant and necessary for computer operations, except that the date on the file showed that the program had been downloaded nine years in the future. A program that denied him access. Hours later, he found a way into program folders that seemed to be completely empty while simultaneously consuming vast resources from his laptop. It fought him time and time again, resisting being moved, renamed, or copied in a myriad of ways. Deletion was definitely not an option. He spent the entire night and most of the early morning stripping that file down to the point where he could at least make a copy of it. With quick hands, he inserted a thumb drive into the USB port and saved the hard-earned reward. He immediately removed the USB so as to avoid losing control of the contents of his thumb drive, feeling fairly certain that any device that was plugged into his laptop was susceptible to manipulation by an external presence that had somehow gained considerable access to his computer. With the memory stick safely in his pocket, he returned to the file chain and found nothing. Nothing there whatsoever. He had spent eight solid hours from eleven o'clock until seven in the morning battling that one file chain. And it had just disappeared. *But I was able to make a copy first. That's something. I was searching for proof of my bank theft, and while this is not that, it is something. It's progress. Finally.*

Remembering the importance of exercise, of maintaining a form capable of self-defense, he dropped into twenty push-ups, brushed his teeth, splashed some cold water on his face, and half-jogged to work, arriving at the familiar stairwell just as the electronic bells tolled throughout the complex signaling the beginning of another school day.

The adrenaline rush of the computer battle began rapidly dissipating and by noon he was exhausted and disoriented and had three classes yet to teach on the history of the first indigenous peoples to the Pacific Ocean islands. The two activities planned were both of his own design and he was looking forward to seeing how they would fair in implementation. Teacher by morning, detective and unpaid computer programmer battling for propriety of his own computer files by night. *Cyber Indiana Jones,* he thought, smiling tiredly. *Oh, but I wish I had that whip.*

He began humming the Indiana Jones theme as he approached the foreign teacher's office. Not quietly, either. He was half-singing the tune as he opened the door and entered in, far more merrily than he had thought possible given the evening he had just had.

"You all right?" queried the fifty-something that sat across from his desk, a fellow social science teacher by the name of Ezekiel. Remy dropped his bag into his seat, still sing-humming.

"Not at all, and also, yes, perfectly fine. Thank you for asking." It was difficult to ascertain the situation with any certainty, but he felt fairly sure that Ezekiel fell loosely into the ally category. He'd displayed kindness and there was just a feel to him that Remy thought of as good. But in the battle zone that was Guangzhou, it was impossible to know for sure and so he kept the man at a respectable distance, reminded that anyone good that got wrapped up in his life would quite likely become jeopardized.

"Feeling adventurous today?"

"Oh, every day is an adventure in this place, Zeke."

There was a flash of something akin to sympathy across his face. "I know," he said, somehow sighing as he spoke the two words.

It was the closest thing to confirmation of the school's connection to his private suffering that he had experienced to date. And it came to him in the form of benevolence. *Everything is upside-down here,* he thought.

He presented a poker face instinctively, a wide smile. 'Well, if you know, then you're one step ahead of me. Probably nine steps ahead of me. And while I'm at it, if you know, then why don't you help me out?"

"Help you do what?"

"Well, that's a fine question. I'm not sure. Retrieve my stolen money, I guess. Help me do that."

"Oh, right. You told us about that."

"Yeah, I told you all about that and more than half of you already knew it as I was saying it. I can read facial expressions like billboards, Zeke. I've been living abroad for a dozen years. So there's that. I'm just one guy over here, up against so many people, seen and unseen. I'm tired but I have to keep at it. I have to see this through."

"The money's gone, Remy. I don't think it's coming back."

"Oh, ye of little faith. Haven't you been listening to all of those Disney songs? Anything can happen if you try hard enough. And anyway, it's not even a choice. Nay sir, not trying isn't even an option. I can't just kick back and let wickedness win." There was a madness to Remy's ever-widening smile, to the cheeriness of his voice, to the glint of his eye.

"Is it even about the money anymore? If you somehow came across a briefcase with the money you lost in it, would that be the end of it?"

He had never contemplated the notion of success. He had sent a message to Interpol two weeks prior, and other than a single cursory anonymous reply stating that the message had been received, no word had followed. The notion that his emails were being redirected at the discretion of some insidious other whom he was battling for control of his own laptop had been pretty much confirmed over the many late nights that had followed. He had lost each of those battles over the past two weeks, each time failing to gather data, failing to reestablish permission over a host of shady files. *But not this time,* he thought, caressing the thumb drive in his pocket, smiling.

"Remy?"

"Yeah? I mean, no. No, it wouldn't be the end of it. I'm set upon bringing down something huge and evil now." The words tumbled out as honest words are wont to do, without thought as to how they would be received.

"I bet that's what it always was."

"I'm sorry, just who the f$*& are you again? I barely know your name. You sit across from me and seem nice but you obviously know a lot more about all of this than you let on. I am immersed in the unknown and malevolent. I'm just dripping wet over here and I don't even know what I'm soaking in. It's maddening. I come to work after a long, hard night and am met with cryptic statements from the only man here who I would begin to put on my side of this struggle. But I don't know much about you. Who are you?"

"I'm Ezekiel. Are you sure you're okay? I teach here at Guangzhou---"

"Come on! Come on. There's more to it than that and you know it."

He looked up and thought to say more. Instead he looked down, straight down to his shoes. "Choose well," he said simply and looked up, and there was that goodness, so out of place among so much deceit. "I like you, Remy."

"Thanks, Ezekiel. I like you, too, but 'Choose well'? Really? You know you just added more complication to my ever-so-complicated life, right?"

They both chuckled at this.

Looking to his left, Remy found the desk and chair catty-corner to his own uninhabited. "Where's Patrick?"

Zeke stiffened. "I don't know. Not here, I guess."

"That's odd. I thought for sure I'd see him this morning." *Unless I wore him out last night. Did I win that battle? Did I actually win one?* The thought was intoxicating. He drew the thumb drive from his pocket as if it were mighty Excalibur. The office was a battle zone full of seeming well-wishers looking for an opportunity to insert their blades into a back, save for the one and only Ezekiel. It was exhausting even without the all-night cyber battles and/or poker games searching for leads. From so much failure, he was eager to collect his prize. *All I have to do is attach this file from the thumb drive to a message emailed to myself. Also, a few family and friends back home in America, the more that I think about it. Better to spread this thing wide in case my own email truly is compromised.*

He inserted the drive into the USB port, relieved to have finally accomplished something after so much turmoil and hardship. He opened the drive to the folder containing the thing, some suffix defining it that he had never seen before. Definitely not jpeg, or doc, or docx, or pdf. He squinted at his monitor to read the file's full name. And then it disappeared.

He looked down at the keyboard in shocked disbelief. He had clicked on nothing, touched no button. A look at the recycle bin showed no file contained therein. His thumb drive held no trace of his prize. It was gone.

And in walked Patrick, not sixty seconds later. The smug smile told the story. Shot through the kneecaps at the finishing line, that's what had happened. Bewilderment faded as Remy put the pieces of the puzzle together. Patrick situated himself into his desk, eyes dark and puffy. *He's just as tired as I am. That's my opponent. At least I walk away with that information.*

"You have no honor." Remy stated plainly.

"What did you say?"

"I said, 'You have no honor.'"

"What is that supposed to mean?"

"Funny you should say that. That explains a lot, you not know-ing what honor is."

"I know what honor is."

"Do you? You look tired. Are you tired today?"

"Yeah, I didn't sleep well."

"Really? I'm just shocked, so shocked to hear that. What were you doing all night?"

"Not sleeping."

"Me neither, Patrick. Me neither."

Both men disengaged. Pompously, Patrick immediately returned to the fray in the midst of opening his bag and settling in to his desk in the morning.

"That's a nice thumb drive. Where'd you get it?"

"Where did I get this thumb drive? Are you seriously asking me that question right now?!" Remy rose from his seat, "You know, it's best that I just come over there and show you this thumb drive. Real close. You should get a good look at this drive." He began march-ing around the collection of individual desks that formed a collective teacher seating area.

"Hey, Remy. Come over here. I want to show you something." Ezekiel disengaged with a student who had just begun a barrage of questions about an upcoming quiz.

He turned to Ezekiel and his true smile and well-rested eyes and that overall glow of goodness and was soothed into compliance. They spoke of things unimportant for as long a time as Remy needed to calm himself and accept the loss. Within the twenty min-utes of dialogue that had followed, Remy hinted that his was a dan-gerous realm and that, while he appreciated the concern, it would be best if he muddled through it alone. Such subtlety was either not understood or rejected by Zeke.

Zeke departed the teacher office late to his own class, a faux pas uncharacteristic of the man, leaving Remy and Patrick seated closely among a handful of foreign staff, mostly composed of teachers that Remy had never seen teach and who acted not as teachers act. Mildly threatening and not cleverly so, and while he didn't feel overly threatened, he was uncomfortable nonetheless. Though names had been doled out, he doubted the authenticity so instead remembered them as: Huey, Dewey, and Louie, in no particular order.

Remy and Patrick both looked like they felt, completely exhausted from a battle of the minds that had again ended in favor of the wicked. *Chalk another one up for the bad guys.*

"Have I ever told you the story of the man who moved a mountain?"

"No, and I don't have time for a story right now." Patrick opened a desk drawer and slid headphones over his ears.

"Are you really hiding from me? You're hiding right now?" Remy jeered causing Patrick to slide the headphones away.

"Good. I'd hate to think I was fighting nothing all night long."

"Talk."

"Once upon a time," Remy began. Immediately Patrick rolled his eyes. "Well, it wasn't that long ago, Patty boy. Do pay attention. Once upon a time, there was a man and a mountain."

"Great story. Finished?"

"No, you tiny bug. Not at all. The man worked hard. He was a merchant, you see, and needed to travel to one town in order to sell goods produced from another town. It's how he made his living." Remy turned his attention outward and found the three ducks -- Huey, Dewey, and Louie -- paying rapt attention. He raised his voice so that it carried over the din of office life.

"At the end of each week, the merchant hauled his goods over the mountain that separated the two towns. Week after week. Year after year. Until one day, he decided that he had had enough."

"'Mountain,' the man said, 'I have been courteous and respectful. But I am growing older now and must ask you to step aside so that I may journey to the village without undue hardship.'"

"The mountain bellowed a laugh that shook the foothills. 'You're just a man,' the mountain roared. 'Why do I care what you ask of me?'"

Patrick was listening, transfixed, as were the three thug/teachers.

"I told you. It's a good story. Where was I? The man says 'move'. The mountain laughs. Ah, so the merchant accepts this indignant response and returns back to his home. The next morning, he visits the mountain again, this time armed with a pick and shovel. He heaves, and strikes, and scoops until day becomes night, barely scratching the surface of the mountain. The next morning, tired and sore, he returns and continues working. The next day, more of the same. After a week, very little had been accomplished. The mountain asked, 'What do you think you're doing?' The man replied, 'I'm digging a tunnel through you since you refuse to step aside.' Well, the mountain found this just the funniest thing it had heard in centuries. It laughed and laughed as the man clanked and clambered. Weeks went by. Then months. Years later, the man has made some progress, though not much, creating a bit of a crevice into the mountain's surface."

"'Why are you still here?' the mountain asks. 'Surely you realize that even if you spend your whole life toiling in this way, you cannot tunnel through my core. You cannot win.'"

"The man looked up, tired and happy to have a break from swinging the heavy pick. 'True,' he said. 'But soon I will teach my son how to swing this pick. And he will teach his son. And my grandson's grandson will come here and dig away at you, mountain.'"

"And then the mountain stood up and walked away. That's the story of how a man moved a mountain."

Huey, Dewey, and Louie had only understood pieces of the tale. It wasn't a volume or vocabulary issue. They just weren't philosophical story connoisseurs. Patrick, however, was impressed and did a fair job of not showing it.

"Mountains don't stand up and walk away."

"Mountains don't talk either, but here you are, flapping your gums."

Remy had spent many long hours trying to secure a file chain that had been immediately intercepted at work by the very same brood that had employed him. Thugs that didn't teach and yet loitered in the office daily, giggled at the loss of Patrick's face hearing Remy's retort. Patrick was miffed and Remy capitalized on the moment.

"Your goof troop is positively bursting with delight over there. I can't find words to voice how lowly I think of the lot of ye. Surrounding a man like this. Trapping him. Cheating. Lying. Stealing. You're wicked and you're in my way and I'll pick and pick away at you until you stand up and leave."

"It's your life."

"No, no it isn't. Not anymore."

He returned to his teaching duties and Patrick was happy to go about the same course of action. By midday it was easy enough to forget the whole event had even happened. Remy ate a sandwich during lunch while Patrick sipped hot ginger tea and without witnessing the morning's event, one would have had no clue how these two men truly felt about one another.

CHAPTER XLVIII

USA

One-hundred ninety, two-hundred ten, two-hundred thirty, fifty, seventy, ninety. Two hundred and ninety dollars. Not awful. And there's a two-week paycheck to accompany these tips that totals about half this amount. Not a ton of money, but a step toward paying the bills. A step toward next month's rent and an electric bill around the corner. A car that needs gas and an oil leak that needs attention. A savings account in need of replenishment. Credit card debt too vast and nonvital to even consider. A retirement account that would keep me living nicely for about a week of retirement.

He chuckled at the hopelessness of it all, having little else to do with the cold dose of reality. If he had given up drinking, he could've saved another one hundred dollars or so each month. An extra $1500 each year was a rather underwhelming choice over not feeling buzzed each day. Alcohol made the memories manageable. Alcohol made the monotony of each day tolerable. Moreover, without the drinking, he was certain he would've been fired for responding unfavorably to a rude customer, so in a way, the drink was paying for itself and then some.

He was giving serious contemplation to leaving America again. Life held no allure. One foot in front of the other. Endless tedium.

"It's Joseph's last day today."

"What?" Remy responded, emerging from the gloomy daydream.

"Yes," the new manager said. "He's moving on. Got a promotion. He'll be a GM and run his own store this week."

"Well, good for him. He works hard. He was always a little cruel to me, but he works hard. That's for sure." Memories of insults and barely contained rage when mistakes were made, of the short-temper and baseless anger. A customer that had ordered a pint and then decided that he didn't want the pint though the order had clearly been placed, insisting it be taken off his bill. Somehow, that had been Remy's fault. Both the customer and Joseph had come to define average Americans to Remy, yet another reason why he maintained a buzz. Not enough to impair bodily functions, but almost. Almost tipsy.

"You can't be nice to everyone and manage a restaurant. That doesn't work."

"Yeah, sure. That makes sense. Certainly not here." Recent memories of cooks intentionally shrugging off their duties, pretending not to hear a server's requests. Of the servers who grouped in circles and gossiped instead of filling ice containers. "Yeah, I'd prefer the carrot but there doesn't seem to be one in this godforsaken place, so the stick, I guess."

"I don't get any carrots either."

"This country needs more carrots. You know, that's how most election campaigns run. So-and-so promises this many carrots, and so-and-so promises those carrots. Mudslinging in between and in the end there are no carrots. Trump. Obama. Kennedy. Whatever. It's all sticks."

"Obama wasn't that great."

"He established Obama-care, which did provide health care for impoverished Americans but at what cost? The private health insurance companies are stronger than ever now. All that taxpayer revenue just funneled directly into them and the coverage provided is negligible at best. Unsurprising when one thinks about where the bulk of election campaign funding comes from: giant corporations like Pfizer, the major insurance companies, corporations, CEOs and the like. Elected officials satisfy the wants of those that fund their campaign, and that's the wealthy cats. It ain't us. The wealthy minority command elected officials and that's a fact. The rest of us never get a fair shake. Never have. Democracy? Nope. Not at all. Nothing even close to that. It's an oligarchy is what it is, and then we point our fingers at other nations and say they aren't 'free' whatever that means. I want to be free. Give me some of that freedom everyone's talking about."

"You're not free?" the manager asked, smiling a bit.

"I don't know. In some ways, I guess. I'm free to voice my opinion but not free enough to better this decrepit system. Look it could be worse. I get that. But it could also be whole lot better."

"That's true."

The words hung, neither Remy nor the manager caring to break the stillness. It was a painfully slow workday. Only two customers sat at the bar, delivering enthusiastic tales to one another.

"We should buy him a cake. Where's the nearest bakery?"

"Not sure if bakeries even exist in America anymore. There's a supermarket near here. A mile and half that way, I think." Remy thumbed southward. "For twenty dollars, they'd probably put a 'Goodbye, Joseph' on there or something."

"I'm not going to pay for that. You guys are here."

"Touché, sir. Touché. Only I have the handwriting of a doctor so the joke's on you. A cake would be a nice gesture, though. Just say the word and I'll go pick it up. I wouldn't be missing out on much business today. But it would be weird to give him a cake. Last month Tiffany left. She'd been working here for over two years and on her last day, hardly anyone even said goodbye to her. It's a cold place. Like the moon but less atmosphere."

"So you're a critic now, huh?"

"I'm just a guy who doesn't belong. Wherever I go."

"Hang in there."

And with that, he thumped Remy hard on the back and walked off, signaling the end of their conversation. Remy flashed back three years: stepping off of a chair in a dilapidated shared efficiency apartment in Los Angeles, noose constricting tightly around his neck, his hands instinctively clutching at the rope as his body began slowly swaying back and forth. Choking and gasping until his legs were close enough for feet to find purchase along the wall. Bracing himself, he created a little slack in the rope, just enough to wiggle the knot loose, and out he fell to the floor, slightly miffed with himself for failing and slightly relieved to be alive. Everything so slight. So terribly slight.

"I don't hang very well," he replied, chuckling at a joke only he understood.

CHAPTER XLIX

CHINA

Two new "teachers" arrived shortly after the day Remy told the story of the man who moved a mountain. One was on the shorter side of five feet, stocky, lean, muscular. The other was Remy's height, around six foot, and quite corpulent. He didn't seem particular agile or strong, but there was something to him, fat though he was. He had seen a scrap or two. Not a push-you, push-me childish confrontation but the real thing. He'd caught a punch or two and had dished out real beatings and he perpetually seemed on the verge of punching Remy in the face.

Remy introduced himself to the two newcomers as no one else in the office seemed to acknowledge their presence. *If they want to be enemies, that's on them, but I won't treat a stranger as an adversary. I'm above such things.* Wolverine and Chunk shook hands with excessively firm grips, wearing smiles designed to bear fangs and little else. *Alright,* Remy thought, *adversary it is.*

"Nice shoes," Chunk smirked.

"Thanks," Remy replied, ignoring the tone. "They're comfortable and semi-professional."

"Yeah, sure."

"You know, it's difficult finding good shoes in large sizes over here. Did you bring shoes with you? You're going to have a devil of a time finding decent kicks out here. How long are you planning on staying out this way?"

"I don't know." And then more angrily for some reason. "Don't worry about that." And then, just to really drive it home, he repeated his opener, "Nice shoes."

"Yeah, you've mentioned that. You don't teach English, do you? Because I'm not sure that would be a great fit."

Wolverine thought this was quite funny. Chunk did not. He took a step forward nose-to-nose with Remy in a high school teaching office, looking more like an elementary school bully than anything akin to an educator. Completely out of place in an office, but there it was.

"What'd you just say?"

"Oh, come on now. We're grown adults. Well, I'm a grown adult. This is just absurd."

Remy slid back, creating space. Chunk grinned wickedly.

"Well, a real pleasure to meet the two of you."

Remy returned to his desk, searching the room for Patrick in the process, but of course he was nowhere to be found just then. *Later. He will sick these goons upon me from the shadows and then subtly gloat about it later.*

Later that same day, Patrick did exactly that, and Remy was so pleased in predicting it correctly that he caught very little of the sentiment. The next morning, he arrived early to work to find a new desk neighbor, Wolverine. Displayed on his computer screen was a very familiar image: Remy's older brother's house on the other side of the planet back in the states.

He set down his bag calmly and rolled his chair into his new neighbor's private desk space, uncomfortably close. It had been another fruitless night of fleeting chances to secure computer files and programs. Frustrated and exhausted and surrounded by enemies, Remy was on the verge of slipping into a rather nasty response upon seeing his family's privacy intruded upon. "That place looks familiar," he said flatly, flashing a pleasant smile while he gauged the best place to sink his jaws into the bodybuilder's throat if need be.

"Yeah, you know where this is?"

"I do. It looks like Florida."

"It is Florida."

"It looks like my brother's house. Can you scroll back a bit? Let me see the block." Remy acted as he spoke, taking Wolverine's mouse into his hand and doing the scrolling while he was asking for it to be done. Google Maps complied with Remy's commands, verifying that it was indeed his brother's home.

"Now what possible reason could you have to be looking at that? And what exactly is your position here again? I'm having a hard time understanding why you're here."

"Quality control. Human services. Something like HR."

"Something like HR," Remy repeated, mulling it over. "Well, you certainly act more like HR than any other division of labor I can think of. The H stands for human, though, so we're a little off already." His lips drew back into a snarl.

Wolverine rolled his chair farther away and pointed to the more distant computer screen, "It's amazing what computers can do nowadays."

Remy didn't follow the man's pointing digit. His eyes remained locked on the whole of Wolverine, preparing to strike. "It's amazing what *I* can do nowadays." He had decided to blind the man by inserting rigid digits into the sockets of the man's eyes. His digits curled into stiff hooks as he computed the distance to Wolverine and compared it to his own speed and reach. Remy smiled, this one not forced at all. His back twitched the beginning of action.

As that twitch moved downward through his arms, a signal bell rang throughout the scene, marking the end of second period and the beginning of an extended break before third period began, completely disrupting a would-be flash of movement. Legitimate teachers, mostly Chinese, filtered into the office with students in tow. Remy's fingers relaxed into normal digits once again.

"*Saved by the Bell*. Do you remember that show? You look old enough. It was an early nineties show."

"Yeah, I know it. Zack Morris."

"Yep. Zack Morris! That's you right now. Mr. Morris. Tell you what, Zack. I'm going to go to the restroom and then I'm going to come back to your desk. If you're here, then we'll talk about why you're looking at my brother's home address in your leisure time. If you're not, then I'll treat your work computer like my own and poke around until I find something of interest and delete what you shouldn't be in possession of."

"Good luck. Its password protected."

"Oh, is protecting privacy important to you? The irony is not lost on me. And if you think I won't stomp-kick the metal frame that houses the inner workings of this PC until it warps an opening large enough for me to pry the CPU from the core and go analyze your files somewhere else, well then, you probably also think that you almost weren't blinded."

"What?!"

Remy sauntered off, feeling in charge of the situation, a rarity in those days. He groomed himself in the mirror until he heard the bell that marked the start of third period classes. The hallway, once flooded with student traffic, was empty. Muffled sounds of teachers beginning lessons leaked from under doors as he walked down the hallway. Returning to the office, he found Wolverine had left. He shrugged and marched forward to his new neighbor's computer, grasped the metallic shell, and heaved it forward, wedging it farther and farther out of its cubby hole, disconnecting wires free from ports in the process. The bulk of the computer frame was far enough removed from its niche to land a proper stomp-kick, and so Remy braced low on his left leg and brought up the right.

"What you are doing?"

He paused, awkwardly balanced on one leg, right knee held high. He'd expected Patrick or Huey, Dewey, or Louie, maybe Wolverine newly returned, or Chunk. Expecting a member of the gang that plagued him, he hadn't given much consideration to actually ceasing the strike. But across the room was a thin teenage boy in dire need of strong facial soap.

"That's difficult to answer, kid. Yikes, this sounds suspicious already." He brought down his leg slowly, deliberately. "I was going to kill a pest." Honest metaphorically speaking but a stretch. "Trying to clean up the office a bit." Truer.

"Yes, sometimes roach are here." Replied the youth in impressively passing English. Patrick emerged from behind the boy, curving around and into the office.

"Yep." Remy replied dully, eyeing his opponent. "Oh, how I miss being surprised."

Patrick slowed as the detached computer came into view.

"Do you have an older brother, Patrick?" Remy asked, unperturbed.

"No."

"Any siblings at all?"

The silence hung.

"Well, I do. I've never mentioned my brother to this school, though I use the word *school* very loosely here. He wasn't an emergency contact. He's not part of my resume. I've made it a point to exclude my family as much as I can from all of this. And yet," Remy walked around the line of desks to where the student and Patrick stood wearing a smile that only a stranger would find warming, "I see my brother's home displayed on the computer screen of one of your thugs, Patrick." He turned to the child, desperately out of place.

"You should go."

"But teacher isn't..."

"Go. Now."

He complied clumsily, leaving the two combatants standing facing one another, taking in one another in cold stillness. The sound of the door shutting sounded throughout the office and then dimmed into tense silence. There were others in the room. Not Wolverine or Chunk, not Ezekiel, but nameless, intent-unknown Chinese seemingly going about normal teaching business, surreal in their normalcy.

Patrick broke the silence, "Your mother's address isn't true, is it? She doesn't live there."

"I don't lie. Work visas require a family contact address from my homeland and so I jotted down the most current address I could remember. Granted, I didn't exactly probe the deep recesses of my memory. She may've moved since then." *I'm sure she's moved since then. A couple of times.* A ploy to remain honest and employed yet keep his family safely out of the picture, while simultaneously searching for justice in shadowy places. "Doesn't explain why you have access to information I provided my employer in order to secure a visa."

"She lives with your sister now," Patrick said with a smirk. A hated pause as he calculated Remy's reaction. "But you didn't know that, did you?"

A wild, wild west stare down ensued. Remy broke the tension by pivoting and crossing the room, keeping his back to Patrick as he spoke.

"You're something of a lieutenant, commanding some while others command you. A glorified middle-man, really. Ending your hold here wouldn't end this new danger to my family that you threaten me with. There isn't just one guy on top, anyway. I've been thinking about it. I've thought about so much these days, so little of it good." Remy turned back to face Patrick, a warm sadness apparent in his features. "I should leave. That's what I should do. I should return to my family to warn them of you and yours and then sleep for a week. Abandon this hunt for justice. Transition to a new job, maybe a new line of work. Tell what I know to the authorities. Hug my family. Run all the way back home, touch home base and scream 'Olly, olly, oxen free!'"

The words rolled out truly, his heart on his sleeve with every utterance.

"But what I want and what I will do aren't the same. They're so rarely the same anymore. I'm so tired of that. So tired..." he drifted off, sorrow spilling out into his voice. "But I'll stay right here instead. I'll collect every last ounce of evidence possible. Everything you throw at me I will endure and absorb and turn against you. You won't kill me because murdering an American in China would add much credence to my story." He paused, finding the right words. "You robbed me. That's undoubtedly true. And you and your goon just threatened my family in Florida. I work in a school that is connected to my own banking theft, crazy as that sounds. Such audacity is difficult to fathom, but here it is. Live and in the flesh. A division of this legitimate Chinese school has robbed me via wire transfer and suppresses my computer's capabilities, ludicrous though that sounds. Moreover, the government here must sponsor this to some degree, for truly this could not go on without the approval, or at least acknowledgement, of some top-level characters. I am aware of much and I will learn more. I'll find evidence and turn it against you just as soon as I can or I will perish in the attempt. Justice will prevail, I swear it. Your threat to my brother this morning has only strengthened my resolve."

There was the beginning of another western stare down, but Remy cut that short.

"I've had enough of all this tough guy stuff, Pat. Either attack me or don't."

A cold smile and a colder voice. "Why Remy, whatever do you mean? You sound like a crazy man. Are you feeling alright?"

"Feeling great. Like a million bucks. Now, if we're finished here, I have some papers to grade."

It was as if a hammer-bell rang, signaling the end of a round of boxing. Each competitor returned to their respective corners, sat down at their respective desks, a little banged up but only just begun.

CHAPTER L

CHINA

Remy was a meticulous man, relatively patient, able to gather data objectively and make decent assumptions thereafter in order to plan and act accordingly. He was at a dead-end, though, and he knew it. He knew he was barking up the right tree when he sat down at the poker tables in the backrooms of the various pool halls and pubs where he played. He knew some of those involved knew more than they let on about his wire theft. Insight served him well. One seemed to be involved with the police force in some capacity, although in what sense he couldn't discern. A few were for the most part unreadable: rarely speaking, earbuds in ears 95% of the time, placing bets, the first to leave the table and call it a night, refraining from socializing altogether. There was an older distinguished couple with a bodyguard permanently affixed. A man in his early twenties, wealthy in a way that went unexplained. Remy felt that one of these characters had the ability to drop names of persons associated with his banking theft but night after night both sides left the obvious unsaid, ignoring the elephant in the room as they squared off, Remy doing his best detecting in moments when the betting was the highest, when the inner wall was turned toward protecting all-ins and raises and not criminal privacy.

Poker. A game of statistics, quick math, and reading people's true intentions, best paired with boldness and humility. According to his gambling ledger, he had profited around four hundred dollars each month, with a mostly steady win ratio of one hundred dollars each week. He would sit down, cash in two hundred dollars in chips, socialize and play defensively, wait until the right moment and then act on a very strong hand with subtlety and gradual pressure which usually amounted to doubling up. He would ride out the rest of the evening in observation, betting little and producing a steady supply of sly questions designed to shed light onto his investigation. His opponents were not easily duped, however, and while Remy knew that valuable information was to be found amongst them, he was unable to procure it. He was barking up the correct tree but the inhabitants of that tree were simply enjoying the spectacle.

It was also just about the only thing Remy could do. He'd taken a break from software exploration, though tearing himself away had proven quite difficult. After realizing there was another acting against his cyber interests, it had become very difficult to sleep. Mistrust of his surroundings began to consume him. Lowering his guard to relax at home and rest became synonymous with a dangerous endeavor. Truly restful sleep began slipping away from him.

Monica and Remy remained in touch throughout this time. Daily phone calls produced far less information about the theft than the poker tables yielded and also had the unfortunate tendency to fill his heart with longing and sorrow. He was on very foreign soil and failing deeply on a fairly regular basis. Interpol had sent a rather bland cookie-cutter email to him asking for a few details of the bank theft. Based on what he had witnessed her do to his computer while she thought him to be showering and the fact that he had found a host of troublesome files on it, he was never certain of the legitimacy of online content, emails included. *Was that actually a reply from Interpol or was my email redirected from the legitimate Interpol account and into the realm of the very same people who robbed me?* Such were Remy's thoughts, night and day. He couldn't trust his own computer and he was surrounded by adversaries.

"So, Interpol wasn't much help. Not sure why you cared so much about me using your name. The email they sent lacked personality or anything resembling concern."

"You should no done that." She sounded genuinely disappointed, not threatening. He paced across a darkened garden at the back of a pool hall during a fifteen-minute poker break.

"I shouldn't have done a lot of things, princess. But here I am anyway. Just losing every single day. But I can't just let them have it. I can't stop. How could I enjoy a mirror then?" He gazed down into the inky waters of a koi pond, seeing only a faint shadow of his reflection in the rippling water.

"You love see yourself." She said, as if she were there.

"I love seeing you more."

"Remy, you are no smart."

"Thank you. That helps. I was feeling low, you know, just trying and failing all the time. So, thanks for that little pick me up."

"I need go now. I call you back." And with that she hung up.

He returned to his table and played a little more poker. When the phone rang a half hour later, he excused himself and took the call outside, back into the shadowy garden once more.

"I come see you," she said. "I come visit you again. I miss you."

Remy, in love and entirely out of promising leads, was overjoyed at the notion of her visit. Complicated and messy though it was, theirs was a romance he had come to cherish. After ironing out the details of her visit during an upcoming one-week holiday -- Golden Week -- they hung up with pleasant voices belying ulterior motives.

CHAPTER LI

USA

"What do you like most about living in America?"

"I don't know, Rem. I don't think about it much."

"Well, I do." He turned to another server at the pub. "How about you? What's the best part about living here?"

"I don't know. Freedom?"

"Yeah, Americans love their freedom. That's part of the problem. All this freedom but no one's making any personal sacrifices, you know. It's all me, me, me. You know how it is: customers running us around, always wanting more, never satisfied. Entitled. Disrespectful. Awful drivers on these roads. Everyone's got a car, drives every day of their lives, and yet, terrible drivers dominate the roads. Just taking, taking, taking."

The server shrugged and began using a newly vacated computer terminal to key in an order. No one seemed to care much about the issue. Remy was quite alone and he knew it. *Once upon a time, I did fantastic things. Important things. And now here I stand, middle-aged, impoverished, and depressed. All this potential just squandered. Every day I wake up and continue down a mind-numbing path of nothingness.* He was drifting aimlessly and finding it difficult to remember why exactly he was supposed to keep his head above the waves any longer.

CHAPTER LII

CHINA

William looked up with a furrowed brow, seemingly disappointed in his master's decision to leave the house at such a late hour. Not disappointment, really. Concern. Like an uncle worried about his teenage nephew's rebellious behavior. It was that kind of look. And then it was gone, leaving just a sleepy dog resting his muzzle atop his front paws.

"You are a very good dog, William. Better than most people I know but that doesn't say much these days."

The shepherd opened only the one eye nearest Remy, glancing over briefly and deciding nothing important was occurring before settling into sleep once again.

"I wish I had more to offer you. A big yard teeming with woodland creatures for you to chase. This can't be comfortable for you: coming in at late hours, furiously clicking away on a keyboard, growling in disappointment until the sun rises."

William, roused awake yet again, stretched his long neck out and raised his wolfish head. He opened his mouth to pant, pink tongue lolling down, curling up across a jaw full of sharp teeth. A typical dog-smile. Remy took a couple of steps over to his sleeping pad, crouched low, and gave the dog a big kiss on the top of his thick skull.

"Be good, William."

Tensions were running high at work, at the poker tables, and with his mixed-up love life. High enough that someone breaking and entering into his apartment while he was away was not beyond the realm of possibilities. In light of this, he had begun leaving triggers on the front door, signs that would show if anyone had entered his apartment while he'd been away. As the door swung shut, he inserted a thinly folded paper, wedging it knee-level between door and frame. If he were to arrive home, open the front door, and not see the paper fall from the appropriate height, there would be cause for concern. All good in theory but after a week of this practice yielding no results, it was beginning to feel like proof of paranoia more than anything.

A ten-minute walk to the subway station. A thirty-five-minute train ride. Another ten-minute walk. Poking around the social crevices of Guangzhou searching for clues had revealed a few black markets throughout the city. One strip of sidewalk shops focused on contraband electronics. Another in pirated software, DVDs, CDs, and the like. The black market that Remy visited an hour after leaving his flat consisted of various African men employed under some false pretense or another -- mainly the clothing trade -- congregating along a stretch of sidewalk alongside and under an interstate bridge behind a prominent hotel. It was along that sidewalk that a host of hushed, conspiratorial voices offered connections to prostitutes in a wide variety of terminologies. But that wasn't why Remy had come. The endless battles with his own network and operating system had taken its toll, denying him sleep and awareness in the classroom. Still, he soldiered on, refusing surrender, intent on crippling the reign of the syndicate that acted against him with such imperiousness.

"What do you need, my friend? I have many, many girls. You like boom-boom, yes?"

"Sure, I guess I do, but no. I'm not here for that. I do believe that would just be adding fuel to a blazing fire." Remy turned to the man who had approached from the shadows, sizing him up as muscular but untrained and therefore not a serious threat. The man stopped short, sensing something disconcerting. Confusion played about his face in perfect clarity to Remy, a man accustomed to reading tells of the most deceitful people the world had to offer.

"I can get you a very pretty girl."

"Yeah, I don't want that. I'm here for something else. Something to keep me awake. If I sleep, I could very well be attacked. I need something to help me stay alert. Can you find anything like that?" And they parlayed and negotiated a price and Remy walked away a little poorer. He was continually threatened, psychologically and physically. His home had been transformed into a battleground in which he feared lowering his defenses. There existed a justifiable need to remain awake in his ongoing plight to prove the existence of the rabbit hole he had fallen in.

He returned a little after midnight, waking the hound who gave him that concerned-uncle glance once again. William stretched out along his front legs, bowing deeply while arching his back before straightening and shaking himself from nose to tail, freeing up a cloud of loose hairs before trotting over to the hanging leash, biting down on the handle loosely, and shaking the leash free from its anchor on the wall. Remy took his cue, picked up the handle and off they went down seventeen floors and through an empty courtyard in which two conflicting groups had squared off against one another the night he'd moved in. That memory helped quiet a restless conscience as the hours zipped along until the sun shone confidently on the horizon and he called another failed night to a close, bathed, and returned to an office full of colleagues that threatened him daily.

CHAPTER LIII

CHINA

The phone in Remy's pocket trembled and buzzed as he approached the seventh stop from the international airport.

"Hello, love."

"I here. At airport."

"You're early. Okay. Well, I'm on my way. Just meet me at the subway platform. I should be there in fifteen minutes." A pause. "I'm very glad you're here. I missed you."

"Yes. I see you soon."

She was pulling her shiny hot pink roller suitcase again and looking wonderful. To Remy, she was the only woman around, though scores surrounded them: boarding, exiting, waiting anxiously, embracing family and friends. *Why me? Of all the men in this world, why is this lovely creature here with me right now?* And then memories of his hacked computer, of stolen money, a thug replacing a decent police officer in Nanchang, all came rushing in and he stiffened his resolve. His expression did not waver as contentment shifted into something sharper. The answer to the question why was lightyears away. The how, the who, and the where were possibilities, however.

They hugged and he nuzzled in for a kiss that she dodged with typical grace. He resigned himself to holding her hand as the train thundered along, jostling this way and that along the stretch of track that led back to the Tianhe subway station. Having forgotten to double-back and find a way to the airport after the initial misleading arrival, meeting Monica had the added benefit of establishing a clear path via subway to the goal of any sensible exit plan: the international airport.

Solidifying his understanding of the way back to the airport had brightened Remy's spirits before her call had come through. Holding her hand was icing on the cake. He almost felt human again as he sat alongside the woman he loved as the train careened around a subterranean bend.

It had been a lonely month. Ezekiel, the one good man in the red-hot mess that was the foreign teacher's office, had been keeping his distance. Not that Remy could blame the man. He likely had family and friends of his own that he didn't want to get sucked up into the cyclonic turmoil of Remy's life. He was a tad relieved Zeke had chosen to separate himself from the fray although this had left him without an ally. He had dutifully continued exploring his computer software for potential proof of wrongdoing, though often stumped at impasses that would as suddenly appear as disappear, taking with it much data that could've been useful if only he'd been able to make a copy; or at impasses that remained, resolute and unmovable, file chains of inaccessible parent permissions; or at impasses that were finally outmaneuvered only to cause a system crash that required a full reinstallation of the Windows operating system. It was a slogfest and he had all but abandoned hope in his quest.

His heart felt heavy at what was to come. Only a slight glimmer of hope shone as he contemplated the possibilities of the immediate future. His stomach churned painfully. *Maybe we should abandon this*, he reasoned with himself inwardly. In response, his mind flashed the memory of creeping around a corner, soaking wet and nude, to find her perched over his laptop, of the strange formulas and grids that were displayed. With new resolve, a grim acceptance washed over him, concealed with the sweetest of smiles.

They made small talk about her flight and of life away from one another. Things to do in Guangzhou while she visited, places to visit. He was a man torn. On the outside, cheerful and on full display. Underneath, grave.

He kissed the back of her delicate hand. "I love you and I'm sorry for what will come. I just don't know any other way to move forward. And it's not like you're totally innocent, you little minx."

She smiled warmly. "What?"

"It's nothing. Forget about it. Hey, I thought we could do something special tonight. Since we haven't seen one another in a while. I bought these." He slid a packet of foil-encased pills from his pocket covered in the Chinese characters for vitality, endurance, love, and energy. She flushed and almost giggled.

"Where did you buy?"

"At a drugstore in downtown." Flirting with the truth.

She took the packet and examined it more closely, putting a fine eye on the ingredients list. Remy assumed it contained elements of ginger, ginseng, cinnamon, stuff like that given the propensity the Chinese had toward usage of natural ingredients. It may contain panda whiskers for all he knew but likely nothing synthetic. She didn't nod, but there was something approving in her demeanor that let him know she found this acceptable.

"Takes an hour, sugar lips. And we'll be back in my apartment in half that time. So, shall we?" He made a show of slipping the foil packet out of its covering and popping two pills out. Not wanting to draw more attention to themselves, Moni followed, snatching up the foil packet and popping two pills out, swallowing them down quickly with a bottle of water she had brought for the trip. *Perfect.*

"Taste bad."

Remy chuckled at this. "Yeah, it is awfully yucky. I'm trying to fix it but I can't."

"What you say?"

"Nothing, sugar pants. Nothing much. I love you. I hope you know that. I love you so much. I missed you. I can't trust you at all but I love you. Head to toe." When she swung her head around to face him, he swooped in and kissed her cheek. She ducked away afterward, grinning.

"No. Not here. Much time soon."

He smiled, in love with the premise. He'd been longing for her for quite some time, and she was ravishing. From her earlobes to her pinky toe, he loved her all. He wrestled with her suitcase and his own shame as they ascended the steps to the sidewalk that led to his apartment building.

CHAPTER LIV

CHINA

"I feel very warm. Very hot."

"Yes. Yes, you are. I've always thought that. From the moment I first set eyes on you back in Nanchang. Hot. Do you even remember that, I wonder? Though the first few dates were tepid, I was quickly overcome with a need to be with you. I'm still overcome. A wiser man would have disengaged long ago. In truth, I wonder if I'll ever be free."

She smiled prettily, "I no understand. Apartment is hot?"

"Well, if you're so warm, you should probably remove some of your clothing. You know, to be more comfortable. Just looking out for you." He grinned wryly.

"You will like that."

"I would." And they kissed delicately and passionately. As their ardent energies swirled, he detached, temptation taking a backseat to obligation.

"I must tell you the truth about what has happened. We're drugged, you and I. We are *drugged*." Repeating the word for emphasis.

"Yes, I know." She stretched luxuriantly across his lap as cats do and they kissed once more.

"Well, you see," he said between kisses, "the thing about that is that I replaced the legal pills you examined with illegal ones."

She stiffened and sat upright as the meaning of the words came together. Her smile lost its warmth. He pressed on, needing the truth to be out. She looked perplexed, and beautifully so. He could only imagine where her mind was taking her, the questions she must have.

"Razor cuts along the edge of the foil. Cheap masking tape to re-seal the foil packets. Practically invisible and easily torn. I'm pretty impressed with the result, actually. Didn't expect the foil to give way and make that *snap* sound. Of course, privately I don't think it would have held up to your scrutinizing eye which is why you were exposed to it in public. I must say it does feel nice to win one."

"Really? I drug now?"

"Oh yes, princess. And I am as well. Fair is fair. Anything else would be too creepy to consider. This is some James Bond stuff we are into these days, no?"

"You no James Bond."

"I am not James Bond. He would have solved all of this in two hours with a magic watch, but I make do with what I have. Actually, I don't make do at all. Which brings me here and now."

"You speak so much fast."

"Duly noted." He began heeding her advice, slowing his speech, replacing difficult terms with easier vocabulary. "James Bond would have sodium pentothal at his disposal. Truth serum. I do not." She draped herself across his lap like a cat. He looked down at the lovely upside-down creature as a wave of euphoria rushed through his senses. A drugged perma-smile stretched across their faces.

"I no understand and I no care."

"That's the spirit! That's exactly what I'm going for here. Man, it does feel nice to win one of these." From atop a nearby table, deep within her purse, a phone lit up and buzzed. Remy's head tilted a bit in acknowledgement. Monica seemed oblivious. He stood. "Babe, I'm going to move our stuff into the bedroom, alright? I'll be right back." The phone buzzed and lit her purse in a dull glow again as he lugged her belongings into the bedroom. He dug through the contents of her sizeable purse and shut off the phone, resisting the temptation to memorize the displayed incoming phone number of her screen. He shut the door firmly behind him and returned to the living room where she was lying on the sofa kicking her feet up in the air pleasantly.

"I love you so much. Forever, maybe, like it or not. But I need the truth. There is so much shade and deceit and I need to clean the air, light up the room if you will."

"No turn on light," she commanded absently.

"Yep, not going to do that. I'm speaking figuratively here. Anyway, you consistently dodge important questions I present to you. You say you don't understand, but sometimes you do, I see it in your eye and in your mannerisms. I repeat the same questions over and over, in different ways, in the simplest of English. I speak or text in Mandarin and still you feign ignorance." He resituated, nestling together with the woman he adored and was simultaneously disappointed in, a woman he respected and distrusted. He kissed her forehead, her cheeks, and lastly her lips. "I love you and I'm sorry about all of this."

Her smile was wide, her eyes half-closed. "I love you," she echoed. Remy was lost for a moment, wanting to believe her words, but remembering.

"That does bring up my first point. *Love.* Let's focus on love. You must love your family but you don't say much about them." That was a vast understatement. "I've never seen photos of your parents.

I want to meet them but you haven't allowed it. I don't even know what their jobs are."

"My father is teacher. Like me." She reached behind Remy's neck and pulled him downward into a long kiss. A kiss leading to more. He woefully detached, dutifully climbing out of her embrace.

"You are drugged. You know that, right? You do understand that, I hope. You've swallowed two pills of ecstasy. I went through the trouble of testing three, no four different batches and found this type to be the most suitable in chemical composition to my needs. This is the only chance I have at pulling some truth from you." His guilt and shame warred with potential triumph. *Means to an end,* he reminded himself.

"I love you dearly but you've hurt me so much. From the theft, to lying about where you go half the nights, to that thug in the police station that chased away an actual police officer. There are some serious issues here."

"No serious." She pulled him close and again they kissed. He was finding it increasingly difficult to disengage. She was warm and sweaty-wet and wonderful. She rose gracefully to her feet and began to dance sumptuously, body gyrating erotically to a tune only she could hear. She bent over, torso low, hips and buttocks on full display and looked back playfully. "Where is tie? You should have tie. Give me tie."

"What? Like a, like a necktie?"

"Yes. You will like."

"Okay." He hurried off and opened the door to the bedroom where her bag continued glowing and buzzing. *I know I shut that off and I'm pretty sure that didn't shine so brightly last time.* The mobile growled angrily as if in response to his inner monologue. Remy smiled. Well, *I must be doing something right.* He snatched a red necktie from the closet and returned. He found her as he had left her, gyrating sensually. When he held out the necktie to her, she shook her head.

"No, you wear."

He twisted the thing clumsily about his neck with fingers that had lost their nimbleness. The knot was all wrong, but he couldn't have cared less as she slinked toward him, straddled his lap, and gently pulled it away from his failing hands. She held an intimate, hypnotic gaze upon him as she loosened the tie, bending forward and whispering in his ear, "You like this, yes?"

"I do. I like you. Whoever you are. I love you, you know."

She unwound the tie from his neck and used it as a dancing ribbon of sorts as she continued dancing erotically, a mating dance if there ever was one, clothes piling up alongside them as she stripped each article away with luscious flourishes. Their bodies melded and spirits soared into euphoria. Afterward, they spoke as lovers do, in hushed voices and subtle movements.

"So that was remarkable. You seem pretty good at that."

"Good. Yes, it good."

"Yeah, but I do have to wonder. See, that did not seem like your first time seducing a man with a tie."

"First time?" she giggled. "No, not first time." She giggled again and immediately caught herself, her eyes showing the beginnings of clarity. *Time is running out, and I will never get this chance again.*

He chuckled to rekindle her giggling, leading her away from second-guessing her own words. Caressing her, he continued.

"You're a stripper than." He couldn't find the real words. *Stripper* was the closest he could muster. She shrugged and smiled. "That makes sense. You're a dancer. I remember you showing me that video of your college exhibition. The exhibition where everyone tied for first, second, and third place." He kissed her bare shoulder. "You Commies. No one wins."

"Everyone win," she replied, reminding him why he loved her.

"Agree to disagree."

"Agree you wrong."

"I disagree." They cuddled closer. "And you teach dance at the school in Nanchang where we met. That's what you've told me this past year, at least. Only I've never seen you teach, or coach, or whatever you want to call it. You never told me where or when you were doing your thing. I couldn't ever pop-in and see you in action."

"I shy," she replied perfunctory.

"Yes, you've said that many times. And it made sense at first. But after a year, it's just odd."

She stiffened to the point that he had to let her go as she wriggled free. "I assist. I assistant to director."

"Right. That's your main job, you say. That's why you needed to leave the apartment half of the time. To assist the director of the school at eight or nine o'clock at night. We brought Tan to justice and things were normal and good, but a month later you began leaving again. Only you didn't go to the school. A black sports car picked you up and drove you elsewhere. And you were awfully dolled-up to be assisting a director, a man I personally verified you were not meeting with."

She spun back around to face him and froze, slowly pondering the words. "You follow me," she remembered aloud, still smiling druggily.

"Oh, yes. And I drugged you, too. Remember? I just did that like an hour or two ago. I also returned to the school grounds a few times feigning forgotten possessions in order to check on your story of assisting the new director. He was rarely on schoolgrounds during those times and never to my knowledge interacted with you in the evenings when you left our home. He checks out. You do not." He smiled lovingly and poked her nose gently. "You are trouble."

"Trouble?" She stiffened and rolled away. "I no trouble."

"You are the worst kind of trouble -- the kind I can't put down." She rolled back and they kissed and squirmed with pleasure once more.

"You trouble," she said between kisses.

"Thank you," Remy replied, knowing a compliment when he heard one.

CHAPTER LV

CHINA

The glowing, humming bag had become pretty difficult to ignore. As she freshened up in the shower, he took it upon himself to reposition the devilish thing. Entering into William's room, the shepherd looked up sleepily as Remy slid inside. "Hush now, boy. I don't mean to wake you. I just need to drop this thing off." The bag throbbed a quick pulse as if resisting the idea. He set it down across the room and, realizing the bag would be just as much if not more of an annoyance for William, cursed quietly to himself and instead tucked it away in the living room.

Monica exited the bathroom, crossing paths with Remy who seamlessly guided her back into bed and away from thoughts of a phone or purse. Sobriety was returning and with it the window of opportunity was closing.

"You're a dancer. Let's call you that. You dance. Like with that necktie just now."

"You like that."

"I did. I do. I will again if I'm lucky."

She relaxed into his arms. They tangled together like old roots and laid still.

"So, you dance. That explains the late hours. The stranger picking you up. Your incessant lies. Explains the American in the karaoke bar whispering into your ear about a newly divorced friend he wanted you to meet."

"You hear that," she stated incredulously. "You hear many thing." On the cusp of a threatening tone.

"Ears don't close, my dear. And some people talk loudly. Bray like donkeys, really, like dogs barking in each other's ears and then shouting blame at those who overhear. You blame me for hearing such vileness? How about, stop being vile? How about, don't be a terrible person? How about that?" The anger in his tone was unmistakable. She looked to him with rapidly clearing eyes.

A change in tactics followed. "Alright." He forced tenderness from a far-away place. "Alright. I love you and have loved you for quite some time. Despite whatever it is you're mixed-up with."

"I love you," she replied, returning to sleepy sexiness. "But you no know me, Rem."

"Okay, I don't know all of you. That's obvious or I wouldn't have drugged us. I know you struggled before you robbed me. I know you wrestled with that decision two weeks before you robbed me because you left us for no reason. You broke up with me just before the heist, and I wouldn't let that be. It was too puzzling. And more to the point, I can't let you go, Moni. I just can't. You and William are all I have. All I want, really."

Her eyes welled and she spun away.

"I've talked to one of the poker people I play with. Not friends. Mates? Poker mates? That doesn't feel like the right word either, though. Anyway, the one I trust the most has offered you a job in Guangzhou as a secretary, an assistant, like what you do now."

The words sunk in as he spoke them. *Like what you do now.*

"Oh." He stopped himself dumbly. An extremely awkward pause ensued.

She rolled back, eyes brimming, her smile sad and for the first time, not pretty at all. "I tell you."

"You most certainly did not. You told me the principal made a move on you, that he locked a door and placed his hand on your thigh. That he sexually harassed you and you hated it. You were the innocent victim in that tale. Where we are now is nowhere close to that." Cold. Bitter. Accusatory.

A stream etched a path down her face. The other eye pooled but did not spill.

"That wasn't it, was it?" he continued. "There was more. F&%*, there was more. You stopped the story halfway and I just filled in the rest."

He was furious. At himself. At her. At those responsible for poisoning such a life.

This time it was Remy who rolled away, and up onto his feet, full of vigor and fury.

"Physically tearing you away from these men would be easy enough. Getting away with it, not so much." He looked back to the bed. Adorned in sheets that half hid her nude form, she met his gaze, clear pain in her smile.

"Who?" she asked in a tone that expressed the impossibility of it all.

He took it a different way. "Exactly, Moni. Let's do this. Where do we begin? Who needs to... be away in order for you to be free?"

"We don't do this thing. You don't."

"Well, maybe you won't, but I..."

"Yes," she half-laughed, the lone tear gone. "You superman. You save me."

"I'll try. I'm trying right now. This isn't impossible."

"You won't. You can't." She reached out and took his hand, oblivious as the sheet fell away and exposed her plaster-white skin in the moonlight. "Go home. Go now. Leave."

"Come with me and I will. Pack your bag. We'll get dressed first, I suppose, but then pack that bag. I'll pack mine. William's on a leash and then we're on our way. Tonight. Like in ten minutes."

She looked up, smiling prettily once again. "And my family? My friends?"

"I doubt you have true friends, Moni. Probably not much of a family either. Leave them and come with me."

"And you forget everything? We live happy after?" She paused, thinking of the right expression. "Happy ever after?"

"Happily ever after, ferret face. And yes."

She gathered up the loose sheet and deftly tucked it into a makeshift toga in one smooth motion, the speed of which took him by surprise. Her tone had become stronger, the effects of the makeshift truth serum no longer so pronounced.

"Where we live?"

"Well, I don't know. I'm flying by the seat of my pants these days. Just trying to solve an international crime all by myself in Triad-infested waters. That's all. No big deal."

"And how we live? You have job?"

"You mean beside the lovely one in Guangzhou with all of these fantastic people that mean me nothing but the best? Beside that one? Nothing."

She looked to him with bemusement.

"But I have some money saved up. I've won more than I've lost in poker. I've saved most of these paychecks. Wait, one paycheck. Wow, has it only been a single month here? It feels like a such a long time."

"You have money in bank?" she asked sharply.

"You know the answer to that. Why're you doing this? Why're you shooting down this thing? It'll be hard. I don't have all of the answers. But it can be done if we're together. Whatever it is." He sat on the edge of the mattress, bent over her, smiled, and rubbed his nose against hers, looking into eyes that hinted of pain and pity. His vision blurred and the moxie left him. "Why can't you just leave it all behind?"

"Family," she answered, as if it were all so simple.

"I left mine."

"They left you. Your family no love you." *Ouch.* "I sorry. But I love my family. They love me. I no leave."

I haven't seen my family in years. We barely speak to one another or bother with emails. I've always put on the brave face, trying to seem like a normal man with a normal family and someone she should definitely spend the rest of her life with. But she saw through it.

His posture slumped. "So that's it, then?" He shot back, straightening. Her body language softened in response, conveying compassion. "Tell me about this marvelous family of yours. The one you cherish so much. The one that loves you, the real you, because they know you and I don't. Tell me about them. The parents you've never introduced me to. Do they know about any of this? The dancing?"

She pulled away, perched nobly on the corner of the mattress, and began staring through the slivered opening of the closed curtains, past the distant, dark skyline and into the past. "I no like dance." A pause. "I no like dancing when I young girl."

"Well, you're quite good at it," he interjected, thinking of both the choreographed video of her college recital and of the recent ecstasy-induced encounter.

She smiled prettily and continued, "I fourteen when I dance first time."

While he had requested her to divulge this part of herself, he nonetheless was finding it far less palatable than he had imagined, "Yep, okay. I was young, too. I was about that age when I had sex for the first time. That sounds about right. Don't worry about your age at---"

She spun about swiftly and calmly placed a solitary finger upon his lips but it was her eyes that silenced him. "My father send me away when I twelve. Study dance. A woman come to school. That week, she visit some girl families. Invite join dance team. Special invite."

Remy, for a very rare instance, was without words.

"I hate it. Two years, all dance. Exercise and dance."

A long pause. Each of her sentences came slowly, each word spoken like walking on thin ice, each sentence requiring a full breath.

"When I fourteen, I have first performance. For older man. At birthday party."

"What the f&^%, Moni. What are you saying right now?"

She continued as if no words had broken the spell. "Government man. Important. He have birthday and there group of us. Dancing."

"All your age? Fourteen?"

She didn't nod but displayed an affirmation nonetheless.

"How many?"

"Maybe five. Maybe six."

"And you just danced?" he asked, unable to give voice to the alternative.

"Yes," she smiled slyly. "We dance. We practice and we dance together. There rice wine. Some men drunk. It very late."

"Your parents sound like awful human beings, Moni. I would have to be killed before such a thing would happen to my daughter. Where was your father? Why do you care about him at all?"

"You no understand. It special invite. What you say? 'No's no option.'"

"Not an option. But yeah, there was an option."

"Fight?" she bitterly snickered.

"Yes. Fight, Monica. Fight the wicked. That's exactly what I mean."

"My father like you. He good man. He say no when woman come." Long pause. "You no understand. You no understand all."

Remy stopped. His face was flush, the blood flowing hot through a pounding heart. She placed her warm palm across his cheek lovingly. He kissed her fingers as he spoke, "Now more than ever, you must come with me. You must leave this behind. Be free."

"Free? With no money? But I Moni." They both chuckled.

"Was that a joke?"

"Money. The government man give money. And present. Snacks. Clothes."

"I really don't want to hear any more of this."

But she continued on absently. Relentlessly. "More dance. Different man. More man. When I fifteen, I go back to high school but still dance. No girl my friend. Only dancing girl my friend. Now I twenty-five. Still dance."

"I'm thinking about knocking you unconscious and dragging you to the airport tonight."

She closed her eyes as if to welcome the blow. He clenched his fist and delicately nudged her fine chin. A joke wholly out of place. He was overcome with her. Of what she had endured. How it hadn't broken her. He swept her into his arms, pressing as much of her against him as possible, his eyes spilling tears with the enormity of it all.

It was then that the shadow entered into his periphery. It was unlike normal shadows that pass through mostly closed curtains. It was not a shadow cast by the headlights of a passing vehicle seventeen stories below. Nor was it a pigeon flitting by searching for temporary lodging. No, this shadow was humanoid and close, extremely close. It slipped passed the window along the tiny lip of a ledge that circled the seventeenth floor, human-sized and swift. More than mere observation, he felt the presence. Felt a person there. Impossibly there.

She calmly looked into his teary, astonished eyes. "I sorry. I told you go home."

(END OF BOOK ONE)